Blood of a Boss

Lock Down Publications
Presents
Blood of a Boss
The Moreno Family
A Novel by *Askari*

DEDICATIONS

This book is dedicated to the memory of my loving mother, Mrs. Edith Annette Farmer. I promised you that I'd do something great, and everyday I'm working extremely hard to fulfill that promise. I love and miss you so much. I wish you were here...I'm pretty sure things would be so much different.

This book is also dedicated to my beautiful babies, Dayshon Kapone Farmer, Keyonti Nikkia Farmer, and Quamar Preston Adams. Daddy loves y'all more than y'all could ever imagine. I need y'all to always love, protect, and support one another, and never allow anything to come in between y'all. Day and Qua, y'all are Kings! Keyonti, you're a Queen! Never forget that! And no matter what, always know that daddy loves y'all!

ACKNOWLEDGEMENTS

To my number one supporter, my beautiful auntie, Mary Dee Broomer. Thank you for always having my back and for being the closest thing to a mother that I could ever ask for. If it wasn't for your love and support, I would've never made it this far. I love you forever and beyond!

To my little brothers, Tyron and Shamar Farmer. I love y'all dudes til death, and I'm extremely proud of y'all. I need y'all to learn from my mistakes, and use y'all God given capabilities to make an impact on this world! All the BS has to get put to the side. We're brothers and nothing can change that.

To my beautiful sister, Chrissia Lindsay. I love you, Twin! And I'm so proud of the woman that you grew to be. Mommy would be so proud of you! I know we don't always see eye to eye, but you're my only sister, my mother's only daughter, and I love you!

To my pops, Earl Preston Farmer III. I love you, Big Dawg! Hold ya head, bul!

Most importantly, I need to give a shout out to my Queen, my everything, my beautiful grandmother, Jeanette Farmer. I love you Mom Mom, and I miss you like crazy!

To all of my family and friends who held me down, I love y'all. It's too many to name, but y'all know who y'all are.

I also want to give a shout out to my first and only love, you know who you are. It's crazy how things turned out between us, but when I told you "21", I meant it. That's something that'll never change!

To the big homey, Cash, and my LDP family! Coffee, JPeach, Ms. Sandy aka My Angel, Linnea, Frank Greaham, Royal Nicole, Forever Redd, Kanari Diamond, Lady Stiletto (THE RAVENS SUCK!!), Mahaughani, Ms.Writer For Life, and my Philly homegirl, Jane Pannella. Thanks for welcoming me to the roundtable and giving me the opportunity to bring my creativity to the world. When one of us pops, we all pop! We got the book game on smash and we not lettin' up! They gon' have to deal wit us! I salute!

Last but not least, I wanna give a very special shout out to my set 400 Block Pueblo Bishops. Our motherland Pueblo Del Rio Housing Projects in South Central, My 52st Bishops. And most definitely my 92st Bishops out in Watts.
BISHOP LOVE!!
Tali Da Don, I told you, brozay. The takeover is officially here!

First Edition January 2015
Printed in the United States of America

Lock Down Publications
Email: rdiordgz@gmail.com
Facebook: Askari TheWriter
Cover design and layout by: Dynasty Cover Me
Book interior design by: Shawn Walker
Edited by: Shelby Lazenby

Chapter One

August 2012

It was your typical summer's day in North Philadelphia, and all throughout the Bad Landz, the shouting of *Weed! Dope! Wet! Crack!* could be heard indiscriminately. The blazing sun was scorching down on the drug infested streets that were no wider than a New York City alleyway. Drug addicts of all races were patrolling the neighborhood. They were dying to spend the money they scraped and slaved for.

Sitting on the hood of his black on black 2012 Chevy Tahoe, Sontino 'Sonny' Moreno was playing his position of caseworker. His job was to secure the block and keep track of the block's revenue. At the age of twenty-three, he was 5' 11" and a solid 205 pounds. He was light skinned with a chiseled baby's face, and he had thick, dark, wavy hair. Although he was considered to be extremely handsome by the women he encountered, he was far from a pretty boy. He was more of a rugged type. Essentially, he was a thoroughbred young bul. The women loved him, and the niggas in the hood respected his gangsta.

"Hey, yo, Sheed, grab ten more bundles from the stashspot!" He ordered as he glanced around, looking at the crowd of crack heads that were itching for a fix. "Yo, y'all mu'fuckas gotta stop crowdin' around. Matter of fact, half of y'all walk around the block and come back. The rest of y'all, get y'all shit and keep it movin'."

Like the majority of the corners in the Bad Landz, Fairhill and York was poppin'. It was 4 o'clock in the afternoon, which meant it was rush hour, and you can bet your bottom dollar that the rush was there. As soon as Sheed returned from the vacant lot with the ten bundles, each containing fifteen dime rocks, Sonny sent him back for twenty more.

"Tom Tom, we closing shop in like fifteen minutes," he

said to his right hand man, Tommy. "We only got twenty bundles left, and I'm try'na get the fuck up outta here."

"Yeah, I'm definitely feelin' you, my nigga," Tommy replied, thinking about spending some quality time with his daughter and her mother.

After knocking off the last of the bundles, Sheed said, "Damn, the week ain't even over yet, and we already moved a whole brick. That nigga Mook gon' be feelin' us somethin' crazy. We got this shit poppin' out here."

"Yeah, I know that's right," Sonny concurred. "I'm a call the big homie right now and let him know we closin' shop for the rest of the day."

He reached inside of his truck and grabbed his iPhone from the passenger's seat. After scrolling through the rolodex and stopping on Mook's number, he pressed the call button and held the phone to his ear.

Ring! Ring! Ring!

"Yo," Mook answered.

"Big homie, what's poppin'? It's Sonny. Where you at?"

"What's bangin', Blood? I just left the sneaker store on the Ave., and I'm on my way to the block."

"Damn, I wish I woulda called you earlier, I woulda told you to grab me the new Lebron's." Sonny shook his head from side to side. "Fuck it, I'm a just shoot up there as soon as we shut down the strip."

"More or less," Mook replied in a nonchalant manner. "What's the block lookin' like?"

"Aw man, everything's good over this way," Sonny assured him. "And we just finished fuckin' that lil' white bitch you sent through the other day."

"Say no more, scrap. I'll be around there in a hot minute. Soowoo!" Mook ended the conversation.

"Bang! Bang!" Sonny replied.

After disconnecting the call, Sheed noticed a light skinned chick with a face like Ashanti's and an ass like K. Michelle's walking down the block, demanding everyone's attention.

"Damn, Flo, is we fuckin' tonight or is you just suckin' my dick?" Sheed shouted loud enough for the world to hear.

She stopped in her tracks and looked at him like he was stupid. "Only if you gon' eat my pussy again like you did this morning!"

"Bitch, ain't nobody eat ya stank ass pussy!" Sheed lied, knowing damn well he had his face up in that twat. "Why you try'na play me in front of my niggas? Don't get ya lil' yellow ass smacked out here."

"Nigga, fuck you!"

"Bitch, fuck you!"

"Will both of y'all *please* shut the fuck up?" Sonny laughed. "Ain't nobody try'na hear y'all ghetto ass soap opera bullshit."

As Sheed and Flo continued their dysfunctional way of flirting, Mook turned the corner in his candy apple red 2012 Bentley Continental GT. His 22" rims sparkled in the sunlight and the sounds of Meek Mills' *I'm a Boss* was thumping from his customized sound system.

I'ma Boss like my nigga, Rozay/Shawty asked me for a check, I told that bitch like no way/'Cause I started from the bottom, there was never no way/And I never had a job, you know I had to sell yay.

He parked in front of his trap house, and then climbed out of the European coupe, all 6' 5" of him. He greeted of his lil' homies with their Blood handshake, and then he leaned against his Bentley and fired up a Vanilla Dutch.

Mook was a big black ugly mutha'fucka, but the crazy part about it was that he kept some bad bitches and whenever the team would grind him up about his appearance, he would always counter by saying, "Yeah, I'm an ugly nigga, but my money make me cute."

If what he said was true, then he was the cutest nigga in the world because his money was longer than Broad Street.

After exhaling a thick cloud of Kush smoke, he smiled at Sonny, “What’s poppin’, Skoobie?"

“That *five* poppin’ and that bix droppin’. Suit dat or shoot dat. If you ain’t Bishop, then move back.” Sonny quickly responded, while throwing up his set.

“More or less.” Mook smiled, and then led him away from the small crowd that quickly formed around him. “So, what’s the count?”

“Well, we just finished the brick you dropped off the other day, and we racked up $45,000. I’ma run in the spot and grab it for you.”

A couple of minutes later, he returned from the house with a gray Nike gym bag. “Here,” he handed Mook the bag. “It’s $35,000 in there. I already took out my $4,000 for the week, and I took out another $6,000 to pay Tommy and Sheed.”

Mook took the bag of money and used his key ring to open the Bentley’s trunk. After laying the bag beside his customized speaker box, he locked the trunk and then took a seat next to Sonny on the trap house steps.

“Let me put you on to somethin’,” he said just above a whisper. “When the time comes, you, me, and the team, we gon’ run Philly. Right now, we got a stronghold on most of the North and Uptown, but once we get our hands on Downtown, Southwest, and West Philly, we gon’ have this shit sewed up, my nigga. Then after that, we takin’ over South Jersey and Delaware. I’m ‘bout to turn this shit up, Blood. You wit’ me?”

Sonny looked at his big homie and smiled. “Come on, bro, you already know.”

*****

Looking out of the windows of an abandoned row home, Detectives Ronald Sullivan and Adam Smith had spent the past three hours watching Sonny and his team sell crack like it was going out of style. The differences between the two detectives were many, but the ones that stuck out the most were their motives and experience. Detective Smith a/k/a 'Smitty' was an overweight, middle aged white man who'd been on the force for the past twenty-five years. He was a piece of shit and was known for being a dirty cop. Over the course of his career, he'd extorted everything from street level drug dealers all the way up to mafiosos, and with his mind set on retirement, he had no plans to stop.

Detective Sullivan, on the other hand, was a rookie detective from Norristown, Pennsylvania. He was a thirtythree year old black man and was known for being an honest and over the edge street cop. A couple of months ago, he transferred to the Philadelphia Police Department where his father-in-law was the police commissioner, and he was immediately promoted to detective. Although he was black, the only black thing about him was his beige complexion. As a small child, he was adopted by a middle class white family, and sadly, they never taught him about his culture. Consequently, he grew to be the type of black man that hated any and everything that reminded him of his race. He preferred to attach himself to the white slave masters that raped their way into his bloodline instead of identifying with his oppressed African ancestors.

"Goddamnit, Smitty! We've been sitting in this shithole watching these bastards sell crack like it's friggin' legal for the past three hours! Why can't we just radio in, and have a unit storm the corner and arrest these fuckers?" Detective Sullivan asked, sounding like Carlton from The Fresh Prince of Bel-Air.

"Because, Sully, it's all a part of my strategy," Detective Smith replied while feasting on a jelly donut. "Right now they're comfortable and that's just the way I want 'em. Sure, we could easily raid the corner and confiscate a few bundles of crack and some chump change, but that's nothin'. They'll just post bond, and reopen the corner in a couple of hours. Obviously, that's not what we want." Detective Smith tried to reason with his young partner.

"Well, what is it that we friggin' want?" Detective

Sullivan shot back. He was full of frustration. “I’ve personally witnessed these son-of-a-bitches rake in every bit of $4,000 in the past two hours, and here I am, struggling to pay my friggin’ mortgage while these drug dealing bastards just blow through money without a care in the world. This is friggin’ ridiculous!”

“I understand your frustrations, Sully. Honestly, I do. However, the fact still remains that the key to shutting down this organization is Michael Brooks. He’s the one that just pulled up in the red Bentley a few minutes ago. He’s the one we want. That cocky sonofabitch right there,” he pointed at Mook.

“Well, what about the other guys? Who are they?”

“The stocky light skinned guy that’s talkin’ to Brooks, his name is Sontino Moreno, and he’s the second in command. The short dark skinned guy with the braids, his name is Tommy Wilson, and the tall brown skinned guy, that’s Rasheed McDaniels.

“According to the Gang Unit, they’re members of the Bloods Street Gang. The Block Boy Bishops to be exact and that fuckin’ Brooks is the ring leader. Do you know that motherfucker supplies weight to damn near every coke block in our district? To make matters worse, our buddies over the bridge in New Jersey are telling me that this bastard is beginning to branch out to Camden and Trenton.”

“Well, shucks, Smitty, that’s interstate trafficking. Isn’t that a federal issue?”

“Sure, it’s a federal issue,” Detective Smith replied, slightly agitated that his partner felt the need to state the obvious. “But fuck the feds! This shit is personal. I’ve been trying to get Brooks off the streets since ‘97, but every time I get my hands on him, that greaseball attorney of his always turn my cases into shit. But not this time, Sully.” He shook his head from side to side and smiled mischievously. “This time around I lucked up and found myself a new friend,” he nodded toward Tommy, “and he’s my ace in the hole.”

*****

The Following Morning...

Sonny was sound asleep, enjoying the comfort of his Tempur-Pedic mattress when he was awakened by the loud shouting of his mother.

"Sontino! Get yo' ass outta that damn bed and pick up the goddamned phone! Riana, I love her to death, but she better stop calling my house so goddamned early."

"Hello," Sonny said, picking up the cordless phone from his nightstand.

"What's up, boo? Why ya mom screamin' on me like that? She be hatin'." Riana stated and then started giggling.

"I don't know," Sonny replied, still bundled under the covers with his face buried in the pillow. "She's always buggin' about somethin'. At the same time, it is early as shit and why ain't you just call my cell phone?"

"Boy, I've been callin' your cell phone since 7 o'clock this morning, and I ain't get nothin' but your voice mail."

"Damn, that's right, I forgot I turned that shit off last night. What's up wit' my baby girl? How you feelin' this morning?"

"I'm good. I was just callin' because me and Erika wanna go and get our hair and nails done, and I need you to bring me some money."

"How much you need?"

"Um, about a stack."

"A thousand dollars? Damn, Riri, what is you try'na do, buy the whole fuckin' salon?"

"No," she laughed. "And you better stop gettin' smart. I wanna buy me a new outfit too."

"A'ight, I'ma give you the money. But that's only because I love you next to ya girl, Erika, you got the best pussy a nigga ever had."

"What?"

"Sike, naw, I'm just fuckin' wit' you," Sonny laughed.

"Yeah, whatever, pussy! Let me find the fuck out! I see the way that you be lookin' at her too."

"Man, whatever. Don't nobody be lookin' at no fuckin' Erika. She ain't even my type." He continued laughing.

"Umm hmm, whatever, nigga. So, when is you comin'?"

"When am I comin'? Do you *really* want me to answer that question?"

"Eeeeew, boy! You are so fuckin' nasty," Riri laughed. "That's all you think about—pussy."

"Naw, I be thinkin' about ya mouth too," Sonny chuckled. "But on some real shit, I'ma be up there in like an hour."

"Alright, I love you, daddy."

"I love you too, ma."

Click!

After placing the cordless phone back on the charger, he rolled over on his back and thought about his future with Riana. She was different from all of the other chicks he was slinging dick to. Riri was his heart. He reached into the ashtray on his nightstand and grabbed the Backwood that he stubbed out the night before. After sparking it up and taking a deep pull, he thought about the day that he first met the love of his life.

January 3, 2008

There was a skating party at the Wow Skating Rink, Tommy and Sheed had gassed him up to go because he wasn't really into the party scene. Especially a party that revolved around roller skating.

On the night of the party, the three of them were fresh to death. They were dipped in butterscotch Timberlands, Seven jeans, white long sleeved shirts, and customized Marc Bucannon leather jackets with 'Bishops' stitched on the back. Sonny's jacket was red with black stitching. Tommy's was white with red stitching. And Sheed's was black with white stitching. The Blood culture was fairly new to the city, so to let it be known that they were Damu, they each had a red bandana hanging from their back right pocket.

When they arrived at the skating rink and saw how jam packed the party was, Sonny was glad that he had came. Unfortunately, none of them knew how to skate, so they posted up at the arcade and played video games.

"Damn, Sonny, lil' buddy over there keep starting at you," said Sheed. He then gestured toward a short, petite, light skinned girl with long, silky, black hair. "She on ya top, bro. You better go over there and bag her."

Sonny smiled at him and used his left hand to lay down his wavy hair. "Nigga, you ain't said nothin' but a mu'fuckin' word."

He casually made his way to the food stand where the girl was waiting for the slice of pizza she had just ordered. He approached her. "What's up, ma? They call me Sonny. Who you?"

He extended his right hand, and she accepted the gesture with a feminine handshake. "My name is Riana, but all of my friends call me Riri."

He smiled, displaying the dimple in his left cheek. "A'ight, Miss Riana, it's nice to meet you. But dig, though, I noticed you was over here looking at me like you knew me or somethin'. So, do I know you from somewhere?"

She looked him up and down. "No, I don't think so, but I was definitely looking at you. I think you're cute, and I'm feelin' the way you and ya mans and 'em is killin' it wit' y'all lil' leather jackets."

"Well, speakin' of cute," he shot back, "you look exotic like a mu'fucka. Whatchu Brazilian or somethin'?"

"No, I'm not Brazilian," she blushed. "My dad is Black, and my mom is Puerto Rican."

"More or less. So, who you here wit'? I know you ain't here by yaself."

"I'm wit' my best friend, Erika. She's over there in the corner talkin' to her boyfriend, Troy." She pointed toward a tall dark skinned girl with an ass like Nicki Minaj and a tall light skinned dude.

"Hold up, you mean to tell me that you come to a party just to to stand around looking cute, while ya home girl in the cut talkin' to her boyfriend?"

She quickly replied with a playful attitude. "I came here to party and have fun like everybody else. I'm just hoping that don't nothin' pop off in here because it's a lot of niggas at this party, and whenever Philly niggas get together for somethin', somebody's always gettin' stomped out or shot the hell up. Especially when they're from different parts of the city, and they all try'na prove who's the hardest."

"Yeah, I know that's right," Sonny concurred. "But we all know that the North get it poppin' the most."

"Oh, so let me guess, you're from North Philly, huh?"

"Without a doubt," he smiled, and then licked his lips seductively. "What part of the city is you from? You look like one of those lil' prissy Mt. Airy chicks."

"Naw, I'm not from Mt. Airy, but you're close. I'm from Crestmont."

"Crestmont? Where the fuck is that?"

"It's the neighborhood right next to the Willow Grove Mall. It's okay out there. It's mostly an all-black neighborhood, and the majority of the people who live there are originally from Philly."

"Oh, a'ight," he nodded his head, and then realized that Riri was looking in the direction of Erika and her boyfriend.

"Ahn ahn, no the fuck he didn't!" she said to herself as she watched Erika crumble to the floor from the blow her boyfriend had just landed on the left side of her face.

She left Sonny at the food stand and skated toward her friend. Unbeknownst to her Sonny was right behind her, and Tommy and Sheed were right behind him.

"Erika, why the fuck is this clown ass nigga puttin' his hands on you like he lost his fuckin' mind?" She helped her off of the floor.

Troy scowled at her, and then folded his arms across his chest. "Yo, mind ya business, Riri. This shit ain't got nothin' to do wit' you."

"It's cool, Riri," Erika said as she rubbed the left side of her face. He's just mad 'cause I quit his cheatin' ass."

"Bitch, you can't quit me!" Troy snapped. "Matter of fact, speakin' of quittin' somethin', you better quit runnin' ya fuckin' mouth 'fore I..."

"Before you what?!" Riri interrupted him, and then got up in his face.

"Bitch, you better back the fuck up 'fore you get the same shit ya girl just got!" Troy snarled, and then he ice-grilled Sonny who was standing directly behind her. "And why the fuck this super save a hoe ass nigga keep lookin' at me like he want somethin'?"

Without saying a word, Sonny pushed Riri out of the way, and hit Troy with a devastating left hook, knocking him out cold. As soon as his body hit the floor, Tommy rushed in and began stomping him in the face, knocking him out and waking him up with every blow.

As Troy laid on the floor blinking his eyes and trying to figure out what had just happened, Sheed spit a straight razor from his mouth, then swooped down and gave him a buck fifty from his ear to his chin. A gory wound appeared on the side of his face and warm blood sprayed everywhere.

The people in the skating rink began to crowd around them, and immediately Sonny thought about the potential consequences of their actions. He looked at Riri, "Yo, I don't know whatchu and ya home girl 'bout to do, but me and my niggas is gettin' the fuck out of here."

She looked at Erika, and then returned her gaze to Sonny. "Shit, we ain't stayin' here either. We going wit' y'all."

From that day forward, Sonny and Riri became extremely close and have been together ever since.

Chapter Two

After getting dressed, eating breakfast, and cleaning his gun, Sonny was ready to start his day. As he was about to leave the house, he stopped at his mother's room to check on her. "Hey, mom, you need anything 'fore I leave?"

"No, baby. I'm good," she replied while smoking a Newport 100 and watching a movie on the Lifetime Network. "Just be careful out there."

She knew the game. Her husband played it well, but just like the majority of the players in the life, it ate him alive. That was a concern she had for her only son, but in the same vein, she knew she couldn't control his actions. He had to live and learn on his own.

When he walked out of the front door and into the blistering heat, he was dipped in a pair of black True Religion shorts, a fresh wife beater, and a pair of black and red Lebron's. An iced-out 'NP' charm hung from his 35" chain, and his iced-out Breitling glittered like a light show. He looked across the street and noticed a dingy individual who resembled a Center City street person was wiping down the 26" rims on his Tahoe. When he realized who it was, he gritted his teeth and ice-grilled the man who at one point in time was the sharpest hustler in the city, his father, Ervin 'Easy Money' Moreno.

"Yo, what is you doin' to my truck?" He barked at his father which broke Easy's concentration.

Easy looked over his shoulder and smiled at him. "Oh, there he go! There he go! North Philly's finest, Lil' Easy Money!" He shouted in a raspy voice and displayed a mouth full of gums.

"Lil' Easy Money?" Sonny retorted. "Look at you, you all dirty and stinkin' and shit. Nigga, I ain't nothin' like you."

Easy dropped the rag he was using to wipe down Sonny's rims and cracked his knuckles. "What the fuck did you just say to me, boy?"

Sonny approached him. "Nigga, you heard me. I ain't nothin' like you."

As soon as Sonny came within reaching distance, Easy wrapped his hands around his neck and applied pressure. "Oh, so ya lil' ass think you a big shot, huh? Ain't got no respect for your own goddamn father? Nigga, I should *break* ya fuckin' neck!"

As he struggled to breathe, Sonny pulled the .357 Sig Sauer that was tucked in the small of his back and pressed the barrel against Easy's temple. "Nigga, you better get the fuck off me 'fore I *rock* ya dumb ass!" He snarled through clenched teeth. "Pussy, I ain't gon' say it again!"

Easy released his grip and with tears in his eyes, he tried to apologize. "Sontino, I'm sorry, man. I'm sorry for everything. I mean, look at me." He held out his arms for emphasis. "I ain't shit no more. I used to run this muthafuckin' city, now look at me. I'm just a *has been* junky." He dropped his arms and shook his head shamefully. "I didn't come over here for this. All I wanted to do was talk to you."

Instead of responding, Sonny removed the gun from his head and used the back of his hand to wipe away the single tear that slid down his right cheek. Easy tried to hug him, but Sonny pushed him away. He hopped in his Tahoe and laid his head against the headrest. Disgusted, he scowled at Easy in the rearview mirror, and thought about the man that he used to be. In particular, his mind traveled back to the day that Easy moved their family out of the hood...

August 18, 1992

It was 2:30 p.m. when a three year old Sonny and Easy pulled up in front of their Reese Street row home in Easy's brand new SL 500. Easy turned down the trunk rattling sounds of Steady B & Cool C's 'The Glamorous Life', and then looked in the back seat where Sonny was playing with his Happy Meal toy.

"What's up, Lil' Easy Money? You good back there?"

"Yes."

"You know that your daddy loves you, right?"

"Yes."

"And you know that your daddy is the boss of the city, right?"

"No!" Sonny laughed and frantically shook his head from side to side.

"No?" Easy looked at him like was crazy. "Well, if your daddy ain't the boss of Philly, then who is?"

"Me!"

"You?" Easy laughed. "Naw, lil' man, we gon' clear this up right now. I'm the boss, and you're the underboss."

Sonny looked at him and smiled from eartoear. "I the underboss, daddy?"

Easy nodded his head up and down, and then honked the horn. A couple of seconds later, his wife, Annette Moreno, emerged from the house in a soft pink Gucci short set and white Gucci Lottos. Her door knocker earrings and gold Rolex sparkled in the Philadelphia sun, and her cinnamon complexion had a natural glow. She was 5' 9", 135 pounds, and had a strong resemblance to the actress, Phylicia Rashad.

She climbed in the Benz and leaned across the center console to give Easy a kiss. She then turned her attention toward the back seat where Sonny was stuffing his mouth with French fries. "Hey, baby."

"Hi, mama. Look." He held up his doll sized Ronald McDonald. "My daddy took me to McDonalds," he bragged.

"I see," she smiled, and then leaned forward to kiss him on the forehead. After stealing a couple of his French fries, she settled into the passenger's seat and returned her focus to Easy. "Alright, now where's the surprise you were tellin' me about?" She asked in reference to the phone conversation they had earlier that day

"Just relax and enjoy the ride." Easy smiled, and then pulled away from the curb.

About forty-five minutes later, they pulled up in front of a huge estate in Upper Dublin, Pennsylvania. "Surprise!" Easy stated with a wide smile spread across his face.

The sight of the 10,000 square foot mansion left Annie mesmerized. Being the city girl she was, she instantly fell in love with the manicured lawn and the tall trees that were spread throughout the property. Her eyes scanned the horseshoe driveway and the luxury cars that occupied the space. She spotted a Range Rover, a Lexus SC 400, a BMW 850, a Porsche 911, and a 5.0 Mustang. Each vehicle was cocaine white and had matching rims and tinted windows.

"Didn't I tell you I was gonna get us out the hood?" Easy smiled at his beautiful wife, and then used the back of his hand to caress her face.

"Yeah, but this—this is just too much. Is this really our new house?"

"Yup," Easy confirmed with pride in his voice. He drove up the driveway and parked behind the Range Rover.

They hopped out the Benz and approached the eight foot high double doors. He placed a key inside of the gold door handle, and led them inside. The first thing to grab their attention was a dual grand staircase that led to a balcony on the second floor and the whitecrystal chandelier that hung from the foyer's twelve foot ceiling.

"Oh, my God! This is so nice." Annie stated, and then stood on her tippy toes to give Easy a kiss.

"Come on," he began walking. "I'm a show y'all around the first floor, and then I'ma take y'all to see the basement. After that, we're going upstairs to the second floor."

When they entered the living room, they were greeted by a black leather sectional that occupied two walls of the room and a 100 inch projector screen that was accompanied by a state of the art sound system. A marble fireplace decorated the third wall and on the forth wall there was a huge fish tank they could look through and see the dining room on the other side. The fish tank was decorated with colorful stones and small castles and three miniature sized sharks were swimming back and forth as if they didn't have a care in the world.

"Look, mama," Sonny pointed at the fish tank. "Do you see the fishies?"

"Yes, baby, I see them. Aren't they nice?"

"Yes."

After showing them the 'White Room', Easy took them into the kitchen where a granite island was positioned in the center of the room. In addition, there were stainless steel appliances, marble countertops, and mahogany cabinets that were stockpiled with groceries.

Next, he led them downstairs to the basement where there was wall to wall carpeting, a fully stocked bar, a regulation sized pool table, and three arcade game systems.

"So, how do y'all like the new house so far?" he asked.

"Bae, I love it!" Annie smiled.

"Me too, daddy." Sonny nodded his head. "I like it a lot."

"A'ight." Easy began walking toward the back of the basement. "Let's go upstairs so I can show y'all the second floor."

"Bae, why are you going that way?" Annie asked, pointing toward the staircase behind her. "The stairs are that way."

'I know, but we ain't takin' the stairs. We takin' the elevator."

'The elevator?" She asked in disbelief.

Sonny raised his hands in the air and playfully shouted, "Yeah, mama! We takin' the elebator." He looked at Easy. "Right, daddy?"

Easy chuckled. "Yeah, lil' man, we takin' the elebator." He mimicked the way his son mispronounced the word.

When the elevator reached the second floor, the doors slid open, and they stepped off and into the exercise room. The floors were padded and the walls were covered with mirrors. There was a punching bag, a speed bag, universal weights, a treadmill, and two exercise bikes.

"Ahn ahn, bae. You got us an exercise room, too?"

Easy nodded his head. "Yeah, so that way I can teach Sontino how to box, and he can grow up to be the next Holyfield. Ain't that right, lil' man?"

"Yes," he laughed, then bounced around, doing his best rendition of Evander as he threw a left hook and a right uppercut.

"A'ight, now I'ma show y'all the bedrooms." He led them to the master bedroom, which was more akin to a small apartment. There was a 'His & Hers' closet and bathroom, a jacuzzi, and sliding doors that led to a balcony overlooking the Olympic sized swimming pool in the backyard. A circular king sized bed sat in the center of the large room, and it was covered with silk sheets and a mink blanket. There was also a 62 inch television, a sound system, and a suede loveseat that was positioned against the back wall.

Next, he led them down the hallway to Sonny's room. The walls were painted 'Ninja Turtle' green, and life sized stickers of Michelangelo, Donatello, Leonardo, and Raphael were stuck on every wall. His bedspread and curtains had a Ninja Turtles theme and a slew of Ninja Turtles action figures were stockpiled in the middle of the floor. As soon as Sonny laid eyes on his new room, he placed his left hand on his forehead, and then fell to the carpet, acting as though he'd just fainted. Easy and Annie burst out laughing.

Back To August 2012

Unfortunately, that was then, and this is now. After becoming a success in the drug game, Easy fell victim to the same drug that made him a millionaire by the age of twenty-five. *Crack!* By 1996, he'd lost everything. He'd lost the money, the cars, the mansion, and ultimately his family.

After coming to grips with his nostalgic memories, Sonny

started the ignition and pulled away from the curb. As he turned the corner and darted up Susquehanna Avenue, Easy wiped away his tears and looked at the impoverished house that his family once again called home. His eyes wandered to the second floor, and he noticed that Annie was staring at him through the window. Embarrassed, he lowered his head and walked away.

*****

When Sonny pulled up in front of Riri's house, he noticed her mother's car was gone. He remembered it was Saturday and assumed she spent the night over at her boyfriend's house. He climbed out the Tahoe and knocked on the front door. A second later, the door creaked open, and Riri was standing before him in her birthday suit.

Damn, this mu'fucka bad, he said to himself as his dick grew rock hard.

Riana was a dime to say the least. Aside from bearing a striking resemblance to WNBA star, Skylar Diggins, she had a perky pair of B cups with pinkish nipples, a toned stomach, thick thighs, and a nice little bubble butt that fit her body to perfection.

"So, what's up, daddy? You just gon' stand there lookin' cute, or are you gonna come inside and let me do somethin' strange to you?" She spun around and bent over to give him a clear view of her fat pussy.

He stepped inside of the house and locked the front door behind him. Riri stood up straight and turned around to face him. "I love you, boo."

"I love you too, ma." He pulled her against his body and kissed her passionately. She led him over to the sofa, pulled down his shorts and boxers, and then pushed him on the sofa. She straddled him across his lap.

While continuing to kiss one another, she reached for his throbbing dick and directed it slowly inside of her creamy tunnel. "Ummmmm!" she moaned from the pleasure and pain she was feeling. Increasing her pace, she rode him like a jockey on a thoroughbred. “Oh, my God! Umm, I love this dick!” She cried out.

The feeling of his 9 inch dick was driving her insane. She grabbed the back of his head and guided his mouth to her right nipple.

“Boo, I’m ‘bout to cum! I’m cummin', daddy! Ahhhhhnnnnn!” She whined as she released her juices all over his shaft.

With his dick still inside of her, he picked her up and carried her over to the wall that separated the living room from the dining room. He slipped out of her, and then put her down.

“Bend over and put ya head between ya ankles.” She did as he instructed. “Now, lean ya back against the wall.”

When she got in this position, her pussy sprouted from in between her thighs, and it was so wet that Sonny could see her vaginal secretions dripping onto the carpet. He knelt down behind her and feasted on her asshole as if it were his last meal on earth. He then buried his tongue deep inside of her pussy, and professionally dipped it in and out and up and down her slit. Simultaneously, he reached his hand around her leg and used his middle finger to massage her clitoris.

“Yeah, daddy! Eat this pussy! Umm!”

After a couple minutes of getting her pussy sucked and licked, she craved the feeling of penetration. “Fuck me, daddy! I need to feel you so bad.”

Obediently, he stood to his feet, crouched on top of her, and buried his shaft deep inside of her pussy. “Damn, I love this shit!” He groaned as he slammed his thighs against her ass like a jackhammer, his long hard strokes were making her cum instantly.

“Ahhhhhnnnnn!” She cried out. “Sontino, why you doin’ this to me?”

“This my pussy, right?”

“Yeeeeeaaaaah!” She moaned. “Fuck yeah, this ya pussy!”

'A'ight, then! I'm a hit it like I wanna hit it!" He replied. His words matching every stroke.

After a hard ten minutes of fucking in that position, his body tensed up, and he squeezed off deep inside of her.

*****

An hour later, they were lying in her bed, smoking a Backwood and watching the movie, *Love Jones*. Her head was resting on his chest, and he was running his fingers through her hair. "Boo, is everything okay?" she asked.

The question caught him off guard. "Yeah, everything's good. Why?"

"Because earlier you was beatin' up my pussy like it stole somethin' from you, and the only time you be gettin' like that is when something's bothering you. So, don't be hittin' me with that everything's good shit. I know you, and I can tell when something's wrong. So, what's up?"

He took a long pull on the Backwood, and then stubbed it out in the ashtray. After taking a deep breath, he began telling her about his confrontation with Easy.

"I ran into my pops this mornin' and we went through somethin'."

"Somethin' like what?'

"Somethin' like that nigga tried to choke me out, and I had to put that mu'fuckin' heat in his face."

"Ahn ahn, boo! Are you serious?"

"Yo, I'm dead serious."

"Well, I'm not gon' get in the middle of y'all beef 'cause at the end of the day he's still your dad."

"Man, fuck that nigga. I shoulda shot his crack headed ass."

She shook her head in disbelief, and then chose her next words carefully. "Alright, I can understand that you and him don't see eye to eye, but at the same time, you gotta consider all the circumstances. From whatchu told me, back in the day, your dad was a major dude, and he gave you and Ms. Annie everything. Now, look at the way things turned out. That shit has to really fuck wit' him, Sontino. It has to," she continued while shaking her head. "Instead of wasting time hatin' him, why don't you do somethin' to help him get back on his feet?"

"Yo, fuck that nigga! Didn't nobody tell his weak ass to start smokin' on that glass dick and lose everything we had!"

Riana couldn't believe her ears. "Hold up, you mean to tell me that your ill feelings toward your dad are based on material shit?"

"Naw, Ri, it's deeper than that. The fact that we lost everything and had to move back to the hood was just the tip of the iceberg. When this nigga started gettin' high, it got to the point that he would whip my mom's ass if she didn't give him her money. On top of that, this nut ass nigga used to steal the food out the refrigerator, and sell it to get high. It's like, what type of mu'fucka would steal the food out the mouths of his own family?" He shook his head in contempt.

"Damn, boo, I didn't even know all of that." She stated in a soft tone.

"Well, *now* do you see why I feel the way I feel about him?"

"I guess so, but at the end of the day that doesn't change the fact that he's still your father.

Instead of responding to her last statement, he just lay back on the pillow and stared up at the ceiling.

Chapter Three

A Week Later

Sonny, Sheed, and Tommy were chilling at Mook's mansion in Dover, Delaware, watching their favorite movie, *Paid in Full.*

"Yo, I love this fuckin' movie, but that nigga 'Po went out like a bitch!" Sheed said to nobody in particular. "I don't even know why Killa Cam played the role of a rat ass nigga!"

"Yeah," Tommy agreed. "But at the same time, that nigga 'Po was on some straight up goon shit. You still gotta give the nigga *some* type of credit."

Sonny screwed up his face. "Yo, what the fuck is you talking 'bout, Blood? That nigga's a rat! Point. Blank. Period! Plus, he killed his mans, Rich, on some snake shit. That nigga ain't gangsta. That nigga's a fuckin' clown." Sonny snapped with pure disgust in his voice.

He also made mental note to keep his eyes on Tommy. He figured if he could give props to a nigga like Alpo, then maybe he possessed some of the same qualities.

Tommy smiled it off and changed the subject. "Anyway. Hey, yo, Sheed, whatchu got in this Backwood, Blood? This shit taste like dirt." He stubbed out the cherry on the spliff, and then looked to Sheed for an answer.

"Well, excuse me balla. Y'all niggas wanna be spendin' all that bread on that loud, knowin' damn well y'all were smokin' that Reggie Bush like everybody else. Now that niggas is gettin' at a lil' bit of money, y'all try'na front. Yo, y'all niggas fucks me up." Sheed laughed, and then reached into the ashtray to retrieve the stubbed out Backwood.

As they continued watching the movie, Mook appeared on the balcony that was positioned above the living room. He smiled down on his little homies in admiration. He loved the three of them to death. There was nothing he wouldn't do for them. Sonny was like the son he never had, and ever since he was seven years old, he raised him to be a loyal soldier, grooming him to be the boss he was destined to become.

He loved Sheed for his aggressiveness and for the loyalty he showed to the team. He loved Tommy because he was a survivor. At the age of two, his father received a life sentence for murdering his mother and although the odds were stacked against him, he made it through the struggle and was now a certified 'Block Boy'.

"Soowoo!" Mook shouted, demanding their attention.

"Bang! Bang!" They replied in unison.

"I called y'all out here to bring y'all up to speed with the latest developments in the family," he stated with a tone of authority. "First and foremost, y'all days of hustlin' on the block are over. From this day forward, everybody in this room is his own boss and will conduct himself accordingly. As for myself, I'll remain at the head of our roundtable, but only as the supplier. It's a new day, my niggas. Operation *Lock the City* starts now. Are there any questions?"

"Yeah," said Sonny. "I've got a couple of questions. First, if we ain't fuckin' wit' the block no more, then I'm assuming we gon' be pushin' weight. Is that right? Secondly, what's new? Why the sudden change of heart?"

These were the exact same questions Mook was expecting him to ask. He walked toward the end of the balcony and descended the spiral staircase. "Yo, come wit' me outside. I gotta show y'all something."

He led the trio out of the front door and over to his five car garage. He reached inside of his Prada slacks and retrieved a remote control. After pressing the open button, three of the garage doors slid open, revealing three snow white Mercedes Benz SL 550s. Mook smiled at his little homies, knowing his next words would change their lives forever.

"For the past five years, y'all niggas stuck by me and believed in my dreams of locking down North Philly. Now, it's time for me to believe in y'all. Together, we gon' lock down the entire city. I never told y'all this, but a couple of years ago I started fuckin' wit' this new connect. He's a Columbian nigga from Miami. He recently made a move that put him in position to sell me bricks at $20,000 apiece. The only catch is that I grab 300 at a time.

"It's 30 bricks inside the trunks of these Benzes. Right now, niggas in the city is sellin' bricks of garbage for $42,000. I'ma front y'all 30 bricks of pure Columbian fish scale for $30,000 a whop, and I suggest that y'all corner the market, and sell 'em for $35,000 apiece. That way y'all can each make a $5,000 profit off of every brick. Once again, do y'all have any questions?"

"Yeah, I got a question," Sheed spoke up. "We ain't never sold weight before, so obviously we ain't got no clientele. How you expect us to move this shit?"

"That's a good question," Mook shot back, then rubbed his hands together like Birdman. "This is how y'all gon' move it. Right now, y'all got 30 bricks of pure cocaine, which means y'all got the best coke in the city. Now, when you add that to the fact that y'all gon' have the cheapest prices, niggas gon' be breakin' they necks to link up wit' y'all. At $35,000, they' gon' be savin' every bit of seven racks, so trust me, the circumstances will dictate the flow of revenue. I can guarantee that y'all won't have any problems movin' the work. It's marketing, baby boy. Straight up marketing."

"A'ight, Mook, I hear you, but did you consider the fact that certain mu'fuckas ain't gon' be feelin' our movement? Especially, when they playas stop callin' to re-up" Tommy pointed out to Mook.

"Of course I considered that, and I came to the conclusion that niggas gon' have to roll wit' the Block Boys or get rolled the fuck over," Mook replied. "Plus, the only nigga in the city that's in a position to really feel the effects of our movement is that ol' head, Grip. I already holla'd at him and made him an offer that he can't refuse. If he accepts the offer, then that's good money. If he doesn't," he shrugged his shoulders, "fuck it! We gon' make him wish that he did."

Sonny remained quiet and absorbed everything that was being discussed. He figured if he moved 30 keys at $35,000 a piece that would amount to $1,050,000, and after paying Mook, he would be left with $150,000. He realized if he ran through a shipment in a month's time, in one year, he would be sitting on $1,800,000. He also recognized the only downside to the equation was Grip.

At the age of seventy-two, Grip had become the cocaine king of Philly, and he ruled with an iron fist. He was the boss of *The Black Mafia* and his young buls, *The Grip Boys*, were ruthless. Their reputation alone was enough to make the average nigga fall in line, but in Sonny's mind, he wasn't the average nigga. For as long as he could remember, he was bred to go hard, and he'd be damned if he let another nigga stand in the way of him getting money.

Mook looked at him and wondered what his favorite young bul was thinking. "What's poppin', Skoobie? You good?"

"Yeah, I'm gucci," Sonny responded. "What's up wit' them Benzes, though? Are they for us?" He asked with a Kool-Aid smile.

"Yeah, they for y'all," Mook answered. "Y'all earned 'em. When you a boss, you gotta look like a boss, and there is no better way to do it than to come through the hood in somethin' super husky. So, yeah," he pulled out three sets of keys. "They a gift from me to y'all."

He handed them their keys, and then watched as they examined their new whips. Each car was sitting on 22" rims wrapped in Pirellis tires and were equipped with an AMG kit. The interiors were fully loaded with black leather and white piping, and the seats had the word *Bishops* stitched into the headrest. They climbed inside of their cars and started the engines.

Vrrrrm!

After adjusting his seat and mirrors, Sonny looked at

Sheed with a devilish grin. “Yo, how you feelin’, Blood?”

“Like a mu’fuckin’ Block Boy, nigga. Brrrrrat!”

“Tommy, how you feelin’, Five?”

“Soowoo!” he replied.

At the sight of them all amped up, the only thing Mook could do was smile.

“Hey, yo, y’all niggas be safe drivin’ up that highway. Remember, from here on out, we takin’ this shit to the next level. It’s either go hard or go hard, there is no going home. Make sure y’all hit me when y’all get back to the city. Soowoo!”

“Bang! Bang!” They replied in unison.

*****

While driving up Interstate 95, Sonny had one thing on his mind, his future. All he had was his mom, Riana, and his team. He knew he was gambling with his life by accepting those thirty keys, but he had a *fuck it* mentality. If that was the only way he could get his family back to where they used to be, so be it.

*****

As soon as Tommy entered the city, he pulled into a gas station, and grabbed his cell phone from the passenger’s seat. He scrolled through his contact list and stopped on Detective Smith’s number. He pressed the call button, and then held the phone to his ear.

Ring! Ring! Ring!

“Hello,” Detective Smith answered.

“Yo, it’s me, Tommy. I just left Mook, and he gave me somethin’ that’s gonna blow ya mind.”

“Oh, yeah? Somethin’ like what?”

“Somethin’ like that nigga just fronted me two keys,” Tommy lied. He figured he could turn in two of the keys and keep the remaining twenty-eight for himself.

"Where are you?"

"I'm in South Philly."

Detective Smith glanced at his watch and saw that it was only 11:30 a.m. "Fuck it, meet me at our spot in an hour."

Click!

*****

When Tommy pulled into the parking lot of The Oak Lane Diner, all he could think about was betraying his team. He didn't want to do it, but in his selfish mind, he had no other choice. About three months ago, Detective Smith pulled him over for a routine traffic stop. However, instead of Tommy enduring the normal procedures, he was removed from his car, handcuffed, and placed in the back seat of Detective Smith's unmarked car.

After two minutes of watching the detective illegally search his car, he rested his head against the back window, and closed his eyes.

This dickhead ain't doin' nothin' but wastin' his time, he thought to himself. *It ain't like he's gonna find somethin'.*

A few minutes later, Detective Smith returned to his unmarked car with a black 9mm clutched in his right hand. "Hey, asshole! Look what I found under the driver's seat." The detective smiled.

"Yo, that shit ain't mines!" Tommy protested.

"Sure it is," the detective shot back. "And your black ass is under arrest."

After being transported to police headquarters at 8th and Race Street sitting in an interrogation room for well over twenty-four hours without anything to eat or drink, Tommy grew weaker mentally. Due to a prior felony conviction for possession of a controlled substance with the intent to deliver, he knew that a gun case would fall under the federal mandatory sentencing statute.

Damn, I'm fucked, he thought to himself.

An hour later, Detective Smith entered the interrogation

room with a huge smile spread across his face. He held up the brown folder that was in his left hand, using it to fan himself.

"Whew, it's hot in here, huh Tommy? It seems as though you done hopped outta the frying pan and landed head first into the fire. According to this rap sheet, you were convicted a few years back for possession with the intent to deliver. Awwww, man, that's a fucking felony," he said sarcastically, then lowered his voice a few octaves. "And now you're being charged with the possession of a firearm." He was doing his best to antagonize Tommy and it seemed to be working. "Now, you know the feds done went and made a mandatory minimum of fifteen years in prison for situations like yours, right?"

"Yo, this is some straight up bullshit! That fuckin' gun ain't mines!" Tommy yelled. "You planted that shit in my fuckin' car!"

"Awwww, come on, Tommy. You know that's not gonna hold up in court. It'll be your word against mines." The detective laughed. "You won't stand a chance," he continued, and then took a seat at the interrogation table. "Look," he said in a controlled voice. "I know all about you. I know about Sontino. I know about Rasheed, and I know about your big homie, Michael Brooks. You niggers call yourselves 'The Block Boy Bishops', and your gang is a faction of the New York Bloods. The sergeant from the Gang Task Force has been keeping tabs on you guys and trust me that's another pile of shit you done stepped in." He shook his head from side to side.

"Have you ever heard of the RICO law? The dectective questioned sarcastically, laughing. Awwww man, you're fucked. Well, not completely fucked. I've got a proposition for you. Now, either you can accept it," he shrugged his shoulders, "or you can spend the next fifteen years in a federal penitentiary getting fucked in the ass by a gang of California Crips. The choice is yours, Tommy. What's it gonna be?"

"What kind of proposition is you talking 'bout?"

"A proposition called Michael Brooks. I want that

sonofabitch nailed to a friggin' cross."

Begrudgingly, Tommy accepted Detective Smith's proposition, and for the past three months, he'd been helping him build a case against Mook.

When he entered The Oak Lane Diner, he spotted the detective sitting in a booth, eating a plate of barbecued ribs, potato salad, and green beans. He approached him, and took a seat on the other side of the table. Detective Smith wiped the corners of his mouth with a napkin, and then gulped down a glass of Pepsi.

"Alright, now what's this shit about Brooks fronting you two keys?"

*****

Later that day, at police headquarters, Detective Smith was sitting at desk, drinking a cup of coffee, and going over his file on Mook.

Knock! Knock!

He looked up from his file and turned his attention to the door. "Who is it?"

"It's Detective Sullivan."

"Come in," he said, and then laid the file on his desktop.

Detective Sullivan entered the office with a goofy look on his face. "I just received your Email. What's the news on the Brooks' case?" He asked, while taking a seat by the door.

"I think we've hit the jackpot, Sully." Detective Smith smiled at him. "I met with my informant. According to him, Brooks fronted him a kilogram of cocaine, and guess what else?" He held up a brown paper bag. "I've got it right here."

"That's excellent, Smitty. Now that we've got our evidence, all we've gotta do is get a judge to sign off on an arrest warrant."

"It's not that simple, Sully. At this point, our case isn't exactly airtight."

"What do you mean it isn't airtight? That piece of shit just gave our informant a key of coke. We've got it right here." He pointed at the bag. "All we've gotta do is present our case to a judge, and he'll have no other choice but to issue an arrest warrant," Detective Sullivan propounded.

"I'm sorry to say it, Sully, but it's not that simple. We don't have any jurisdiction over that particular transaction. According to the informant, Brooks gave him the cocaine in the State of Delaware. Therefore, no judge in his right mind is gonna sign off on a warrant for a crime that was committed outside of his jurisdiction."

Detective Sullivan rubbed his forehead, exuding frustration. "Alright, well, what's the next step?"

"I told the informant to lay low for about a month, and then we'll give him the buy money to pay Brooks. All he has to do is get Brooks to come back to the city to collect his money and bring him an additional kilo. If he does," Detective Smith smiled and rubbed his hands together, "we're gonna tar and feather his ass!"

"Now that, Smitty, is one hell of a plan. I've got one question, though. Why are you still holding on to the cocaine? Shouldn't it be tagged and processed into the evidence room?"

"Sure it's gonna get tagged and processed." *However*, Detective Smith thought to himself, *the other key that you don't know about is getting tagged and processed into my retirement fund!*

Chapter Four

In Crestmont, Riana was sitting on her mother's front porch staring at the results from her home pregnancy test.

Damn, I can't believe I'm knocked up. Sontino gon' have to slow his ass down 'cause I ain't raising no baby by my lonesome. Fuck that! she thought to herself. She loved the shit out of Sonny, but the way he was living had her afraid. *Either he gon' slow his ass down and leave these streets alone, or I'm getting an abortion. It's as simple as that!*

While she was caught up in her thoughts, a snow white Mercedes Benz SL 550 pulled up in front of her house and just sat there with the engine running.

Who the fuck is that? she asked herself, while admiring the hottest car she'd ever seen. *Whoever it is, why they stop in front of my house, and why are they just sittin' there wit' the engine running? Ahn ahn, this shit don't seem right. I'm takin' my black ass in the house.*

As she stood to her feet and reached for the doorknob, a familiar voice said, "Damn, beautiful, where you going?"

She spun around just as the tinted driver's side window retracted into the door. "Sontino? Boy, whatchu doin' in that car?"

Sonny didn't respond. Instead, he opened the driver's side door and hopped out the Benz in a white linen Gucci set and a pair Gucci soft bottoms. His ears were decorated with five carat diamonds and an iced-out Rolex was wrapped around his left wrist. As Riana approached him, the fragrance of his CK cologne coupled with his GQ appearance made her pussy moist.

"Damn, boo, you lookin' sexy as shit. Whose car is this?" She asked, giving him a kiss as she wrapped her arms around his waist.

"This my new shit. You like it?"

"Hell yeah! This jawn husky as shit." She broke their

embrace, and then gave the car a thorough inspection. “Now, you know I'm gettin' the Tahoe, right?”

"Yeah, you got it. It’s out in Delaware, though. I left it at Mook's house. But dig, mommy, I got somethin’ for you.” He led her to the back of the Benz and popped the trunk. “Those three boxes right there, they for you.”

She looked at the boxes and couldn't decide which one to open first. The box that was bigger than the other two was covered in gray Gucci print, it sparked her interest. However, another one of the boxes was from Jimmy Choo, and the smaller box was from Tiffany’s.

She looked at him and asked, “Which one should I open first?”

“I don’t know.” He shrugged his shoulders. “Open the big one.”

She did as he suggested and was blown away by a white, one piece strapless Gucci dress. “Awwww, Sontino, I love it!” she said as she held it up to her body. “This is so pretty. Thank you.” Next, she opened the shoe box and discovered a pair of white Jimmy Choo shoes with spaghetti straps. “Ahn ahn, Sontino, these ain’t even out yet. They don't come out ‘til the fall.” She kissed him on the lips, and then gave her new pumps a closer examination.

“Yo, that shit ain’t ‘bout nothin’,” he replied in a nonchalant manner, even though he was happy to see his queen with a smile on her face. “But yo, you ain’t even open up the box from Tiffany’s yet.”

When she opened up the rectangular jewelry box, she was momentarily blinded by the white diamonds that smothered a heart shaped pendent and a platinum necklace.

“Oh, my God! Oh, my God! Oh, my God!” She screamed as she hopped up and down. “This is so beautiful, Sontino. Thank you!”

Sonny smiled. “It’s beautiful like you, ma. Now, go in the house and get dressed. We ‘bout to party like rock stars.”

As she carried her gifts into the house, he grabbed the gym bag with the thirty keys from his backseat, and then crept to her bedroom. He opened the footlocker that was at the bottom of her closet, and stashed the work inside. He then went over to her dresser and pulled out the bottom drawer, where unbeknownst to Riana, was $100,000. He counted the ten stacks of money, each containing $10,000, and then put the drawer back in its place.

*****

Later That Night…

The people standing in front of the Plush Nightclub were interrupted by the thumping sounds of Lil Wayne and Cory Gunz's *6 Foot, 7 Foot*, and the sparkling white Benz that pulled up in front of the entrance bumping the sound.

"Damn, who the fuck is that?" A thick, dark skinned girl asked her friend.

"Girl, I don't even know, but that Benz is doin' the pussy," her girlfriend replied. "Okaaayyy!" They both smiled and gave each other a high five, straight up hood rat style.

Inside of the SL 550, Riana killed the ignition and climbed out looking immaculate. Her new dress was hugging her body as if it were painted on. It lifted the bottom of her ass and stopped mid-thigh, making the spaghetti straps on her Jimmy Choo shoes look ten times hotter. She casually walked around the front of the Benz and opened the passenger's side door for Sonny. When he stepped out of the car, the lights from the club's sign made the diamonds in his ears shine so brightly that the people waiting in line could hardly see his face.

"Oooooh, ain't that the bul that play for the Eagles?" The dark skinned girl asked her friend.

"Naw, that's the bul, Sonny, from Reese and Susquehanna," her girlfriend shot back. "Damn, that fine ass nigga done stepped his mutha'fuckin' game up!" She looked at him and waved. "Okay, Sonny. I see you, booboo."

He smiled at her, and then locked hands with Riana. Together, they walked past the line, around the metal detectors, and headed straight for the V.I.P.

*****

The Following Morning…

Back at the Marriot, in the presidential suite, Riana was sound asleep. She was exhausted from a night of clubbing and receiving the best sex she'd ever had in her twenty-one years of living. That was until Sonny awakened her with the texture of his tongue sliding across her clitoris.

"Uhhhhnnn!" She moaned as he gently licked and sucked on her love button. "I'm 'bout to cum, daddy!" She moaned out after just a few minutes of his talented swirl action. "Put it in me. I wanna feel you inside of me," she whined.

He obeyed her command and buried his manhood deep inside of her. After twenty minutes of intense love making, they laid in bed, holding one another. Her head was resting on his muscular chest, and his fingers were running through her silky hair and massaging her scalp. She lifted her head and looked him in the eyes.

"Boo, you know I love you, right?"

"Yo, why would you even ask me somethin' like that? Of course I know you love me."

"Alright, well, what I'm about to say is straight from the heart, so don't take it the wrong way."

He sat up and rested his back against the padded headboard. "A'ight, I'm listening."

"Yesterday, while I was getting dressed, I found the gym bag that you put in your footlocker. When I looked inside, and yes I looked inside of it, I saw all of that work. I was like, damn. When is enough gonna be enough? I know you got enough paper put up, so why do you keep fuckin' wit' this shit? Why do you insist on gambling wit' ya life?"

He sighed, "Look, I dig where you comin' from and all that, but I gotta plan. All I need is a year to do my thing, and I can get my family back to where we used to be. I just need for you to trust me on this, Riri. All I need is one year, and I'm done."

"Boo, I'm not try'na overstep my boundaries or nothin', but how much paper you got saved up?"

"Naw, you ain't oversteppin' ya boundaries because we in this together. You my mu'fuckin' dawg. What's mines is yours. But to answer ya question, we got a lil' over $100,000 in the tuck."

"A *$100,000?* You mean to tell me that's not enough for you to walk away from this shit now?"

He shook his head and looked at her like she was crazy. "Yo, $100,000 ain't shit! I can't hold us down the way I want to wit' no punk ass $100,000!"

"Sontino, I don't care about none of this material shit. Especially at the cost of losin' you. All I need is you, can't you see that? All *we* need is you!"

"*We*? Whatchu mean *we*?"

She grabbed his hand and placed it on her stomach. "I'm pregnant, Sontino. I found out yesterday, and I'm afraid that I'ma end up in this situation by myself." She laid her head on his lap and began to cry.

"Come on, bae, don't cry." He lifted her head and wiped away her tears. "I'ma always be here for you. I promise." He kissed her on the forehead, and then wrapped his arms around her. "Just give me one more year, and I swear to God, I'm done."

*****

After sleeping most of the day away, they drove to his house to tell his mom the good news. When they walked through the front door, they were immediately blown away by the smell of lasagna and garlic bread.

"Hey, y'all." Annie smiled from the kitchen. "I hope y'all

are hungry 'cause I'm in here doin' the damn thang."

Sonny and Riana laughed.

"And Riri," she looked at Riana and placed her hand on her hip. "I hope you ain't mad at me for diggin' in that ass the other day, but you know I don't like nobody callin' my house early in the mornin'."

"My bad, Ms. Annie," Riana replied with an embarrassed smile. "It won't happen again."

"Yeah right," Annie laughed. "Now, I know you don't expect me to believe that? Sontino got yo' ass floatin' on cloud nine, and you got to nerve to stand here talking 'bout you ain't gon' be callin' here at all hours of the night lookin' for his ass. Shit, I was young once. I know how y'all young girls get."

Sonny and Riana continued laughing at her.

"Now, come in here and get ya'selves somethin' to eat. I hope y'all are hungry."

"Oh, she's hungry a'ight." Sonny smiled, and then placed his hand on her stomach. "She's eatin' for two."

"Riri, you're pregnant?" Annie asked with a voice full of excitement.

"Yeah!" She smiled and nodded her head up and down. "I found out yesterday."

Annie walked over and gave her a big hug. "Congratulations, y'all!" She kissed Riana on the cheek, and then felt her stomach. "I hope it's a girl. Now, don't get me wrong, I'll take whatever God gives us. I'm just prayin' it's a girl. Lord knows I've always wanted me a daughter."

*****

An hour later, Sonny and Riana were lying on his bed watching the movie *Jason's Lyric*. As Allen Payne and Jada Pinkett were rolling around in the grass butt ass naked, Sonny's iPhone vibrated on his nightstand.

"Yo," he answered.

"Sonny, what's bangin', Blood? It's Mook. Where are you at?"

"That Five, you already know. But yo, I'm at the spot right now. What's up?"

"I holla'd at the ol' head, Grip, this mornin' and we havin' a sit down at the T.G.I.Friday's on City Line Ave. I need you to roll wit' me."

"A'ight, like what time?"

"Around eight o'clock."

"A'ight, well, where are you at right now?"

"I'm at the house, relaxin'."

"A'ight, I'm 'bout to slide through so I can pick up the Tahoe, and I'm bringin' Riri wit' me so she can drive it back."

"A'ight, my nigga, I'ma see y'all when y'all get here. Soowoo!"

"Bang! Bang!"

*****

It was a little after eight o'clock when Sonny and Mook pulled into the parking lot of T.G.I.Fridays. After smoking the remainder of their Kush filled Backwood, they climbed out of the Bentley and casually strolled into the restaurant. They requested a seat in the back corner, and were immediately accommodated. From this position, they had a clear view of the entire dining room, most importantly the restaurant's entrance.

"Would you gentlemen like anything to drink until you're ready to place your orders?" Their waitress asked.

"Yeah," Mook answered. "Lemme get a pina colada."

"And you, sir." She turned to Sonny and smiled. "Would you like anything to drink?"

"Yeah, lemme get the same thing my mans just ordered, and you can get me some mozzarella sticks, too."

The waitress wrote down their orders. "Coming right up," she smiled, and then walked away from the table.

"So, whatchu think?" Sonny asked while cracking his knuckles. "You think this nigga gon' take the offer or what?"

"I ain't sure, Blood. If he does, then everybody gon' be able to get money in peace, but if he doesn't, then you already know what it's hittin' for."

"Hey, yo, there the nigga go right there." Sonny nodded his head in the direction of an older light skinned man with slicked back wavy hair and a salt and pepper beard. At 72 years old, with a strict diet and workout regimen, Grip appeared to be closer to his late fifties. He was 6'2" and approximately 165 pounds, and his broad shoulders and chest gave him the look of a retired prize fighter. He was draped in a French vanilla linen suit and a pair of chocolate crocodile boots. A huge diamond ring was sparkling on his right pinky, and a cocky expression was written on his face. As he stood at the entrance with two of his goons directly behind him, he scanned the room until his eyes locked on Sonny and Mook in the far corner. He adjusted his pinky ring, and then headed toward their table with his goons following closely behind.

When he reached the table, Mook gave the old man the respect he deserved. He stood to his feet and embraced him with a firm handshake. He knew that Grip was cut from a legendary cloth, *The Black Mafia*, and had undeniably paved the way for hustlers such as himself.

Throughout the sixties and seventies, The Black Mafia not only controlled the streets of Philadelphia, they also had a strong influence on other cities such as New York, New Jersey, Chicago, and Detroit. However, when the eighties rolled around, the majority of them were either dead or serving life sentences, and in this day and age there were only a handful of them still on the streets. Grip was one of them. A stone cold gangster. He was as sharp as tack and as vicious as a wolverine. He maintained a stronghold on Philadelphia's underworld, and he felt that after five decades of putting in work, he'd be damned if he let some young niggas alter the way he made his money.

"Grip, I'm glad you could make it." Mook greeted him, and then gestured toward a seat at the table. "Here, have a seat. I was hopin' we could relax a lil' bit, and then get down to business."

Sonny looked him up and down. He was sizing him up from his salt and pepper hair to his blue eyes.

Man, I hope this old mu'fucka accepts our offer. It'll be a goddamn shame if he survived in the game for this long, just to have me exterminate his old ass, he thought to himself.

Grip locked eyes with Sonny, and his heart skipped a beat. *Nah, it can't be*, he thought to himself. He then returned his gaze to Mook, "Who's this?"

"That's my young bul, Sonny. He's my number one soldier."

"Yeah," Grip replied in his deep, raspy voice. "Well, these are two of my street generals. This is Smack," he gestured toward the medium built, brown skinned man that was standing to his left. "And that's Biggs," he turned to his right where the tall, chubby, brown skinned man was standing with a blank expression on his face.

Grip took a seat at the opposite end of the table and folded his arms across his chest. "Alright, let's get down to business. There's no time for pleasure. What's this deal of a lifetime you're so eager to tell me about?"

"A'ight, Grip, it's like this—I know you been doin' ya thing for the longest, and I respect that. However, it's a new day and time, and I was hopin' you could assist my movement." Mook stated, while staring him in his unflinching eyes.

"I'm listening."

"I'm in a position to supply you at $28,000 a key, but I would need you grab nothin' less than a 100 per shipment.

Is this nigga crazy? Grip thought to himself. *Shit, I'm getting my keys for $20,000 a piece, and that's including what I pay to have them shipped into the country. And 100 per shipment? I wouldn't waste my time with nothing less than a*

1,000. He cracked his knuckles. "So, what's the quality of the product?"

"It's pure Columbian raw. It's never been stepped on. You could easily put a one on one, and still have the best product in the city."

Grip calmly removed himself from the table, and motioned for Smack and Biggs to follow suit. "Give me some time to think it over, and I'll get back to you as soon as I reach a decision." He turned his attention to Sonny. "Hey, young fella, is Ervin Moreno your father?"

At the mention of Easy's government name, Sonny tensed up and instinctively became defensive. "Yeah, that's my pops. Why?"

"Humph, you just look familiar that's all." Grip replied, and then turned to leave.

When they exited the restaurant, Sonny looked at Mook. "So, you think he's gonna accept the offer?"

"I don't know, Blood. That ol' mu'fucka's so crafty that I couldn't really read the nigga. But at the same time, who in they right mind would turn down $28,000 a key?"

*****

While driving back to South Philly in Grip's money green Escalade, Biggs asked him, "So, whatchu gon' do, Mr. Moreno? You gon' accept the nigga's offer?"

Grip looked at him like he was retarded. "Fuck no! Who the fuck does this lil' dirty mutha'fucka think he is? Trying to indirectly dictate some shit to me like he's running something? I run this shit! I'm the boss of this mutha'fuckin' city!"

"So, whatchu want us to do about him?" Smack asked from behind the steering wheel. "If you want, I can have them niggas missing by the morning."

"No, that's not necessary," Grip responded in a calmer voice. He placed a Cuban cigar in his mouth, and then settled into the backseat. “We’re gonna slow walk him, and then strike when the time is right. If he’s offering to supply me with a 100 keys, then the lil’ nigga must be doing good for himself. Therefore, I’m gonna give him a little more time to fatten up, and then we’ll lead him to slaughter. For now, all I want you to do is keep your eyes on the young bul that was with him. Find out any and everything you can about him, and then report back to me.”

“Say no more, Mr. Moreno. We got it covered.” Smack assured him, while stopping the SUV at a traffic light. He looked at Biggs, who was sitting in the passenger’s seat, texting somebody on his Samsung Galaxy. “Did you hear what Mr. Moreno said about the young bul?”

“Yeah, I heard him.”

“A’ight, well, I’ma need you to get wit’ Murder and Malice. Tell ‘em I said to suit up and go do what they do.”

“I got you,” Biggs confirmed, and then continued texting. “I just don’t see why this lil’ nigga’s so special.”

Grip chuckled, and then lit the tip of his cigar with a gold lighter. He took a deep pull and blew out a thick cloud of smoke.

“He’s special because he’s my grandson.”

Chapter Five

Tommy was a nervous wreck. He knew he was in a fucked up situation, and his paranoia was getting the best of him. The only thing that improved his feelings was the fact that Detective Smith had set him up with an apartment out of town, and the fact that he had twenty-eight kilos of cocaine and $24,000 saved up. He figured all he had to do was fulfill his obligation to Detective Smith, and then move on with the rest of his life.

"Come on, Imani, hurry up and eat the rest of your food so when can go to the movies to see *Cloudy with a Chance of Meatballs*." Tommy said to his four year old daughter. They were at the McDonalds on Stenton Avenue. It was him, Imani, and his baby's mom, Nahfisah.

"Yeeeeeaaaaah, mommy. We're going to the movies." Imani beamed, and then stuffed her face with French fries.

Nahfisah ice-grilled him, and then folded her arms across her chest. "Out of everywhere in the State of Pennsylvania, why we gotta move to Lebanon? What the fuck is so special about Lebanon?"

"Ooooo, mommy said a bad word!" Imani said to her father, while shaking her head in disappointment.

Tommy ignored his daughter's hereditary snitching and responded to Nahfisah. "Because it's a lot of shit goin' on, and I don't want us to be no where near the city when this shit hits the fan."

"I'm sayin' though, out of all places, why Lebanon? We don't even know nobody out there."

"Yo, we've been through this shit a thousand times, Nahfisah. Damn. I already told you that it's money out there, and I'm try'na get it." He calmed himself down, and then returned his attention to Imani. "Are you all done, lil' mama?"

She nodded her head up and down. "Yes, daddy, I'm all done. Can we go to the movies now?"

"Without a doubt." He kissed her on the forehead, and

then used a napkin to wipe the ketchup from the corners of her mouth. "Do you love your daddy?"

"Yes."

"How much?"

"This much." She stretched out her arms and started laughing.

*****

For the past week, Easy had turned a new leaf. After the last confrontation he had with Sonny, the look of disgust he saw on his son's face was enough to motivate him to clean up his act. He left North Philly, and moved to West Oak Lane to stay with his mother. He knew that in order for him to change his life around, he would need a change of scenery, and his mother's house was the exact change he needed.

When he arrived at her doorstep and announced he wanted to get his life together, she fell to her knees and thanked God. For the past sixteen years, she had to stand by and watch her only son destroy himself. Now that he was ready to get clean, she was ecstatic. She'd always known him to be a man of his word, so when he professed he wanted to stop getting high, she had no reason to doubt him.

The first thing she did was make him take a shower, and then she gave him some fresh clothes from her husband's closet. Next, she made an appointment with her dentist to get his teeth fixed, and then took him on a shopping spree for new clothes. After acquiring a wardrobe and getting a fresh haircut, Easy looked like a new man. Now, all he had to do was find a new source of income, and working a nine to five wasn't going to cut it. His mother gave him $500 and loaned him her spare car to look for a job, but Easy had other plans. He used the money to buy a Glock .40 and a box of bullets, and began his climb to the top of the food chain.

He was always known for being a keen individual, and

during his days of getting high, he noticed that the hustlers on the corners, where he copped his crack, always kept their product stashed in a vacant lot. He reasoned if they didn't keep their drugs on them while they hustled, then nine times out of ten, they didn't keep their guns on them either. He also recognized the way they handled business. They used a caseworker and two runners. The caseworker would collect the money from the runners, hold it until the end of his shift, and then pass it along to the owner of the block, who usually lived within a two block radius. Now, there he was, parked on Indiana Street, sizing up a group of Spanish hustlers.

Gordo, the caseworker on 4th and Indian, looked at his watch and saw that it was 5:45 p.m. *About time,* the fat Spanish man thought to himself. *I'm hungry as shit. All I gotta do is take this money to Fernando, go to the Chinese store to get me some pork fried rice, and then take my fat ass home.*

He looked up the block and saw his cousin, Angelo, coming his way. "Hey, cabrón," he called out. "For once in ya life, you came outside to do some work. Lemme guess, ya mom kicked you out the house so we can be alone when I'm bangin' her back out?"

Angelo, the boss' nephew smiled. "Fuck you, punto. The only reason I'm out here is because I was fuckin' ya fat ass wife, and she tried to stick her finger up my ass like she be doin' you. I had to get the fuck outta there," he joked back, and then adjusted the book bag full of bundles he was carrying on his shoulder. When they finally approached one another, they shook hands.

"But listen," Gordo told his cousin. "Esataban and Alex are in front of the bar waitin' for you. I would stick around and shoot the shit wit' y'all, but I gotta go fuck ya baby mom." He laughed, and then continued walking down the block.

Two blocks away, Easy was sitting behind the steering wheel of his mother's Ford Taurus, watching the exchanges between the two men. As Gordo continued walking toward him, he hopped out the car. He left the door open, and the engine running. When Gordo was a half of a block away, he pulled out his Glock .40 and held it by his right leg. Had Gordo been more aware of his surroundings, opposed to thinking about feeding his fat face, he would've noticed that Easy was watching him the same way a lioness watches a gazelle. As soon as he came within arm's reach, Easy grabbed him by his shirt and placed the barrel of the Glock to the side of his neck.

"Pussy, you know what it is?" Easy snarled through clenched teeth. "Say one word, and I'ma blow ya fuckin' head off!"

"Please, poppy, don't lay me. Here," he extended the book bag full of money. "You can have this shit, poppy. Just don't lay me."

"Didn't I just tell ya stupid ass not to say nothin'?" Easy barked, and then smacked him in the face with the side of the gun.

Whop!

Gordo fell to the ground and held his hand to the side of his face. As Easy reached down to grab the book bag full of money, he heard Angelo yelling in Spanish. He looked up, and saw three Spanish men running toward him. Without an ounce of hesitation, he raised the Glock .40 and fired.

Boc! Boc! Boc! Boc!

The first bullet burned through Angelo's face, sending a chunk of his left cheek out the back of his skull, and the last three bullets ripped through his chest, folding him like a lawn chair.

At the sound of the Glock .40 firing, Angelo's brother, Estaban, and their friend, Alex, dove behind a parked car. Gordo, on the other hand, was still lying on the ground, paralyzed with fear. He prayed to God and begged Him for protection, but unfortunately God wasn't listening. Easy aimed the Glock .40 at his forehead, and then squeezed the trigger.

Boc! Boc! Boc!

With no time to waste, he hopped back in mother's Ford Taurus and sped away from the scene.

*****

It was 5:59 p.m. when Easy pulled up in front of the check cashing store on Germantown Avenue. He killed the ignition, and then grabbed the book bag off of the passenger's seat. He opened it and to his astonishment there were approximately twenty separate rolls of money. After counting them out one by one, the total came to $18,550. He placed the money back inside of the book bag, and then tucked it under the passenger's seat.

Damn, I hope these mutha'fuckas got some serious bread, he thought to himself as he watched a middle aged Arab woman leave the check cashing store and pull off in a red Volvo wagon. He stubbed out the Newport 100 he was smoking and climbed out the car.

Inside of the store, the proprietor, Abraham Erdogan was standing behind thc bulletproof counter eating a turkey sandwich and counting the $20,000 he just removed from the safe in his office.

"Tomorrow is the first of the month, and I've gotta be ready for the social security and welfare checks, Insha Allah." Nobody was there except for him, but for some strange reason, he was in the habit of talking to himself.

The bell rang on the front door, alerting him that a customer had just entered the store. Unfortunately, he didn't look up fast enough to see Easy lock the door behind him.

"I am sorry, sir, but we are closed for the evening," he stated in a thick Arab accent.

Easy held up a white envelopc and fanned it back and forth. "I'm sayin', though, I need you to cash my check real quick."

"No. I cannot," Abraham replied with an annoyed expression. "The sign on the door says we are closed. The door should have been locked, but my employee must have forgotten to do it when she left. I am sorry for the inconvenience, but you need to leave my store."

"A'ight, well thanks anyway," Easy responded.

As he was about to leave, a painful expression appeared on his face, and he clutched his chest.

"What the hell is wrong with you, man? Get out of my store!"

Instead of responding, Easy fell to the floor and acted as if he were having a seizure. His body convulsed, and the Alka Seltzer that he inconspicuously threw in his mouth produced a white foam on the side of his face.

"What is going on?" The little Arab cried out. "Do not die in my store. Please, do not die in my store!"

He ran from behind the bulletproof counter and came to the front of the store. As he hovered over Easy's shaking body, he noticed he was foaming from the mouth.

"Oh, no. This can't be happening in my store." He knelt down beside Easy. "Don't worry, buddy. I will call for help." He pulled out his cell phone and began dialing 911.

"Nah, Osama, you better drop that mutha'fuckin' phone." Easy dictated, while aiming his Glock .40 at Abraham's face.

Stuck in a state of shock, the little Arab dropped the phone. "I am sorry, buddy. I will cash your check. Here, give me the check, and I will cash it. Just calm down," he nervously stated.

Easy stood to his feet and placed the barrel of the gun to the back of Abraham's head. As he led him to the back, he thought about asking him if anyone else was in the store, but disregarded the thought based on the fact that nobody followed him to the front of the store. When they got behind the bulletproof counter, Easy spotted the stacks of money, and nodded his head in approval.

"Yo, where the rest of the money at, Osama?"

"That's all the money I have. That is all of it."

"*Pussy*, you wanna die?"

"No!" Abraham cried.

"Well, stop fuckin' lyin', and give me the rest of the money!" Easy snapped.

"But, I already told you, buddy, that is everything."

Boc!

"Aaaaggghhh! You shot me in the fucking stomach!" Abraham screamed in pain.

Easy aimed the Glock .40 at his face. "Fuck ya stomach. The next bullet I gon' rip through ya mutha'fuckin' face if you don't give me the rest of that money!"

"Okay, Okay! I will give you the rest of the money. Just please, buddy, do not kill me." Abraham continued crying.

He staggered over to the closet in his office and showed Easy the two foot high safe that was screwed into the floor.

"Don't stand there lookin' stupid, bitch. You better open that safe 'fore these hollow points open the back of ya fuckin' head."

Still crying and coughing up blood, Abraham punched in the combination numbers, and then opened the safe. At the sight of his $80,000, a surge of courage spread throughout his body, and he decided to wrestle the gun away from his attacker. He sprang forward and grabbed the barrel of the gun. Easy stumbled backwards, but quickly regained his balance. He then landed a short left hook to the right side of Abraham's face, knocking him into the closet. Abraham was dazed and growing weaker by the second. In a fit of desperation, he shot past Easy and darted for the door.

Boc! Boc! Boc! Boc!

His heart and lungs reached the door before he did.

Without missing a beat, Easy removed his shirt and tied the sleeves together to make a napsack. He bent down and took the stacks of money from the safe and placed them inside of his shirt. He then went over to the money on the counter and did the same thing. He looked around for any additional assets, and noticed a security camera.

"Damn." He shook his head from side to side. "That

woulda been a bad look if I ain't run across this mutha'fucka." He walked over to it and removed the tape. After that, he wiped down everything he touched, and then quickly left the store.

Chapter Six

"Damn, this cheesecake poppin'." Sonny said to himself, referring to the mouthwatering pastry he was eating.

He was parked outside of the Tiffany's Diner on Roosevelt Boulevard, waiting to meet his man Diamondz. For the past three weeks, he'd been making money like never before, and he was loving every minute of it. One brick here, two bricks there, three bricks here, and a half of a brick there. Out of the thirty bricks he started out with, he only had four of them left, and his man Diamondz, was about to cop at least two of them. *Damn, I gotta call Mook and order another shipment*, he thought to himself. He turned down the sounds of Peedi Crakk's mixtape, *The Crakk Files,* and called Mook.

Ring! Ring! Ring!

"Mook, it's Sonny. Where are you at?"

"I'm at the spot," Mook replied. "What's up? Everything good?"

"Awwww, man, these streets are lovin' a nigga right now. I need to holla at you. The sooner the better."

"Say less, you already know I'm on top of it. Plus, I holla'd at the ol' head Grip, and he agreed to our terms, so I'ma have to come to the city today anyway. Be on the lookout for me."

After disconnecting the call, he lay his head against the headrest and let out a sigh of relief. By Grip accepting Mook's offer, that was one less bridge he had to cross. Now, he could focus on getting money without the threat of a potential war.

A couple of minutes later, Diamondz pulled into the parking lot in a metallic blue 2012 Lexus LS 460 and parked beside his Tahoe. The two of them had been friends since 2002 when they did a juvenile bit together at Glen Mills. However, being as though Sonny was from the Bad Landz, and Diamondz was from Frankford, they didn't hang out much, but whenever they did, they did it big.

When Diamondz stepped out his Lex, he was fresh to death as usual. He was dipped in a pair of Rock Republic jeans, a white Chanel For Men button up, and a pair of cinnamon Mauries. He grabbed a black gym bag from his back seat, and then climbed inside of Sonny's Tahoe.

"What's up, my nigga?" He greeted Sonny, while shaking his hand.

"Ain't shit, Dia. Another day, another dolla, you know how I do," he responded, and then glanced around the parking lot. He was looking for any suspicious activity.

"Yo, that shit was some straight up buttah." Diamondz smiled. "My phone is poppin', my block is poppin', and my young buls have been four and a halfin' the shit out me. I know niggas is too young to know about that '88 money, but if it was anything like this..."

"Yeah, I know, right. My shit been lookin' a'ight, too. But whatchu try'na do, dawg?" Sonny replied in a tone that was all business.

"I got $100,000 in here." He held up the gym bag. "What's up wit' a play for three of 'em?"

"I'll tell you what. I can't do three for $100,000, but this is what I'ma do for you." He reached into the back seat and grabbed the black duffle bag that was holding his last four keys. "I'ma bless you wit' four. Just make sure you hit me wit' the other $40,000 as soon as you get it."

"That's a bet." Diamondz smiled as they exchanged bags. Just give me like two to three days, and I got you. But dig, though, whatchu doin' tonight? My homie, Shiz, just came home from the feds, and I'm throwin' him a party at *The Name Of The Game*. You should slide through."

"I don't know, dawg. Lemme holla at my boys and see what they doin'. If they try'na roll, then it's whatever."

"A'ight, my nigga." Diamondz shook his hand, and then opened the passenger's side door. "Be safe out here. And if I don't see you at the party, I'ma get wit' you in a couple of days."

"More or less."

After watching Diamondz drive away from the parking lot, he started the ignition, and pulled off. He drove down Roosevelt Boulevard, and then banged a left on 6th Street. He drove all the way up until he reached Susquehanna Avenue. He then made a right, and drove eight blocks until he reached Franklin Street, and then made another left. When he pulled up on the corner of Franklin and Diamond, he spotted Sheed standing in front of the Chinese store talking to his homies, Nice and Stubbs.

"Yo, scrap, come here for a minute."

Sheed looked in his direction and smiled. "Sonny Money, what's poppin'?"

"That Five, you already know," Sonny replied, and then looked at Nice and Stubbs. "What's up wit' y'all niggas? Y'all good?"

"Yeah, Sonny, we good," they replied in unison, and then continued their conversation.

When Sheed approached the Tahoe, Sonny reached his arm out the window and grabbed the iced-out 8th Street charm that hung from his necklace.

"Damn, nigga, I see you out here all shined up and all that."

"Come on, dawg, you know this shit ain't 'bout nothin'." Sheed laughed, and then held up his left hand to give Sonny a clear view of his iced-out watch. "But dig the big face Rollie, though."

"Yeah," Sonny nodded his head in approval. "That thing definitely doin' the pussy. I see you shinin', nigga."

"So, what's up wit' you? Where you comin' from?" Sheed asked, and then took a pull on his Backwood.

"I just came from servin' one of my playas. These birds been movin' like a mu'fucka. But, um, what's up wit' the homie, Tommy? Have you seen him lately?"

"Naw. I ain't seen the nigga since the day Mook hit us off wit' this work. I spoke to him the other day, though. He said he was goin' up the Poconos or somethin' like that. He was talking 'bout it's money up there."

"Yeah, well I need to holla at him. Matter of fact," he grabbed his iPhone from the passenger's seat. "I'ma call this nigga right now."

Ring! Ring!

"This subscriber is unable to receive calls at this time. If you would like to leave..."

Click!

"Yo, this nigga got his phone off. How the fuck is he 'posed to be gettin' money, and he ain't even got his phone activated?"

"I don't know, Scrap. Maybe he's usin' a different number while he's up there," Sheed reasoned.

A second later, Flo emerged from the Chinese store with a bag full of food in her hands. She walked over to the Tahoe, "Boo, I ain't know if you wanted soy sauce or duck sauce, so I got you both." She then looked at Sonny and smiled, "What's up, Sontino? When you get here?"

"What's goin' on, Flo? I just pulled up a couple of seconds ago."

She nodded her head, and then returned her gaze to Sheed. "I'ma go wait in the car."

"A'ight," Sheed replied, and then licked his lips at the sight of her fat ass jiggling toward his Benz.

"But dig, though, I holla'd at my man, Diamondz, from Frankford, and he told me he was throwin' a party tonight at *The Name Of The Game*. You try'na ride out?"

"No doubt." Sheed smiled. "You know it ain't a party unless the kid up in da building."

Sonny smiled at him. "I holla'd at Mook today, too. He told me the ol' head supposed to be hoppin' on board."

Sheed nodded his head up and down. "That's a good thing, 'cause I was definitely about to put some holes in that mu'fucka." He lifted the bottom of his Gucci Tshirt, exposing the pearl handle on his .50 caliber Desert Eagle. "But dig, though. I'ma 'bout to slide off wit' lil' buddy. Hit me up later, and let me know whatchu try'na do about that party situation." He embraced Sonny with their Blood handshake, and then strolled toward his Benz.

As he pulled off, Sonny picked up his iPhone and called Riana.

Ring! Ring! Ring!

"Hello," she answered in the voice he loved so much.

"What's up, baby girl? How you feelin'?"

"I'm a'ight, but I would feel a lot better if you were here wit' me."

"Come on, Riri, you know a nigga out here try'na make shit happen. Why you stressin' me?"

"I'm not. I just wish you were here, so I could sexually harass you," she giggled.

"Well, I'm all yours in a couple of days." He smiled at the thought of playing in her tight pussy.

"A'ight, but I swear to God, Sontino, I ain't try'na hear none of that you gotta make a run shit. Dat ass is *mines*."

Sonny laughed, "Yo, you crazy as shit. But I ain't doin' nothin' except chillin' wit' you. Plus, I was thinkin' we could do a lil' shoppin' for the baby."

"That would be nice. I saw some stuff at the baby's section in Strawbridge's too. Awwww, I can't wait for her to get here." She smiled at the thought of holding their baby.

"She? Naw, lil' buddy, we ain't doin' no shes. That's my lil' man you carrying in there."

"Nah ahn," she playfully shouted. "I'm not carrying a boy. I'm carrying a girl, so stop try'na jinx me."

"A'ight," he continued laughing. "If you say it's a girl, then it's a girl."

"That's better. I'm the queen, and I get whatever I want." She responded in a soft voice.

"Yo, you so goddamn spoiled. I see I'ma have to start

slowin' down wit' ya lil' ass. You lucky you're pregnant, 'cause if you wasn't…"

She fell out laughing. "And if I wasn't, then what? Don't make me fuck you up, Sontino."

"Yeah, whatever. But look, I gotta cut this short. I love you, and I'll see you in a couple of days."

"A'ight, daddy, I love you too, and make sure you call me later."

*****

When Sonny pulled up in front of his house, his mom was sitting on the stoop smoking a Newport 100. He climbed out of the Tahoe and gave her a kiss on the forehead.

"What's up, mom?"

"Ain't nothin', baby. I'm just tired as shit from working a double shift at the hospital last night. I wish these next ten years would hurry up so I can finally retire."

"Don't even worry about it, mom. If everything go the way I'm plannin', you'll never work another day in ya life."

"Humph. I've heard that before. You sound just like your father."

"Dizzamn. Why you had to go there? You know how I feel about dude, and you know how I hate it when people be comparin' me to that nigga."

"I'm sorry, Sontino. It's just that you remind me of him when he was your age. You know, before he started gettin'…

"Yo, I'm outta here."

"...high." Her words trailed off.

When he reached his bedroom, he turned on his stereo system, and the sounds of AR-AB's latest mixtape thumped from the speakers. He dumped the money from the gym bag on his bed, and counted it out stack by stack. He trusted Diamondz whole heartedly, but in the same vein, he wanted to make sure everything was in order. When he finished counting, it came out to exactly $100,000. He went to the closet where a pile of sneaker boxes were hiding the small vault that was built into the floor. After removing the boxes and pulling back the carpet, he punched in the combination numbers, and then opened the door. Inside, there were 91 stacks of money, each containing $10,000. He removed 90 of them and placed them inside of the duffle bag he grabbed from the top shelf. This was the money he owed Mook. Next, he removed the $100,000 from his bed and stashed it in the vault with the remaining $10,000. That, plus the $40,000 that Diamondz owed him, along with the $100,000 that was stashed in Riana's dresser, he was sitting on $250,000. *Damn, this was a crazy month*, he thought to himself. *I can get used to this shit.*

After locking the vault and placing the carpet and sneaker boxes back in position, he rolled up a gram of *Sour Diesel* and got his smoke on. At $250,000, he was sitting on more money than he'd ever had in his life, and he was beginning to develop mixed feelings. On one hand, he felt invincible, but on the other hand, he felt as though his new fortune was too good to be true. As he lay on his bed enjoying the effects of the *Sour Diesel* and nodding his head to AR-AB's mixtape, his bedroom door creaked open and his mom stuck her head in the room.

"Here," she held out a white envelope, "you got a letter from Breeze yesterday."

He got up from the bed and grabbed the envelope. "Hey, mom, you know I love you, right?"

"I know, baby," she smiled, and then closed the door.

He lay back down on the bed and examined the envelope. Breeze was his first cousin on his mother's side, and he was currently incarcerated at SCI Camp Hill for a gun case. Growing up, he always wanted a little brother and Breeze was the closest thing to it. Ever since they were little kids, they always looked out for one another, and now that Breeze was serving a one-to-two, he did everything in his power to make sure he was as comfortable as possible.

He opened the envelope and found a one page letter, and a

picture of Breeze posing in his G stance.

"Look at my fuckin' boy!" He smiled, while examining the 6X9 picture. He opened the single sheet of paper, and began reading.

Date: September 20, 2012
Time: 4:05p.m.
Mood: G Makkin
Song: Picture Me Rollin
Artist: Pac

Dear Damu,

What's poppin', homie? I got that bread you sent me last week. I got them flicks too. Good lookin', scrap. Kongrats on the baby, and tell Riri that I send my unkonditional. Oh, yeah, you know me and Erika have been talking 'bout gettin' married, right? I ain't gon' front, yo, that's my bitch, Blood! She been holdin' a nigga down like brazy! But yo, when was the last time you took a trip up top? I need you to shoot through Southside, and holla at my baby moms for me. I tried to kall my daughter the other day, and some bird ass nigga answered the phone. I'm try'na tell this bozo to put shorty on the phone so I kan bark at my drop, and this bird ass nigga talkin' 'bout she ain't there. She went to the bodega to get some soups and Slim Jims to make him a cook up. Then, this nigga gonna start laughing and tell me to hurry up and bring my bowl. Yo, word to Blood, this pussy ass nigga had me tight, son! I need you to shoot up there, and show this nigga how much he been on my mind lately.

More or less, I got my green sheet yesterday, and they gave me a date for December 5, 2012. Yo, Blood, I kan't wait, my nigga. As soon as I touch down, I'm a link up wit' you. I love you, brozay.

Breeze a.k.a. Infamous Balla

As soon as Sonny finished reading the letter, he picked up a pen and a piece of paper.

Date: September 24, 2012

What's poppin', homie?

As always, I open this letter wit' love, loyalty, justice, freedom, and peace. I pray you're mentally uplifted, and thinking far beyond those oppressive walls that kurrently konfine you. As for myself, I'm just try'na make sure that today was better than yesterday, and doing everything in my power to put our family in a better situation.

*More or less, your letter was a successful head shot, and I'ma definitely shoot up top in the near future. Matter of fact, kall ya baby moms as soon as you get this letter, and I guarantee you ain't gon' have no problems. As far as you and Erika thinkin' about gettin' married, that's a good look. Just make sure when you touch down, you show her the same love and loyalty that she showed you while you was stuck behind that G*wall! Til' then, stay up, ola!*

Phantoms & Maybachs

After placing the letter inside of an envelope, he grabbed his iPhone and called Mook.

Ring! Ring!

"Yo," Mook answered.

"It's Sonny, scrap. What's poppin'?"

"You already know," Mook replied while sitting behind his steering wheel, enjoying a ferocious dick suck. "I just left my apartment in Chester, and I'm on my way to the city right now.

"A'ight." Sonny nodded his head. "What's the word on this nigga, Grip? You make that happen yet?"

"Nizzaw. I just talked to that pussy like twenty minutes ago, and now he talking 'bout he don't know if he wanna fuck wit' niggas, and that he needs more time to get his thoughts together."

"More or less. Me and Sheed supposed to be goin' out tonight. Is you kickin' it wit' us or what?"

"Shhhh, Ummm!" Mook groaned as he bust a nut in the back of the girl's throat.

"Hey, yo, Mook, what the fuck is you doin', Blood?"

"Awww, man, I got one of my lil' mommies wit' me, and she got a nigga feelin' like a *Block Boy* right now."

Sonny laughed. "Yo, you'sa wild bul! But dig, though, I'm at the spot right now, so as soon as you hit the city, slide through and holla at me."

"Yeah, yeah."

Click!

Chapter Seven

After meeting with Mook, Sonny hopped in the shower, and got dressed for the party. Not wanting to overdo it, he kept it simple and wore a pair of Levis, a gray Champion hoody, and a fresh pair of white on white Air Forces. He also threw in his diamond earrings, and for a finishing touch, he placed his .357 Sig Sauer in the small of his back. He thought about rocking his *NP* chain, but quickly dismissed the notion. *Nizzaw, the less attention the better.*

*****

When Sheed pulled up in front of Sonny's house, he was puffing on a Backwood, and nodding his head to the sounds of Beanie Siegel and Omillio Spark's *Tales of a Hustla.*

In this life, you're not promised tomorrow, so take the bitter wit' the sweet, and maintain/ In these vicious streets, carry ya heat and keep ya mind on ya money/ Life's a gamble, everybody got a number homie.

He beeped the horn, and a couple of seconds later, Sonny stuck his head out of his bedroom window.

"Yo, hurry up, nigga! You fake ass pretty boy." Sheed shouted, and then pulled down his visor to check out his own reflection in the mirror. "Niggas wanna be like me and shit. He knows I'm the one that pull all the bitches." He laughed to himself.

When Sonny finally emerged from the house and climbed in the Benz, Sheed asked him, "Yo, you strapped?"

"Without a doubt," Sonny responded, while adjusting the passenger's seat.

"Yo, what the fuck are you in here watching?" He gestured toward the monitor on the dashboard where two white girls were eating each other out in the 69 position.

Sheed smiled. "Oh, those my lil' Temple bitches."

Sonny burst out laughing. "Nigga, stop fraudin'. You

don't know them bitches."

"Oh, yeah," Sheed challenged. "Watch this."

The camera spun around and captured Sheed's face with a big ol' Kool-Aid smile. Apparently, he was the one shooting the footage. He laughed, and then returned the lens to the two white girls.

"My fuckin' boy." Sonny snapped, and then gave his man some dap. "Yo, fuck a party. I'm try'na slide up in these Temple bitches. Where they at?"

Sheed laughed. "Yo, chill, nigga. Damn! I got you as soon as I'm finished wit' 'em."

"Awww, that's fucked up, Blood. You always was a stingy ass nigga when it came to some pussy."

"And you know this maaaannnn." Sheed shot back, imitating Smokey from the movie, *Friday.*

When they reached the club on Margaret and Orthodox, the strip looked like a car show. Niggas was hopping out of Benzes, Beemers, Range Rovers, and one nigga even hopped out of a Maserati. Basically, hustlers from all over the city were out to pay homage to one of Frankford's finest. For the past month, the majority of them were either copping their work from Sonny and Sheed, or copping from the niggas who copped from them.

As they parked and approached the club's entrance, Sonny called Diamondz to let him know they were outside. A minute later, he came out to meet them. "Sonny, what it do, my nigga?"

"Ain't shit, dawg. But, yo, this my homie, Sheed. Sheed, this my mans, Diamondz." The two of them shook hands and then together, they entered the club.

When they reached the second floor, the dance floor was jam packed with bitches and niggas wildin' out to Chris Brown's new hit *Look at Me Now.*

"Yo, this that shit," Sheed said, while nodding his head to the music. "But dig, though, the Ciroc and the Spades is on me tonight. I'ma be right back." He left Sonny and Diamondz at the entrance and headed toward the bar.

"Yo, Dia, where you went, dawg?" Shiz slurred. He was obviously high and drunk.

"I stepped outside to get my nigga, Sonny. He's the one I've been tellin' you about."

"What's poppin', fam? I heard a lot about you." Sonny shook his hand.

"Hey, no doubt. I just did a pound in the feds, but the kid is back and I'ma definitely be gettin' wit' you. But excuse me, fam." He grabbed the arm of a thick, brown skinned girl. "I'm 'bout to slide up in some pussy real quick."

Sonny laughed, and then looked at Diamondz. "Yo, ya mans feelin' hisself right now. That's what's up, though. My lil' cousin about to come home too, and I know that nigga gonna be showin' his ass."

"No doubt, but yo, let me introduce you to a few of my niggas."

"Naw, fam, I ain't try'na meet nobody on no hustlin' shit. If niggas is try'na grab, have 'em holla at you, and then you holla at me."

"A'ight, but still." Diamondz shrugged his shoulders. "These my niggas. It's only right that I let 'em know you in the building."

"More or less."

While heading toward the V.I.P. area, the deejay started mixing, and Young Jeezy's *Go Crazy* exploded from the speakers.

When they play the new Jeez, all the dope boys go craaazy/ Now watch the dope boys go craaazy...

The club went wild and hundreds, fifties, and twenties were tossed in the air. Gold bottles of champagne were raised up high and clouds of weed smoke hovered above the dance floor.

As they approached the roped off area, Sheed approached them from behind. He was accompanied by two scantily clad Spanish women and was carrying a case of Ace of Spades.

"Yo, they ain't have no Ciroc, so I got us a case of

Spades." He handed both of them a bottle, and then gestured toward the curvy Latina in the red Prada dress. "This is Maria" he introduced her, then turned his attention to the other woman who was wearing a black sheer dress that exposed her perky titties and black G string. "And this, Michelle. I met 'em at the bar, and they rollin' wit' us tonight."

"More or less." Sonny approved, already choosing the woman in the see through dress. "What's good, mommy? They call me Sonny," he introduced himself, and then rested his hand on her firm ass. "Where you in ya girl from?"

"We from Camden, poppy." Michelle answered in a thick Spanish accent.

"Damn, where mines at?" Diamondz joked, while staring at Michelle like he wanted to eat her pussy in front of the entire club.

Sonny laughed. "We *Block Boys*, my nigga. You ain't know?" He looked at Sheed. "Yo, take 'em out to the car, and I'ma be there in a minute. I need to holla at Diamondz real quick."

"More or less," Sheed said, and then turned his attention to Diamondz. "Yo, it was nice meetin' you, fam. Hopefully, we can do this again, but right now niggas got business to tend to, feel me?" He shook Diamondz's hand, and then led the two women outside to his Benz.

Again, the deejay switched songs, and Tyga's *Rack City* erupted from the sound system.

Rack City, bitch/ Rack Rack City, bitch/ Ten tens, ten twenties, and a fifty bitch.

The beat was thumping. It was so hypnotizing that one chick even got down on all fours and started popping her ass until her white Coogie dress flipped up and exposed her neatly trimmed pussy.

"But like I was sayin', Dia, I know you got ya team and all dat, and I know niggas is try'na get down, but I don't fuck wit' niggas I don't know. So, if them niggas is try'na grab, just have 'em holla at you, and then you holla at me." He shrugged his shoulders, "It's as simple as that."

"Fuck it, my nigga. I can dig it." Diamondz replied, and then shook his hand.

"A'ight, then I'm outta here."

As he was leaving the club, he noticed a light skinned dude at the bar staring at him. They locked eyes for a brief moment, and then the man turned his attention to the bartender.

*****

When they arrived at the Clarion Hotel in Center City, they rented two rooms that were connected to one another. Sonny's room was 708 and Sheed's was 709. Each room came equipped with a bedroom, a Jacuzzi, a living room, a mini bar, and a small kitchen.

When Sonny and Michelle entered their room, he passed her a pack of Backwoods and a sandwich bag of *Sour Diesel.*

"Yo, roll this up." He removed his Champion hoody and threw it on the couch.

He then picked up the remote control to the 50 inch plasma and pressed the *on* button. After flipping through the channels and not finding anything to watch, he turned it off. He went to the kitchen and grabbed two flute glasses for the bottle of Ace of Spades he brought from the club. He then looked at Michelle, who was sitting on the couch rolling them a spliff.

"You good, mommy?"

She smiled at him. "I'm good, poppy. What's up wit' ju, though?"

"Awww man, I'm feelin' that lil' dress you wearin'."

"Umm hum. It's not de dress ju feelin', it's what's underneath it." She replied in a suggestive tone, and then licked her juicy lips.

Sonny smiled at her, and then nodded his head. "More or less." He walked over to the couch, removed his .357 from his waist, then sat down beside her and laid the gun on his lap.

"Here," she handed him the neatly rolled cigar. He put it to his lips and sparked it up. Without taking a puff, he handed the wrapped leaf back to her. "Here, you smoke. I'ma go in the bedroom and turn on the Jacuzzi."

She took a deep pull and enjoyed the taste of the exotic smoke. After exhaling, she reached inside of her Birkin bag and pulled out two blue pills.

"Ju do Molly?"

"Nizzaw. You go ahead and rock out, though." He got up from the couch with the .357 in his left hand and disappeared into the bedroom.

As he turned on the Jacuzzi, he could hear Maria moaning in the room next door. He heard footsteps behind him and turned around to see Michelle standing in the doorway with the bottle of Spades in her right hand. The Backwood dangled from her lips as she walked toward him. She sat the bottle of Spades on the edge of the Jacuzzi, and then began to undress. As soon as her dress hit the floor, she pressed her body against his and then began kissing on his neck. She patted him on the ass.

"Take ju clothes off, poppy." She then climbed in the Jacuzzi, and let the jet bubbles massage her body.

As he removed his clothes, she played with her pussy and admired his physic and dick size.

"Damn, poppy, why ju still holdin' ju gun?"

"Don't take it personal." He shrugged his shoulders. "I'm just a firm believer in the word *security*." He grabbed his fully erect dick and moved closer to the Jacuzzi. "Yo, handle that for me."

Without any hesitation whatsoever, she leaned forward and began sucking his dick like Superhead in the flesh. As he enjoyed the feeling of her warm mouth, he laid the gun on the ledge, and then picked up the bottle of Spades. After popping the top with the corkscrew on his keychain, he raised the gold bottle to his mouth and took a gigantic swig. *Goddamn! This lil' bitch is suckin' the shit out my dick!* He thought to himself as he gripped the back of her head with his right hand. He took another swig from the bottle, and then poured the bubbly liquid over her head as she continued sucking him off without missing a beat.

"Ummmmm," she moaned and made slurping noises.

She took a deep breath, and then swallowed his dick until his balls were resting on her bottom lip.

"A'ight mommy, that's enough." He tapped out, and then took a couple of steps backwards.

She looked at him and laughed. "Damn, poppy, I thought ju could hang?"

"Oh, I can hang a'ight." He shot back, while climbing inside of the Jacuzzi.

He reached over the ledge and grabbed a Magnum Trojan from his pants pocket. After sliding the rubber down the length of his shaft, he positioned his body behind her body, and then slipped inside of her hot, wet pussy.

"Ummmmm shit." He groaned as he gripped her ass and started stroking. He started slow, then picked up his pace.

"Ay, poppy! Aaaaayyyy!" she cried out, loving the feel of his dick.

While throwing his back into every stroke, he growled, "Say Big B's poppin'!"

"Aaaaayyyy! Big B's! Big B's poppin'! Ay!"

"Say Soowoo!"

"Ay, poppy! Aaaaayyyy!"

"That ain't what the fuck I said! I said say Soowoo!" He snapped, and then pumped her pussy even harder.

"Aaaaayyyy! Soowoo! Soowoo! Soowooooo!"

Chapter Eight

The Following Morning...

After sending Michelle and Maria back to Camden in a taxi and leaving the Clarion Hotel, Sonny and Sheed drove back to the hood. When they pulled up on the corner of Reese and Susquehanna, they sat in the car and smoked a Backwood.

After exhaling a thick cloud of smoke and flicking the ash off the tip of the cigar, Sonny looked at Sheed, "Yo, this nigga Tommy is playin' games Blood. Niggas been callin' his ass, and he ain't even callin' niggas back. That nigga better get on his mutha'fuckin' job."

"I'm sayin', though, you think he try'na burn the big homie?" Sheed asked, knowing deep in his heart that Tommy had already committed an irrevocable act of treason.

"I don't know, scrap. I just don't understand why he talkin' this outta town shit all of sudden. On top of that, this nigga ain't answerin' his fuckin' phone. I'm tellin' you, scrap," Sonny shook his head slowly, "somethin' ain't right."

Sheed took a pull on the Backwood, and then exhaled a cloud of smoke. "Well, I know one thing," he flicked the ashes in the ashtray, "it's only a matter of time before Mook starts to lose his patience, and you know what that means."

"Yeah, I know." Sonny responded in a disappointed tone. Him, Tommy, and Sheed had been best friends since the fifth grade, and the thought of Tommy betraying them left a bad feeling in his stomach.

Sheed sighed, "A'ight, my nigga, I gotta go take care of somethin', but I'ma link up wit' you later on tonight."

"More or less," Sonny responded, and then saluted him with their Blood handshake.

Sonny got out of the car and walked over to his Benz. He climbed inside, and then pulled his iPhone from his hoody pocket. After scrolling through the contact list, he stopped on Nahfisah's number. Although she was Tommy's baby's mom, the two of them had been close friends since they were seven years old, and they playfully considered themselves brother and sister. He pressed the call button, but after a few rings, her phone went to voice mail.

"Fisah, what's up, boo? Where you at? How's my goddaughter? I ain't heard from y'all in a couple of weeks, and I'm a lil' worried. Get at me as soon as you get this message. I love you, sis."

He tossed the phone on the passenger's seat, and then laid his head against the headrest. He took a deep breath, and then thought about the fateful night that brought the two of them together.

Feburary 1, 1996

It was a week after his family moved back into their Reese Street row home, and it was the night of his seventh birthday. Despite the fact that his parents didn't have the money to provide him with the lavish birthday parties he'd grown accustomed to, he was more than happy to have the fresh pair of Air Jordans he received from his mother. He was lying in his bed, sound asleep, until he heard his bedroom door creak open and could feel the energy of someone else in the room. He lifted his head from the pillow and wiped the sleep from his eyes. He sat up in his bed and was disturbed by the sight of Easy ransacking his closet.

"Yo, pops, whatchu doin' in there?"

Easy spun around, realizing he was caught red handed. "Huh?"

"I said, whatchu doin' in my closet?"

Easy was sweating profusely and his eyes appeared as though they were about to pop out of their sockets. His bottom jaw was sporadically moving from side to side, and the stink of malt liquor was seeping through his pores.

"Don't worry about it, Sontino. Go back to sleep," he

slurred.

"Naw, I ain't goin' back to sleep. I wanna know whatchu doin' in my closet?"

Easy ignored his last statement and continued rummaging through his son's belongings. When he found what he was looking for, he turned to leave but Sonny's shouting stopped him in his tracks.

"Mom, he's stealin' my new Jordans!"

Easy bolted through the door only to find Annie at the top of the steps with a curling iron in her right hand. "Ervin, you better put those goddamn sneakers back!"

The crack head side of him told him to shoot past her and run down the steps, but the gangsta side of him told him to stand his ground.

"Nah, Annie, fuck that! These mutha'fuckas cost too much. I'm taking 'em back to the store." He attempted to walk past her and down the steps, but she grabbed him by the back of his collar and yanked him backwards.

"Nah, mutha'fucka, you ain't leavin' wit' them sneakers!" she shouted, and then cracked him upside the head with the curling iron.

Whack!

Easy growled like a caged animal. He balled up his fist and struck her in the face with a right hook. The blow knocked her unconscious.

"Pussy, I'ma kill you!" Sonny shouted, and then charged him with a barrage of haymakers.

He desperately tried to bring the drama, but his seven year old punches were no match for a grown man. Easy gripped his face and mugged him backwards. His little body tumbled over his mother, and he banged his head against the wall.

Thump!

As he lay on the hallway floor trying to shake away the dizziness, Easy ran down the stairs and shot out the front door. Sonny hopped up and ran down the steps behind him. After grabbing a butcher's knife from the kitchen, he darted out the front door, looking to kill his father.

An hour later, after vigorously searching the neighborhood with the butcher's knife concealed in his pajamas' pants, he ended up at the playground on 8th and Diamond, leaned against the fence and crying his eyes out.

"Hey, you! Boy across the street!"

He quickly wiped away his tears, and then looked in the direction of the voice. A couple of houses down from the poppy store on the corner, a little light skinned girl was standing in her doorway. She was dressed in a long white Tshirt, and a pink scarf was wrapped around her head.

"Yeah, you," the little girl confirmed. Her voice was full of concern. "Aren't you the new boy at my school?"

"Yeah," Sonny answered in a shaky voice.

"Well, I was layin' in my bed, and I heard you out here cryin'. Are you okay?" She asked in a softer tone.

"Yeah." He lowered his head. "I'm a'ight."

The little girl walked across the street and entered the caged basketball court. She walked up and stood directly in front of him. There was something strangely familiar about her, but he couldn't put his finger on it. "You don't look a'ight." She pointed at his left hand. "You're bleeding."

He looked at his hand and spotted a gash between his thumb and index finger. She grabbed his hand and examined it closely.

"Eeeewwww, that's a nasty cut." She scrunched up her face and released his hand. "Come on." She turned around and began walking toward the opening in the fence. "Follow me to my house, so I can clean your hand and get you a BandAid."

"Naw, I'm good," he quickly replied. "What I look like going over ya house? I don't even know you."

The little girl stopped walking and spun around to face him. She placed her hand on her boney hip and snapped her neck in sistagirlstyle.

"Boy, you better stop playin' wit' me. My name is Nahfisah Thompson, and your name is Sontino Moreno. I know that's your name 'cause like I said, you're the new boy at my school. All the girls at my school know your name. So there, now we know each other." She grabbed him by his wounded hand and led him inside of her row house. Unknowingly, this was the beginning of their life long bond.

Back To September 2012

"Damn, man, this nigga better not have Fisah and my goddaughter caught up in no nut shit," Sonny said to himself as he started the Benz and pulled away from the curb.

*****

An hour and a half later, while driving through the Holland Tunnel, he thought about his cousin Breeze and the foul treatment he was receiving from his daughter's mother. He hopped on the Brooklyn Queens Expressway and headed toward Southside Jamaica Queens.

While driving up Guy R. Brewer Avenue and approaching 120th Street, he noticed a familiar face in a crowd of females. He pulled up beside them and rolled down the passenger's side window. "Omeisha!"

A slim brown skinned girl looked in his direction. "Excuse me, but do I know you?"" She asked with a flirtatious attitude.

"It's Sonny. I need holla at you for a minute."

She took a closer look, and then smiled at him. "Oh, hey, Sontino. I didn't know that was you. Whatchu doin' in Queens? I thought you only dealt with Harlem and Brooklyn niggas?"

"I was in the area, so I figured I'd stop by and check on you and the baby." He leaned over and opened the passenger's side door. "Yo, take a ride wit' me." She climbed in the car, and he continued driving up Guy R. Brewer. "So, what's up wit' you

Miesha? How's the baby doin'?"

"Oh, she's good. Looking like her father and swearin' she's grown." Omeisha smiled. "She's at my mom's house right now. We can go see her if you want."

Sonny pulled out his .357 Sig Sauer and aimed the barrel at her stomach. "Yo, fuck all dat! Why you ain't been takin' her to see Breeze?"

"Huh?" Omeisha replied, shocked and afraid.

"Bitch, you heard me? Why ain't you been takin' that little girl to see her father? And why the fuck you're not acceptin' his phone calls?" He stated in a cold tone of voice.

"Sonny, can you please put that gun away?" She pleaded, while eyeing the large pistol. "I swear to God, I'ma take her to see him. Just please put that gun away."

He pulled over on the corner of Baisley and Guy R. Brewer and pressed the barrel against her left cheek.

"The next time I get a letter from my lil' cousin sayin' you ain't acceptin' his calls and you ain't bringing the baby to see him, I'ma come up here and park ya stupid ass!" He snarled through clenched teeth.

"Sonny, I swear to God I'ma…"

"Bitch, get the fuck out my car!"

As she climbed out of the Benz, she heard somebody calling her name. She looked up to see her boyfriend, Ryan, approaching the car at a rapid pace.

He snatched her up by the arm, "Bitch, who the fuck is *this*?" He pointed at the Benz, then crouched down to look in the passenger''s side window. "Damn, son, what the fuck is you doin' wit' my bitch in ya car?"

Sonny threw the transmission in park, and then hopped out with the .357 clutched in his left hand. He scowled at Omeisha.

"Yo, is this the nigga that was on the phone poppin' shit to Breeze?"

When she didn't respond, he cocked back the top of the

pistol.

Click, Clack!

Stunned and fearing for his life, Ryan quickly pleaded his case. “Son, I wasn’t poppin’ shit to nobody. I don’t even know nobody named Breeze.”

“Naw, nigga, fuck that. I *know* you were the one that was talkin’ all crazy on the phone,” Sonny retorted, and then aimed the barrel at his torso.

“Nah, son, you got me mixed up wit’ somebody else. I don’t even know whatchu talking ‘bout.” The tall, brown skinned man responded.

“Oh, so you don’t know what I’m talking ‘bout?” Sonny barked so fast Ryan could barely decipher what he’d just said. “You don’t know what I’m talking ‘bout. Nigga, this what the fuck I’m talking ‘bout.” He squeezed the trigger.

Boc!

Ryan stumbled backwards and fell. A burning sensation permeated his stomach, and he lost his bowels. Shocked, he felt for his gunshot wounds, and then examined the warm blood on his hands. He looked up and saw Sonny was standing over him with the smoking barrel aimed at his forehead.

“Nah, son. Don’t kill me please.”

Sonny kicked him in his face.

“Pussy, stop bitchin’.” He kicked him one more time, and then walked over to Omeisha. He grabbed her by the hair and pressed the hot barrel against her right cheek. Despite the fact that her face felt like it was on fire, and warm urine was running down her legs, all she could do was stand there looking stupid.

“I swear on my flag, if you don’t take that lil’ girl to visit her pop or start acceptin’ his calls, I’ma *fuckin’* kill you!” He smacked her in the back of the head with gun, causing her to fall on her face.

As she lay on the ground crying, he hopped back in his Benz and pulled off.

Chapter Nine

By the time November rolled around, Sonny's hustle had elevated to a whole new level and he made the proper adjustments. His man, Diamondz, established a coop between himself and the major hustlers from Kensington, Uptown, and Northeast Philly, and together they purchased a shipment of 25 keys at the price of $875,000. Sonny took the money straight to Mook and being that Mook was no longer dealing with the block, he gave Sonny the green light to open up shop on Fairhill and York.

Sonny took advantage of the opportunity and to make a larger profit, he stretched the remaining 5 kilos to 8 and broke them down to grams. He then appointed three of his young buls to work the block and had them move the grams at $40 apiece. Not only were the crack heads happy, but the low level hustlers in the neighborhood reaped the benefits as well. By the end of October, his young buls moved every gram and generated a total of $320,000. After paying Mook the $25,000 he owed him and his young buls their monthly salary of $60,000, his profit was $235,000. Now that November was here, he planned to do it all over again.

"Hey, Sonny! Ya man Diamondz is outside!" His young bul, Nasty shouted from the bottom of the steps, and then he went back to playing Madden on the Xbox 360.

"Yo, let him in! I'll be down in a minute!"

Outside, sitting on the front steps, Diamondz was intrigued by the sight of the stocky built, dark skinned, twin brothers who were tearing up the block and hustling for Sonny. The front door of the trap house opened, and a tall, chubby, brown skinned young bul ushered him inside.

What's up, Nasty?" Diamondz greeted him, while shaking his hand.

"Ain't shit, dawg. I'm just try'na fall back and get this money." Nasty replied, then took a seat on the couch and picked up his Xbox controller.

A couple of minutes later, Sonny descended the steps in a fresh wife beater and pair of gray Polo sweatpants. He greeted Diamondz, and then led him over to the dining room table. “So, how we lookin’,” he smiled, knowing the duffle bag Diamondz was carrying contained the money from the coop.

“You already know, my nigga. It’s the same as last month,” he replied, while laying the duffle bag on the table. Sonny opened the bag and pulled out the rubber banded stacks of money. He looked at Nasty.

“Go around the block and get my money machine from Ms. Sonia. Tell her I gave it to Spank last night, and it should be upstairs in Meeka’s room.”

Obediently, Nasty pressed the pause button on his controller, and then left the house. A few minutes later, he returned with the black and gray machine. He handed it to Sonny, and then returned to his video game. In total, there were eighty-eight stacks of money lying on the table, and one by one, Sonny ran them through the machine. The first eighty stacks amounted to $10,000 a piece, and the remaining stacks amounted to $5,000.

“A’ight, my nigga.” He nodded his head in approval. “That’s good money right there. Here,” he handed him a car key. “The work is in the white minivan at the bottom of the block. You gotta turn on the ignition, press the brakes two times, and then hit the hazard light. The left wall in the back compartment is gonna slide open, and that's where I stashed the 25 bricks.”

A’ight, but dig though, since I got the Lex parked outside, I’ma take the van to my crib and unload the work. As soon as I’m done, I’ma shoot straight back to pick up my wheel and drop off the van. He placed the key in his jacket pocket, and then headed toward the front door. Sonny followed him out the house and watched as he drove away in the van. He looked at the twins and smiled.

“Yo, whatchu smilin’ at?” Egypt, the one with the dreads asked him.

“You and ya brother Zaire, y’all some thorough young

buls, that's all. I fucks wit' y'all niggas."

The twins, Egypt and Zaire, were from Marshall and Montgomery which was known as *Ice City*. At the age of sixteen, they were known for putting in work and would soon be known for getting money.

"Hey, yo, Sonny, why you don't be drivin' the Benz?" Zaire asked. "It seems like you only be drivin' the Tahoe. You don't never push the Benz no more."

"Nizzaw, I still push the 550 from time to time." Sonny continued smiling. "It's just lately, a nigga been on some under the radar type of shit, you feel me? The streets be watchin', and a nigga gotta move accordingly."

"Man, fuck all dat," Egypt interjected. "When I get me a Benz, I'm drivin' my shit everywhere." He laughed, and then used his right hand to turn the steering wheel on his imaginary Benz. "I'm tellin' you, just wait!"

As they stood around laughing and joking, a money green 2012 Cadillac Escalade turned the corner, and parked a few houses up the block. The passenger hopped out and walked over to them.

"Yo, you the bul Sonny, right?"

Sonny looked him up and down, and then pulled out his Sig Sauer. "Yeah, I'm the bul, Sonny. What's poppin'?"

"Damn, cowboy," the man smiled nervously. "This ain't that type of party. I'm the bul, Smack. I met you a couple of months ago at the sit down between Grip and Mook." He gestured toward the Escalade. "The ol' head wanna holla at you."

"What the fuck he wanna holla at me about?" Sonny ice grilled him. "My big homie offered the nigga the deal of a lifetime, and he didn't even have the decency to keep it a hunnid wit' niggas. He shoulda been holla'd at Mook by now," he continued his rant, and then cocked back the top of his pistol.

Click, Clack!

"Listen, fam," Smack held up his hands in a defenseless posture. "All I know is that the ol' head wanna holla at you. He's sittin' in the truck, and he wants you to come over and check him out."

"Yo, why the fuck would I would I walk up on that mu'fuckin' truck?" Sonny scrunched up his face. "If that nigga wanna holla at me, then tell his ol' ass to get out the truck and holla at me."

Smack returned to the Escalade and delivered the message. A second later, Grip emerged from the SUV in a charcoal gray Louis Vuitton suit, a pair of black ostrich skin shoes, and a black Bossalini hat with a red feather stuffed inside of the band. He walked over to Sonny and extended his right hand, but Sonny just stared at him.

"Ol' head, you got about two minutes to say whatever it is you gotta say." He stated, while looking in his blue eyes.

"Oh, yeah?" Grip adjusted the diamond ring on his right pinky. "And if I take longer than two minutes?"

Sonny nodded toward the front door of his trap house where Nasty was standing with an AK-47 clutched in his hands.

"My young bul gon' tear ya fuckin' head off."

Grip looked at him and smiled. He was certain the fireball of a young man had no idea that he was speaking to his own grandfather. *Yeah*, he thought to himself. *He's definitely got my blood runnin' through his veins.* He brushed away a piece of lent from his shoulder, and then continued speaking as if the young man had never even threatened his life.

"All I want you to do is ask your father about me." He reached inside of his suit jacket and retrieved a white business card. "Here," he handed him the card. "As soon as you talk to him, I want you to give me a call."

He tilted the front of his Bossalini, old school style, and then returned to his SUV. After climbing in the backseat, he ordered his driver, Muhammad to pull off. As the Escalade left the block, Sonny put away his Sig, and then took a seat on the steps.

"Hey, Sonny, who was that?" Egypt asked. "That nigga

looked like a black John Gotti."

"That was the nigga, Grip." Sonny replied, while cracking open a Backwood.

"You mean Grip from the *Grip Boys*? The nigga from back in the day that started The Black Mafia?"

"Yeah, that was him."

"And you was comin' at *him* like that?"

Sonny scowled at him. "Man, fuck that nigga. That pussy bleed like anybody else, so what the fuck is you talking 'bout? You better never say no pussy ass shit like that again." He stood to his feet and threw the Backwood on the ground. "As a matter of fact, get the fuck off the block. Ya ass is done for the day."

"Naw, Sonny, I didn't mean it like that. I was just…"

"Nigga, you heard what the fuck I said. And don't bring ya ass back 'til you ready to let ya nuts hang."

*****

Later that night, Sonny and Sheed met up with Mook at his Delaware estate. At that point, none of them had heard a peep from Tommy since the day Mook fronted them the work and gave them their new Benzes, so obviously he was the topic of discussion.

"So, Sheed," Mook said, while nursing a glass of Pineapple Ciroc, "the last you heard was that he was going out to the Poconos?"

"Yeah," Sheed answered, and then took a deep pull on his Backwood.

Mook directed his attention to Sonny. "You think this nigga went against the grain?"

Sonny nodded his head up and down. "Yeah, I do. The reason I say that is because his phone is disconnected, and he ain't holla'd at niggas in over two months. Plus, I stopped by Nahfisah's house the other day to drop off some clothes and shit for my Goddaughter, and the house was empty. I think the nigga took the work, packed up Nahfisah and Imani, and got ghost."

"Well, I guess it is what it is then," Mook said, while lounging back on the sofa. "From here on out that nigga's food. Disloyalty is a crime that will never be tolerated in my family, and I want y'all to spread the word that Tommy's to be shot on sight." He sparked up a Newport and took a deep pull. "A'ight, let's move on. Now, Sonny, what's this shit you was tellin' me about the bul, Grip?"

"Yo, this nigga came through the block earlier, and was tellin' me to ask my pops about him. Matter of fact, now that I really think about it, remember when we met up the nigga at T.G.I.Fridays?"

"Yeah, I remember." Mook nodded his head.

"A'ight, well the nigga asked me about my pops back then. I think they used to run together or somethin'."

"Well, from here on out, that nigga's an enemy, him and whoever he got ridin' wit' him. I offered this pussy my friendship, and he spit in my face. It's no mystery that dude be on some egotistical bullshit, and by him not acceptin' the offer, it's only a matter of time before he decides to make a move. So, therefore the next time that ol' mu'fucka steps foot in North Philly, y'all terminate his ass."

"A'ight," Sonny nodded his head. "But what if we catch him outside of the hood?"

"Honestly," Mook shrugged his shoulders, "I could care less. Our situation is rooted in North, from Fairmount to Butler Street. That's our mu'fuckin' hood, and our hood is our mu'fuckin' hood, period." He looked both of them square in the eyes. "Him and his family are no longer welcome in our hood. Do I make myself clear?" He continued in a calm voice. The Xanax and syrup that he ingested about twenty minutes ago were beginning to kick in.

"Say no more, big homie." Sonny assured him.

Mook directed his attention to Sheed. "Did I make myself clear?"

"Crystal." Sheed smiled, and then massaged the pearl handle on his Desert Eagle.

*****

Lebanon, Pennsylvania was a new experience for Tommy, and he loved every bit of it. To him, being in a new town where nobody knew him was the equivalent to a kid in a candy store with a pocket full of money. The hustle game in the small town was nothing like the hustle in North Philly. Although the flow of money was extremely slower, his sales came in lump sums. Instead of the constant flow of loud mouthed crack heads he was accustomed to, in Lebanon his clientele consisted of small business owners, doctors, lawyers and accountants.

When his family first moved into the house that was provided by Detective Smith, him and Nahfisah went to the local furniture store, and it was there he met his first customer, the store's owner. At first glance, the skinny white man appeared to be a little antsy, and Tommy assumed the man was just excited to be selling $4,000 worth of furniture. But when he took a closer look and noticed the man's nose was red and moist, he immediately knew he was high on coke.

The next day, he returned to the store with a gram of raw and a piece of paper with his new number scribbled on it. When he offered the man the coke, to Tommy's surprise, he declined. Tommy, however, was persistent in his approach, and he used the white crystals in the potent powder to demonstrate its purity. He assured the man it was the best cocaine on this side of the equator, and the skinny man's armpits began to sweat. He looked at the cocaine, and then looked at Tommy. He returned his gaze to the white powder and licked his lips anxiously.

"How much?"

"A hunnid a gram, but this time it's on the house."

"Alright, buddy." The man nodded his head. "I'll try you out." He extended his right hand. "By the way, the name's Don."

Tommy accepted the gesture with a firm handshake. “And you can call me Tommy.”

It didn’t take long for Don to become a loyal customer, and eventually he spread the word to all of his friends. A couple of weeks later, he invited Tommy to a party he was hosting and introduced him to his best friend, Dr. Randolph Perry. His lawyer, Larry Santiguida, and his accountant, Ronald Propst. They each had an expensive habit and purchased nothing less than an ounce at a time. At $2,800 a piece, rat ass Tommy had stumbled on a goldmine.

While sitting at their dining room table, Tommy and Nahfisah were weighing ounces of yolk and counting the money he made throughout the week.

“Fis, don’t you know these crackas done snorted damn near a whole brick in the last month?” Tommy asked, while tying a knot in the sandwich bag he’d just filled.

“What? You mean to tell me these rich ass white people don’t do nothin’ but snort they life away?" She laughed, and then wrapped a rubber band around the $10,000 stack she’d just finished counting.

“Without a doubt.” He smiled, while examining the stacks of money on the table. “So, how much did you count?”

“Umm, one, two, three, four, five. That’s $50,000," she answered, and then placed the rubber banded stacks into a green book bag.

“Awwww, man. We ain’t even been out here for a full two months, and we already stacked up fifty gees.” He bragged, and then snorted a line of fish scale. “Here,” he passed her the rolled up hundred dollar bill, and slid the plate of cocaine across the table. “Rock out.”

As she inserted the bill up her left nostril and snorted the white powder, Tommy's cell phone vibrated on the table.

Vrrrrrm! Vrrrrrm!

“Yo, who dis?” he answered.

“Tommy, it’s me, Larry.”

"Larry, what's up, man? Where you at?"

"I'm at the courthouse. Me and my firm just beat a high profile murder case, and to celebrate I'm throwin' us a party."

"A'ight," Tommy replied, while wiping coke residue from the tip of his nose. "How much y'all gon' need, and when and where is the party?"

"Umm, just stop by my house around seven o'clock, and bring us four."

"A'ight, Larry, I'll see you around seven."

"Alright, buddy. I'll see you then."

"No doubt." He laid the phone down on the table, then snorted another line.

"Who was that?" Nahfisah asked.

"That was the lawyer bul, Larry. I gotta go see him around seven." He replied, and then snorted the last line on the plate. His cell phone vibrated again.

Vrrrrrm! Vrrrrrm!

He lifted his head from the plate, wiped his nose, and then held the phone to his ear. "Yo."

"Tommy, it's Smitty. I need to see you."

"A'ight. When?"

"Tomorrow. Meet me at our spot at five o'clock sharp."

Click!

Although he was enjoying his new life, he was still burdened with the dilemma of either telling on his big homie or going to jail. He knew that the only way to get close to Mook was to pay him his money, and that wasn't an option. He also knew he had to come up with something to appease the detective, but up until this point, he hadn't gotten that far.

While he was caught up in his thoughts of deception, he failed to realize Nahfisah had removed her clothes and was standing beside him massaging her swollen clitoris.

"Boo, this yolk got me horny as shit," she whined. "A bitch try'na get her shit off!"

He spun around to face her, and then he lifted her right leg over his shoulder. He looked up at her blue eyes and bit his bottom lip seductively. He then lowered his head and sucked on her pussy until she came on his tongue.

*****

Around seven o'clock that evening, Larry Santiguida and a host of friends were sitting in his living room snorting the last of the cocaine he purchased from Tommy two days ago.

"Well, I'll be goddamned, Larry. This is the best shit I've tasted since the seventies. Where in the hell did you get it, and how in the hell can I get some?" Mark Rudenstein asked, and then gulped down the rest of his Corona.

"Yeah, Larry," his colleague, Bruce Hagan, cosigned, while wiping coke residue from the tip of his nose. "This shit is friggin' phenomenal."

"Well, fellas," he snorted a line of coke, and then threw his head back. "The man of the hour should be here any minute now."

A couple of seconds later, soft knocking sounded the front door. Larry looked around the room and gave his colleagues two thumbs up.

"That should be the candy man right now." He hopped up from the couch and wiped the powdered residue from his pointed nose. He waltzed over to the front door and looked through the peephole. "Yup, it's the candy man!" He opened the front door and ushered Tommy inside. "Hey, fellas. This is my guy, Tommy, the man of the friggin' century." He smiled, and then wrapped his right arm around Tommy's neck. "And, Tommy, these are my partners from the firm." He pointed toward the skinny man at the end of the couch. "That's Bruce Hagan. And the brilliant man sitting next to him," he gestured toward the fat white man with the lazy eye, "that's Mark Rudenstein."

"Hey, Tommy, it's nice to meet you." Bruce Hagan smiled.

Tommy nodded his head.

"It sure is," Mark concurred, and then saluted him with an empty Corona bottle. "And you'll definitely be seeing a lot of me."

"A'ight," Tommy nodded in his direction. He then turned to look at Larry. "Here," he handed him a sandwich bag that contained three ounces. "I'ma need $8,400 for that."

Larry took the sandwich bag and sat it on the coffee table. He reached inside of his Tommy Hilfiger slacks and pulled out a thick wad of hundred dollar bills. After peeling away ninety of them, he handed them to Tommy. "Keep the change."

Tommy wrapped a rubber band around the stack of money, and then shoved it inside of his coat pocket. He turned his attention to the two lawyers on the couch.

"Y'all can get my number from Larry, and whenever y'all need to get right," he held up his right hand as if it were a telephone, "just give me a call."

The three lawyers were too busy divvying up the white powder to respond. Tommy shrugged his shoulders, and then left the house without saying another word.

Chapter Ten

For the past two months, Easy kept a low profile, and patiently put his plan together. The first thing he did was lease a two bedroom loft in Center City, which set him back $5,000. He spent another $10,000 on furniture, and $60,000 on a wardrobe that consisted of tailor made suits, alligator shoes, and a black full length mink. After that, he went to a car dealership on Roosevelt Boulevard to meet the man, who in the late eighties and early nineties, supplied him with his fleet of luxury vehicles. He used $8,000 to lease a black on black 2012 Range Rover Sport, and left the lot feeling like his old self. Although, he spent $83,000 of the $118,000, in his mind it was more than necessary. He knew that in order for him to get big money, it had to appear as though he already had it. With the right connect and the $35,000 that he had left over, that was more than enough to put him back in position. All he had to do was buy a kilogram of raw, put his whip game to work, and bag up nothing but dimes. His only problem was that he didn't have a block to move the work, and most importantly, he didn't have a connect.

He thought about paying a visit to his old supplier, Columbian Poncho, but his pride wouldn't allow it. I mean, how could he bring Poncho a punk ass $35,000 to buy one key, when he used to purchase a hundred at a time? After deep contemplation, he realized that the only person he trusted enough to get him back in the game was Sonny. He doubted that Sonny was capable of providing him with a whole brick, but at the very least, maybe he could point him in the right direction. All he had to do was convince Sonny to fuck with him, and that in and of itself was going to be a daunting task.

Today he planned on speaking to Sonny, but first he took a trip to his favorite restaurant, The Oak Lane Diner. After placing his order, he took a seat at the back of the restaurant, and fiddled with the features on his new cell phone. For some strange reason, he felt the urge to look to his left, and when he did, he spotted a middle aged white man talking to a young black man. He took a closer look and realized that the young black man was Sonny's friend, Tommy, and that the middle aged white man was a detective. He did his best to eavesdrop on their conversation, but due to the distance he could only hear bits and pieces. He did, however, hear enough to know that Tommy was lining somebody up to get pinched, but he didn't know who. *This lil' rat ass, nigga,* he thought to himself while shaking his head from side to side. Disgusted, he went to the camera app in his phone, pointed the phone at Tommy and pressed *record*.

*****

An hour later, on Fairhill and York, Egypt and Zaire were serving a crowd of customers, and Nasty was sitting on the front steps smoking a Newport and cautiously watching their backs.

"Nast, we need about five more bundles to get this crowd out the way." Zaire informed him, and then sold the last gram in his possession.

Nasty nodded his head, and then disappeared inside of the house. When he returned, he handed Zaire a zip lock bag that was stuffed with bundles, and then fixed his eyes on the black Range Rover that was parked across the street. *Damn, where the fuck that jawn come from?* He thought to him. *It wasn't there when I went in the house.*

He looked at the Range Rover skeptically, and when Easy climbed out the truck and walked toward him, his jaw dropped to the ground. This wasn't the crack head Easy that he was used to seeing around the hood. No sir, this Easy was different! This was the Easy that he grew up hearing stories about. His fresh baldie and neatly trimmed goatee gave him a refined look. A black mink was draped over his shoulders, and underneath, Nasty could see the gold Versace buttons that accessorized his white dress shirt. His Versace blue jeans were extra crispy, and his black wing tipped alligator shoes had a glossy shine.

"What's goin' on, youngin'? You seen my son?"

"Naw, Mr. Easy. He ain't been on the block all day," Nasty responded, while looking at him from head to toe.

"Whatchu mean you ain't seen him all day? Don't he hustle out here wit' y'all."

"Nizzaw." Nasty shook his head from side to side. "He don't hustle out here no more. You must ain't get the memo."

"The memo? What memo?"

"Man, they callin' that nigga 'The Prince of the City'. He dis shit on lock 'round here."

"Naw, I ain't heard," Easy said as he reached inside of his coat pocket and pulled out his Samsung. "Here," he handed the phone to Nasty. "Call him for me."

Nasty did as he was told, and a couple of seconds later Sonny was on the line.

"Big homie, what's poppin'? It's Nasty. I'm on the block right now, and it's somebody out here that wanna holla at you." He handed the phone back to Easy.

"Sonny, where you at? I need to see you about something." Easy spoke into the receiver.

"Yo, who the fuck is this?"

"Who the fuck is this?" Easy pulled the phone away from his ear and looked at it as if it were a poisonous snake. "Umm, umm, umm. I forgot you don't know how to talk to ya pop!"

"My pop? Nigga, I ain't got no mu'fuckin' pop."

"Hey, yo, Sonny, I'm gettin' tired of this disrespectful shit. You better calm the fuck down."

"Yeah, whatever pussy. I'm on 8th and Diamond, and when I come around there, ya ass better be gone."

Click!

Riri was sitting in the passenger's seat, and listening to their conversation. She sucked her teeth and rolled her eyes. "Sontino, why do you keep comin' at him like that?" She asked after he disconnected the call.

"Yo, first of all, slow ya roll." He checked her. "This is

between me and my pops. This ain't got nothin' to do wit' you." He started the Benz and gunned down Diamond Street. He banged a left on Fairhill Street, and drove three blocks until he reached his trap house. He jumped out the Benz and went straight at Nasty. "Yo, why the *fuck* you give that nigga my number, dawg?"

Nasty was speechless. He shrugged his shoulders, then looked at Easy for help.

"Nigga, I *made* him give me ya number." Easy stated.

Sonny couldn't believe his eyes. When he jumped out the Benz a few seconds ago, he shot right pass the man in the mink coat. He would've never imagined in a million years that the man was Easy. As he stood there looking at his father from head to toe, his mind traveled back to a time when Easy was the closest thing to Superman. But then, his heart reminded him of all the years that he and his mother had to struggle while Easy was running the streets getting high. At the thought of all the nights that his mother cried herself to sleep because Easy had stolen her money to buy crack, he became enraged. He balled up his left hand and punched his father square in the face. Easy shook it off and returned a blow of his own. He caught Sonny in the mouth. He followed up with a right hook, but Sonny dipped it and caught him with a right jab and left hook that knocked him a few steps backwards. Simultaneously, they both pulled out guns and aimed them at each other's face.

"Pussy, I'm a blow ya fuckin' head off!" Sonny shouted, and then spit blood from his mouth.

"Well, shit nigga, if you got it like that, then do ya thing!" Easy shot back with his hand firmly gripped around his pistol.

Riana leaped out the passenger's side of the Benz and ran over to Sonny. "No Sontino, don't do it!" She cried and wrapped her arms around him

Sonny snapped, "Get ya ass back in the car, Riri!" He looked to his right, and noticed that Nasty was standing by his side with an AK-47 aimed at Easy's face. To his left, Zaire was holding a .44 Bulldog, and out the corner of his eye, he peeped Egypt creeping up behind Easy with a machete clutched in his right hand.

"Hey, yo, y'all niggas fall back," he ordered, and then lowered his Sig. The trio did as they were told, but maintained their positions around Easy.

Riri was still holding on to him, and tears were streaming down her beautiful face. "Sontino, this shit is gettin' out of hand. This is the shit that I been talking 'bout."

He wrapped his arms around her and held her tightly. "Yo, stop cryin' ma. It's a'ight. Just go wait in the car, and I'ma be there in a minute." He kissed her on the forehead, and nodded toward the 550.

Easy put away his gun, and then told Sonny about Tommy. "Listen Sontino, I'm just try'na look out for you. Earlier today, I was at The Oak Lane Diner, and I saw ya man in there bustin' it up wit' a detective."

"My man? Who?"

"I don't remember the lil' nigga's name, but here." He showed him his cell phone. "Look."

At the sight of Tommy talking to the detective, Sonny wanted to vomit. He shook his head in disbelief, and then returned his gaze to Easy.

"I'm sayin' though, how you know what they was talking 'bout? They coulda been talking 'bout anything."

"Naw Sonny, that rat ass nigga was talking 'bout settin' somebody up. The reason I say that is because I heard the detective tell him that he needed to have his connect front him another brick, and that he would give him the consignment money to pay for the last two bricks."

"Damn." Sonny shook his head. "They must have been talking 'bout Mook. He's the only nigga I know that fronted Tommy some work."

"Well, whatever the case," Easy shrugged his shoulders, "I knew the bul was ya man, so I had to let you know what was going on. It's some other shit that I need to talk to you about too, but now ain't the time. My number's in ya phone, so just get at me when you get a chance."

"A'ight, pops. I need to holla at you about some shit, too."

An awkward feeling washed over them because they didn't know whether to shake hands or what. They each noticed the other's uneasiness, so they settled on a mutual head nod, and climbed back in their cars.

*****

After taking Riri home, Sonny drove around the city thinking about everything that happened. He smiled at the thought of his father getting his act together, and he reached for his iPhone to give him a call.

"Hello," Easy answered on the second ring.

"Yo, pops it's me. I need to see you."

"A'ight, where you at?"

"I'm on my way to the block."

"Say no more. I'ma meet you there in like twenty minutes."

Click!

When Sonny pulled up on Fairhill Street, he parked the Benz in front of his trap house, and then hopped out. He walked up to Nasty, who was sitting on the next door neighbors steps, and greeted him with their Blood handshake.

"What's poppin', big homie?" Nasty greeted him.

"That Five, you already know." Sonny shot back. He noticed that the strip was relatively empty, and he asked, "Yo, where the twins at?"

"We ran outta work about an hour ago, so I told them niggas they could bounce for the night."

"A'ight, well tomorrow is Sunday, so when you see them lil' niggas, tell 'em to stop by my house so I can pay 'em for the week." Sonny said, then reached inside of his pants pocket and pulled out a brick of hundred dollar bills. He removed the two rubberbands that held the money together at both ends, then peeled away fifty of them and handed them to Nasty. "That's ya $5,000 for the week."

Nasty placed the money in his back pocket and said, "Yo, I got about $40,000 and some change in the house for you. Want me to grab it?"

"Yeah, lemme get that." Sonny replied, while wrapping the rubber bands back around his brick of money.

As Nasty got up to go in the house, Sonny thought about his young bul, and smiled. He'd known Nasty ever since he was thirteen, and watched him grow up to be a strong and loyal soldier. At that moment, he decided that as soon as he reached his financial goal, he was gonna hand his operation over to Nasty, and give him the opportunity to make a better life for him and his family.

When Nasty returned from the house with the duffle bag full of money, he handed the bag to Sonny, and watched him as he stashed it in the trunk of his Benz. When he returned to the trap house's front steps, Easy's Range Rover turned the corner and parked directly behind the Benz. He hopped out, and with tears in his eyes, he wrapped his arms around Sonny.

"I'm back, baby boy. I'm back."

Sonny took a step backwards and searched his eyes for any signs of weakness. He found none. He looked at Easy's clothes, and then he looked at his Range Rover. *Damn, this nigga really bounced the fuck back,* he thought to himself.

"Hey, yo, pops come take a ride wit' me." He pressed the automatic start button on his key chain, and the SL 550 came to life.

"Damn, boy." Easy ran his hand across the back fender. "This is a nice lil' Benz you got."

Sonny smiled. "Aww man, this shit ain't 'bout nuffin'. I remember when you used to keep a Benz for everyday of the wee," he shot back, while settling behind the steering wheel. He rolled down the window and called out to Nasty, "Yo, be safe out here Blood. Don't forget to tell Egypt and Zaire to holla at me in the morning."

"I got you, bro," Nasty replied as the Benz pulled away from the curb.

"Hey Sonny, I've been meanin' to ask you this for a while now. How the fuck did y'all young buls get turned out on this gang shit?" Easy asked, not understanding how the Blood movement had made its way to the streets of Philly.

Sonny shrugged his shoulders. "For the most part, I guess you could say it started in the jails. In about 2007, a lot of niggas from New York and New Jersey were comin' to these lil' towns like Allentown, Reading, and York. They was out there on some hustlin' shit, and when they came, they brought the movement right along wit' 'em. Eventually, them niggas started goin' to jail, and the second Blood hit them cell blocks that shit spreads like wildfire. Now, as for me and my set, my big homie Mook, he's originally from Richard Allen. When he was younger, he moved to Brooklyn to live wit' his grand mom. He got locked up in '93, and while he was on Rikers Island, him and the niggas he was rockin' wit' gave birth to the movement on the east coast."

"I can dig it." Easy nodded his head up and down. "I just never thought it would make it all the way from Los Angeles to the streets of Philly. Now I'm seeing young buls wit' red bandanas hangin' out they back pockets, and they throwin up gang signs and shit."

Sonny chuckled, as Easy threw up a fake gang sign that made his fingers look like the crazy white dude's from Scary Movie 2. "Hey, yo, pops, you crazy as shit."

"Naw, Sonny, that's how they be givin' it up," he laughed, and then continued making all types of crazy twist with his fingers.

"But on some real shit pops, it was a time when niggas in New York swore up and down that Blood wouldn't take over the city. Look at it now, Brooklyn is Blooded out. Harlem is Blooded out. The Bronx is Blooded out. Do I need to keep goin'?"

"Naw, man, you don't need to keep goin'." He shook his head and laughed to himself. "Y'all young mutha'fuckas is crazy!"

"So, what made you wanna get clean, and how the fuck you get all this bread?"

Easy took a deep breath. "Man, I ain't touched that shit since the last time I saw you. When you snapped on me like that, it was one of the lowest moments in my life. Matter of fact, it was the way you looked at me. It was like, the sight of me repulsed you." Easy shook his head in shame. "I knew I had to get my shit together. I went to my mom's house, and just focused on gettin' back to where I'm supposed to be." He explained with tears in his eyes.

Sonny didn't respond. He just continued driving, and allowed Easy to tell his story.

"I went back inside of myself and reconnected with who I used to be, you dig? After two weeks of going through the detoxification stage, I reverted back to my first hustle, takin' money. After gettin' my financial situation straight, I got me a loft in Center City. I put some money down on my Range Rover and splurged on a new wardrobe. Oh, yeah, and before I did all of that," he smiled, showing off his new teeth, "I went to the dentist, and got my choppers fixed."

Sonny burst out laughing and looked at his father in amazement. After everything Easy had been through, he somehow found the strength to straighten up and put all the pieces back together again.

Sonny stopped at a traffic light on the corner of Germantown and Erie, and then turned to look at Easy. "So, what's ya next move?"

"Well, as far as gettin' money, the only thing I know is the streets. I was kinda hopin' that you could plug me in wit' ya connect."

"You want me to plug you in wit' my connect? Yo, you

funny as shit," Sonny chuckled. "Nigga, I *am* the connect."

Easy laughed. "Oh, that's right, I forgot the young bul told me you had shit on lock, and that niggas was callin' you *The Prince of the City*." He reached over and massaged the back of Sonny's head. "Now, you know why they call you that, right?"

"Lemme guess, 'cause you're the king huh?" Sonny smirked, and then gave him a look that said, "*Get the fuck outta here!*"

"Yeah, I'm the king young bul! As a matter of fact, fuck that, I'm the mutha'fuckin' *boss*! I thought we already established that twenty years ago when you was a snot nosed brat sitting in the back seat of my Benz, playin' wit' ya Happy Meal toy? I was the boss back then, and I'm still the boss now! I'm just fallin' back and lettin' my underboss do what he do."

Sonny smiled at him. "Damn pops, I'm glad you back man. Whatever you need, just let me know."

"Well right now, I need you to hold me down wit' this work. I'm sittin' on $35,000, and I'm try'na get my hands on a brick. Is that too much, or can you handle that?"

"Can I handle that? Man, stop playin'."

"Damn, well excuse me *Prince of the City*. Since you got it like that, what's up wit' tonight?"

"A'ight, but if you get ya hands on a brick, how you gon' move it?"

"Honestly, I was hopin' that you could help me wit' that, but since you ain't fuckin' wit' the block anymore, I don't know how I'ma move that shit."

"Listen pops, I done stepped my game all the way up, and I'm seeing money like never before. But lately, my girl been buggin' me about fallin' back."

"Hold up," Easy interrupted him. "You mean that lil' chicken tender that was wit' you earlier today? Awwww man, that's a baaaaad mutha'fucka. You better lock that thing down."

Sonny laughed. "Yo, you funny as shit. But yeah, that's my wifey. She's three months pregnant."

Easy smiled. “Congratulations, man! Hopefully, it’s a little girl. I know ya mom wants it to be a girl.”

“Yeah, I know right. But dig though, I’m try’na fall back, and I think you can help me.”

“I’m listening.”

“My block is moving about two bricks a week, and the reason it’s poppin’ so crazy is because I’m sellin’ grams of raw for $40. All I want you to do is run the block for me, and I’m a pay you $15,000 every Sunday.”

Easy nodded his head. “I can roll wit’ that. I just need to know exactly whatchu mean by, ‘Run the block’.”

“It’s simple. All I want you to do is be the liaison between me and my young bul Nasty. Every Sunday, I’m a hit you wit’ two bricks, and all you gotta do is feed ‘em to Nasty and the twins. Nasty’s the caseworker, and his job is to manage the block. The twins, Egypt and Zaire, they the runners and they gon’ turn all the money over to Nasty. Like I said, the blocks movin’ every bit of two bricks a week so that’s $80,640. Nasty and the twins get $5,000 a piece every Sunday. So you gotta pay them niggas, take out ya $15,000, and then pay me the remaining $50,640.”

“Yeah, I can definitely roll wit’ that.” Easy replied, while rubbing his beard. “So when do I start?”

“The beginning of next month.” Sonny answered as he continued driving through the slums of North Philly.

He remembered the conversation that he had with Grip, and asked Easy what he knew about him. Easy pulled out a pack of Newports, and sparked up a smoke. After taking a deep pull and exhaling, he looked at Sonny and said, “He’s your grandfather.”

The news caught him by surprise, and he pulled over on the corner of 18th and Dauphin.

“My *grandfather*? Whatchu mean he’s my grandfather? That nigga ain’t my grandfather.”

“Yeah,” Easy corrected him. “He’s definitely your grandfather.”

"How? My mom's dad died ten years ago and Pop Pop Eddie is probably home wit' Mimom right now. So, how the fuck is Grip my grandfather?"

"Because he's *my* father. Well, my biological father anyway."

"But what about Pop Pop Eddie? He's been wit' Mimom my whole life. I always thought that he was your dad."

"Naw." Easy slowly shook his head from side to side. "He just raised me ever since I was two years old. Before I was born, Grip was the boss of *The Black Mafia*, and being as though they conducted the majority of their business in South Philly, they ended up bumpin' heads wit' the Italians. I'm not exactly sure about what happened, but all I know is that they went to war, and in the process the Italians kidnapped my mom while she was six months pregnant wit' me. When word got around that they had her, and wanted a $500,000 ransom, although Grip was a millionaire he refused to pay them the money," Easy explained.

"Well, how did Mimom get away?"

"The Italians took pity on her because she was pregnant wit' me. They let her go, and ever since that day she vowed to never speak to Grip again. She divorced him, and then moved to North Philly, where Eddie was from. Eventually, they got married and he's been in my life ever since."

"Well, how did you find out that Grip was your real dad?"

"It was the summer of '88, and I was down in the Richard Allen Projects serving my man, Beaver Bushnut. I was parked up on 10th and Poplar, chillin' in my new Jag, and outta nowhere those *YBM* niggas ran down on me. They snatched me out the Jag, and threw me in the trunk. The next thing I knew, I was butt ass naked in a warehouse on Delaware Avenue, and strapped down to a workshop table. After being there for a few hours, this light skinned nigga wit' blue eyes came inside of the warehouse, and the second he laid eyes on me, he ordered them niggas to untie me. He gave me back all of my shit. He gave me my clothes, my money, my jewelry, my gun, and the brick of coke that I was takin' to Bushnut. Then, he gonna tell me to ask my mom about him, and to tell her that he still loved her."

"Later that night, I went to my mom's house, and that's when she told me that Grip was my dad. She broke down the situation between him the Italians, and because she was still married to Grip at the time I was born, she gave me his last name which is Moreno."

"Damn, that's some deep ass shit!" Sonny shook his head, and then sparked up a Newport. "All these years, y'all had me believing that Eddie was my grandpop. What else did y'all keep from me?"

Easy took a deep breath, and then looked out the passenger's side window. After a few seconds of gathering his thoughts, he returned his gaze to Sonny.

"Fuck it, it's about time that I told you this shit anyway."

"Yo, hold up," Sonny interjected. "Man, I hope you ain't about to tell me you got that monster or somethin' like that."

"That monster?" Easy scrunched up his face. "You mean, AIDS? Hell no! I was gon' tell you that you've got a little sister and a little brother."

"I've got a little sister and a little brother?" Sonny asked in disbelief. "Yo, why is you just tellin' me this?"

"Look man, I was livin' reckless, and you already know what I was doin'. I was fuckin' around, and I had a daughter by Rosie from 8th and Diamond, and in '93 I had a son by this chick from 24th and Somerset."

"Hold up pops, Ms. Rosie? That's Nahfisah's mom. You mean to tell me that Fisah's my lil' sister?"

Easy nodded his head. "Yeah, but all the way up until now, I've been denyin' her."

"Pops, you outta pocket. Me and Fisah been rockin' wit' each other since the second grade. What if we woulda started fuckin'? Then what? Yo, that's some nut ass shit."

"Look Sontino, I know I fucked up. Now, I'm doin' everything in my power to make shit right," Easy responded with sincerity in his voice.

"What about my mom? Does she know about any of this?"

"Hell no," Easy quickly replied. "She had her suspicions about Rosie's daughter because you and her were only a few months apart, and resembled each other. Now, ya little brother on the other hand, by the time he was born I had already moved y'all away from the city. She was mostly kept out the loop in regards to what I had goin' on back in Philly."

Sonny reached in the ashtray and grabbed the Backwood that he'd rolled prior to meeting with Easy. He sparked up the Kush filled cigar, and took a hard pull. After exhaling a thick cloud of smoke, he asked, "Well, what's up wit' my lil' brother? What's his name?"

"Rahmello. He just turned nineteen back in October, but I haven't seen him since he was 6 years old."

Sonny looked at him and shook his head. "Pops, you need to fix this shit."

"Trust me Sontino, I have every intention to do just that."

Instead of responding, Sonny turned up the radio, and pulled away from the curb.

Chapter Eleven

Sonny and Sheed drove to Mook's mansion to tell him the news about Tommy. He offered no response. Instead, he just cracked his knuckles one by one, and gritted his teeth. His body language said everything, and that meant that Tommy was a dead man.

*****

Later That Night...

On the corner of 4th and South, an overweight black man dressed in a Santa Claus suit was standing beside a Salvation Army station ringing the bell, and encouraging the holiday shoppers to leave a donation. A brown Dunkin Donuts cup was clutched in his right hand, and the hot steam that seeped from the cracked lid carried the aroma of roasted coffee beans mixed with Hennessey. He took a sip of the scorching liquid.

"Umm umm umm. Now, that's what I'm talking 'bout," he said to himself, and then did a shimmy with his shoulders to shake off the chilly November weather.

As he took another sip, a pearl white Mercedes Benz SL 550 pulled up on the corner, and the heavy baseline that rattled the car's trunk, coupled with the effects of the Hennessey laced coffee made *Santa* nod his head and do a little two step.

Inside of the Benz, sitting comfortably behind the tinted windows, Sonny and Sheed were smoking a Vanilla Dutch, and discussing the conversation that Sonny had with Easy the night before.

"Damn, Blood, Nahfisah's your sister?" Sheed asked, and then exhaled a cloud of Kush smoke. He passed the Dutch to Sonny, and continued talking. "I'm sayin though, y'all do look alike. Y'all both light skinned and y'all both got that curly hair. The only real difference is y'all eyes. Yours is brown and her's is blue."

"Yeah," Sonny nodded his head. "And we always had that

brother/sister type of bond."

"A'ight, now what's the situation wit' ya lil' brother?" Sheed asked.

Sonny shrugged his shoulders. "I don't know, scrap. Last night, me and my pops went through 24th and Somerset to check on him, but his mom said she ain't seen the nigga in two weeks. So basically, my lil' sister's laid up wit' a rat, and my lil' brother's runnin' around the city doin' only God knows what."

"It is what it is, scrap. But yo, I'm a change the channel for a minute. I know you just found out that the ol' head's ya grandpop and all dat, but the big homie gave us the green light, and we gotta follow his orders. Plus, you already know the ol' head be on that *Black Mafia* shit, shakin' niggas down and imposin' his will. These pussy ass niggas in the city be goin' for that shit too, but I'm not. Just so you know, the first chance I get, I'm parkin' this nigga," Sheed stated, indirectly checking Sonny's temperature.

Sonny remained quiet. Although he'd just found out that Grip was his grandfather, Mook was the one who practically raised him, and therefore his undivided loyalty was to Mook.

As he killed the ignition and looked across the street in front of the Dr. Denim's clothing store, he spotted a money green Escalade.

"Speakin' of Grip." He pointed toward the SUV. "Ain't that the nigga's truck?"

"I don't know," Sheed shot back, but instinctively gripping the pearl handle on his Desert Eagle.

A couple of minutes later, Biggs, one of Grip's street captains emerged from the store with shopping bags in both hands. He cautiously glanced up and down South Street, and then made his way toward the Escalade. He tossed the bags in the backseat, and then climbed his 6'4" frame behind the steering wheel. He started the engine, and the sounds of Tupac's, *Hail Mary* erupted from the 12 inch subwoofers in the back compartment...

"I ain't a killer, but don't push me/ revenge is like the sweetest joy nextcto gettin' pussy/ Picture paragrahs unloaded, wise words being quoted/ I peeped the weakness in the rap game and sewed it..."

Slowly, he pulled away from the curb and cruised down the crowded block. He was oblivious to the fact that Sonny's Benz trailed closely behind. He made a left turn on 3rd Street, and the white Benz followed suit.

After trailing the SUV for a few blocks, Sheed looked over at Sonny. "At the first red light, I'm a hop out and park this nigga."

"A'ight, just make it quick so we can hurry up and get outta here," Sonny replied, and then reached inside of his center console and grabbed his red flag. "Here," he handed the bandana to Sheed. "Tie this 'round ya face."

At the intersection of 3rd and Snyder, a red traffic light caused the Escalade to ease to a stop. As Biggs sat behind the steering wheel nodding his head to the music, he spotted a shiny gleam in the corner of his left eye. "What the fuck?" He turned to his head to get a better view of the shiny object.

Doom! Doom! Doom!

The tinted driver's side window exploded in his face, and the bullets missed his head by centimeters. Despite the fact that he was momentarily blinded by the muzzle flash, he mashed down on the gas pedal, and fishtailed into a black BMW that was parked on the opposite corner. Wounded and disoriented, he opened the driver's side door and attempted to flee. Again, Sheed squeezed the trigger.

Doom! Doom! Doom!

A burning sensation spread throughout his body as the three .50 caliber slugs ripped through his back, spun him around, and slightly lifted him off of his feet. He tried to scream for help, but the only thing that came out his mouth was a thick glob of blood. As he lay on his back struggling to breathe, the sight of a man creeping toward him with a red bandana tied around his face made him tremble with fear. Sheed pressed the triangles haped barrel to the center of his forehead, and squeezed the trigger.

Doom!

Biggs' head burst open, and bloody brain matter shot up in Sheed's face. It caused him to stumble backwards. As he frantically wiped the warm flesh away from his eyes, he was caught off guard by the eerie sound of screeching tires.

Scurrrrr!

Initially, he thought it was Sonny coming to scoop him up, but when he noticed the Philadelphia Police Cruiser his heart fell into his stomach. A uniformed officer hopped out the cruiser with his service pistol aimed at Sheed's head.

"Drop the fucking weapon, now!"

Sheed didn't respond. Instead, he glanced over the officer's shoulder, and spotted Sonny crouched down, and sneaking up behind him. Somehow, the bright muzzle flashes of the Desert Eagle had elicited so much of the officer's attention that in his quest to apprehend a murder suspect, he overlooked the white Benz that was parked on the corner with the lights off and the engine running. Unbeknownst to the newlywed and father of three, his oversight would prove to be fatal.

"You've got three seconds to drop your weapon, or I swear to God I will fucking kill you! One! Two!"

Boc! Boc! Boc! Boc! Boc!

"Agh shit!" The officer screamed in pain as he stumbled forward, and then spun around, only to find Sonny aiming a Sig Sauer at his face. Again, bright muzzle flashes erupted from the barrel of the .357.

Boc! Boc! Boc! Boc! Boc! Boc! Click! Click!

Satisfied that the cop was no longer a threat, Sonny and Sheed ran back to the Benz. They hopped inside, and then sped away from the scene.

*****

It was 10:45 p.m. when Grip, followed by Murder and Malice, entered the large storage room inside of his warehouse. His street captains and lieutenants were sitting around a mahogany conference table discussing Biggs' murder. The second they noticed the old man and his two enforcers their discussion came to a halt, and an eerie silence filled the room.

Grip removed his Bossilini hat, and handed it to Murder. He then circled the conference table with an agitated look on his face. Finally, he reached his chair at the head of the table, and took a seat. He retrieved a Havana Cuban cigar from his jacket pocket, and then reached inside of his slacks and pulled out a solid gold cigar cutter. He clipped the ends off the cigar, held it to his nose, and inhaled the sweet tobacco scent. After placing the stogie in his mouth, he glanced to his right where Malice was icegrilling his captains and lieutenants.

"Gimme a light," he demanded.

Without an ounce of hesitation, Malice held a gold lighter to the tip of the cigar, and a small cloud appeared in front of his face. He looked at the men sitting around the table, and then spoke in a no nonsense tone of voice.

"As you all know, Biggs was murdered on 3rd and Snyder, and whoever killed him, they literately blew his head off. It's not a mutha'fucka in this city that doesn't know who we are, so therefore whoever's responsible, they were sending us a message." He paused and fiddled with the diamond ring on his right pinky. "Does anyone have an idea as to who would be brave enough to send us such a message?"

Feeling as though he was the second in command, Monster, the capo from the 5th and Washington crew, spoke up.

"I think it was them niggas from 7th Street. Ever since we raised our prices two months ago, them mutha'fuckas been actin' funny."

"Naw, Unc, I don't think so," his nephew, Lil' Buggy dissented. "Them niggas been gettin' money wit' us for years. When we raised our price to $42,000 they knew it was strictly business."

Grip considered Monster's suggestion, but just like Lil' Buggy he disagreed. He looked at Smack, his capo for the 22nd and McKean crew, and asked him what he thought about the situation.

"I think it was them *Block Boy* niggas. When you rejected their offer, and refused to have another sit down wit' the bul Mook, I think they took it as a sign of disrespect. Plus, that nigga Sonny, according to the information I got from our people in North Philly, that lil' mutha'fucka think he a gangsta. I can honestly see him doin' some shit like this. Especially after the way he was actin' that day we went to his block. I'm tellin' you, Mr. Moreno, that lil' nigga think he ready for war. So, if I had to bet my last dollar on who killed Biggs, it would have to be them *Block Boy* niggas."

Grip puffed on his cigar and nodded his head. "I'm wit' you on this one, Smack. I think Mook's behind this shit, and for that," he blew out a cloud of smoke, "I want that dirty mutha'fucka dead. But first, I want y'all to bring him to me. I want the satisfaction of watching his stupid ass beg for his life.

"Now, as far as my grandson, he's off limits. All I want y'all to do is focus on Mook." He flicked the ash off the tip of his cigar, and then continued. "Oh, yeah, y'all already know that Biggs' funeral is gonna be hot due to the fact that a cop was murdered in the process so just fall back. The cops are gonna want answers, so expect the streets to be uptight for a little while. However," he took a pause, and one by one, looked each of them in the eye, "Make no mistakes about it, as soon as the heat dies down, it's *murder season*."

Chapter Tweleve

Aside from the fact that Nahfisah and Tommy were still missing in action, everything else for Sonny was going according to plan. His man Diamondz was waiting on his December shipment, and after counting the money that he stacked up in the past three months, he was sitting on a little over $700,000. He knew that his cousin Breeze, was getting out of jail in a couple of days so to welcome him home accordingly, he put $100,000 to the side for him. He also realized that Christmas was right around the corner so he set aside another $250,000 to buy Riana the gift that their family deserved, which was a new house. He rubber banded the remaining $350,000 in denominations of $10,000, and stashed the money in the small vault that he had built in his mother's basement. The $25,000 that he owed Mook was already waiting to be collected so essentially, all of his affairs were in order.

As he lay on his bed smoking a Kushfilled Backwood and watching the movie, *Goodfellas*, he heard his mom calling him from the bottom of the steps.

"Sontino, Mook is down here!"

"A'ight, mom! Send him up!"

A few seconds later, Mook entered the room with a black gym bag hanging from his right shoulder.

"Peace, Blood."

"Mook, what's poppin' big homie?"

"That Five," Mook shot back, while embracing him with their Blood handshake. "What's up wit' you, though?"

"Ain't shit, dawg, I'm just gettin' this paper," Sonny responded, and then handed him the duffle bag that contained the $25,000.

Mook nodded his head, and then handed him the gym bag that contained his December shipment.

"Hey, yo, Mook, I've been meaning to ask you about ya real estate agent. I'm try'na get a new house for me, Riri, and the baby."

"A'ight, just holla at me when you're ready, and I got you."

"Nigga, I'm ready *now*. I'm try'na have the house by Christmas."

Mook shrugged his shoulders. "More or less. The housing market is poppin' right now, and it's definitely the right time to buy. How much you try'na spend?"

"Somewhere around $250,000."

"A'ight, you can definitely get somethin' nice wit' that type of bread. If I was you, I would snatch up one of these houses that was foreclosed."

"Foreclosed? What the fuck is that?" Sonny asked.

"That's when a mu'fucka wasn't payin' their mortgage, and the bank that they was dealin' wit' repossessed that shit. Now, once that happens the bank reclaims ownership of the house, and they put that mu'fucka back on the market. The majority of the time they price the house for cheaper than what it's really worth."

"A'ight, my nigga, I need you to get on that for me as soon as possible."

"Say no more, I got you. I'ma have lil' buddy holla at you by tomorrow. But look, I got a lot of shit to do today so I'ma get wit' you later on tonight." Mook said as he extended his right hand.

"A'ight scrap, be safe out there. You know the streets is watchin'."

"Come on, nigga," Mook smiled, and then lifted his Gucci sweater, displaying his Kevlar bulletproof vest. "And I keep one of these too." He pulled out a chrome 9mm.

Sonny smiled and nodded his head in approval. After Mook left the room, he grabbed his iPhone and called Easy.

Ring! Ring!

"Hello," Easy answered.

"Yo, pops, it's that time. Meet me on my block in an hour."

*****

An Hour Later...

Sonny, Nasty, and the twins were sitting at the dining room table in his trap house, weighing and bagging up grams.

"Yo, this shit stank like a mu'fucka," Egypt stated, while placing a rock on the digital scale that sat before him.

"Yeah, I know right," Zaire concurred. "This shit smell like, man, I don't know what the fuck this shit smell like. The best I can come up wit' is Vicks vapor rub mixed wit' some stale ass candy."

As Sonny looked back and forth between Egypt and Zaire, he heard a soft knock on the front door.

"Yo, Nasty, go answer that, and don't let nobody in here unless it's my pops, or somebody from the team."

Nasty got up from the table and walked over to the couch where a sawed off shotgun was tucked underneath the cushions. He grabbed the gun and tucked it behind his left leg, and then slowly cracked the door open. When he saw Easy standing on the on the stoop, he motioned for him to come inside, and then stuck his head out the door and looked up and down the block. Satisfied that nothing was out of place, he closed the front door, then put the shotgun back in the couch, and returned to the dining room table.

As Easy removed his mink coat and hung it on the coatrack, Sonny's pitbull ran over to him and sniffed his leg.

"Ohhhh shit! Yo, what the fuck is this?" Easy asked, scared to death.

"Damu!" Sonny addressed the muscular pitbull in a dominant voice. "Take ya ass upstairs."

The snow white, red nosed pit looked at Sonny, and then returned his gaze to the stranger. Reluctantly, he obeyed his master's order and ran up the steps.

"Don't worry about Damu. He's just doin' his job," Sonny

assured him.

"That's a big ass dog!" Easy exclaimed, and then wiped away the sweat from his brow. "What the fuck is you feedin' him? Steroids. That mutha'fucka got a head like a grizzly bear. And he almost made me shit on myself." He laughed, and the rest of them laughed too.

"Shit," Nasty interjected. "Damu's still a puppy. If you think he's big, just wait 'til you see his pop, Mousillini. He's in the backyard. That mu'fucka's so big that we can't even walk him."

"Well, y'all just keep his big ass in the backyard, then." Easy continued laughing as he walked over to the table.

Sonny grabbed all the bundles and gathered them into a pile.

"A'ight, this is what we're gonna do. As of now, my pops is the one runnin' the block. For the most part, everything's gon' stay the same, except that y'all gon' be answerin' to him, and he is gon' report back to me." He looked at Easy and continued, "Pops, is there anything that you wanna tell 'em?"

"Naw, Sonny, I'm good." Easy shrugged his shoulders. "It's just like you said. Everything is gonna stay the same. At the beginning of every week, I'm a give," he pointed at Nasty, "what's ya name again youngin'?"

"Nasty."

Easy nodded his head. "I'm a give Nasty two bricks for y'all to move, then on Sunday when I collect the money and drop off the next two bricks, I'm a pay y'all $5,000 a piece."

"A'ight Mr. Easy." Zaire nodded his head assuredly. "We got you, ol' head."

"Well then, that's what I'm talking 'bout." Easy smiled. "There is one condition though."

"What's that?" Nasty asked.

"Y'all gotta keep them big ass dogs as far away from me as possible!"

They all burst out laughing.

*****

Later That Day...

Sonny and Easy pulled up in front of his house on Reese Street. "Aye, Sonny, I don't think ya mom is gonna wanna see me man." Easy stated as butterflies filled his stomach.

"Nizzaw, I ain't feelin' you on that one pops. After all those years she sat around prayin' that you'd stop gettin' high." He held up his hands for emphasis. "I know she would love to see you back on top of ya game!"

"A'ight man, I can dig it." Easy shook his head in defeat. "I guess I'ma have to face her sooner or later."

They exited Easy's Range Rover, and went inside of the house. The sounds of Keyshia Cole's, *Love* was thumping from the second floor, and the aroma of Annie's Clinique perfume permeated the air. Easy took a deep breath, and then sat on the couch. *Man, she's probably gonna curse me the fuck out!* He thought to himself.

"Hey, yo, mom!" Sonny called out from the bottom of the steps.

"What, boy? Can't you see I'm up here jammin' wit' my girl Keyshia Cole?" Annie yelled from the second floor.

"I need you to come downstairs! It's somebody down here that wanna talk to you!"

"Hold on! I'm gettin' dressed. I'll be down there in a minute."

Sonny turned his attention to Easy. "Yo, you want somethin' to drink?"

"Yeah, lemme get some water."

As Sonny headed toward the kitchen, Annie descended the stairs in a pink and blue nurse's uniform. When she entered the living room and saw Easy sitting on the couch, she stopped in her tracks. She rubbed her eyes and took a closer look.

Easy stood to his feet and asked, "How are you doin'

Annie?"

Instead of responding, she just stood there with tears welling up in her eyes. He grabbed her by the hand, and gestured for her to take a seat on the couch. She looked at her estranged husband, and attempted to speak.

"How? What? When? How long have you been like this?"

"About three months now. I'm back to the old me Annie. My days of gettin' high are over," he proclaimed with sincerity in his voice.

Sonny returned from the kitchen with a glass of water in his left hand. He handed the glass to Easy, and then leaned forward to kiss his mother on the forehead.

"He looks good, right? I made him come over so you could see him all cleaned up."

She didn't respond. Instead, she just stared at him, and then returned her attention to Easy.

"This shit is too much for me to handle right now. I need to get outta here." She got up from the couch and headed toward the front door. As she grabbed the door knob she took a deep breath, and then turned toward her husband.

"I'm glad that you finally got your shit together, but if you think that after all these years you can just walk back into my life like ain't shit happen, then you got the game fucked up!" She stormed out the house and slammed the door behind her.

*****

The Next Day...

After meeting with Diamondz, and receiving a phone call from Mook's real estate agent, Sonny was parked in front of a townhouse in Cheltenham, Pennsylvania and waiting to meet her. As he sat in his Benz, he looked at the house and nodded his head in approval. The two story townhouse had beige siding and brown window shutters. The front lawn was well manicured, and the newly paved driveway led to a three car garage. He looked at his diamond encrusted Rolex, and saw that it was 3:45 p.m. *Damn, where this chick at?* He asked himself.

A couple of minutes later, a champagne colored 2012 Porsche Panamara pulled up behind him and a beautiful black woman hopped out in full diva regalia. Her cinnamon waist length fox matched her Ugg boots to perfection, and her skin tight Chanel jeans displayed the thickness of her hips and thighs. Her smooth chocolate skin resembled a melted Hershey's Kiss, and her Chanel #5 perfume reached his Benz before she did. To make matters worse, she had almond shaped, hazel eyes and a cute little button nose. Her silky, black hair was freshly cut into a Mohawk, and heart shaped designs were etched on the sides.

Goddamn, she bad! Sonny thought to himself as he climbed out the car.

"Hello," she said as she extended her right hand. "You must be Sontino Moreno."

"Yeah, but you can call me Sonny. You must be Daphney Rines?"

"The one and only." She smiled. Her beauty killing him softly. "So, do you like whatchu see?"

"Well, I guess it depends." He licked his lips seductively. "Are we talking 'bout you or the house?"

She blushed. "The house, silly."

"A'ight, well since you put it like that, I guess you could say that I like the house too."

She laughed at him and began walking up the driveway toward the front door.

Damn, mommy got an ass like one of them Kardashian bitches. I wonder if that thing is real. He thought to himself, while trailing behind her.

"Yes," Daphney laughed.

"Huh?" Sonny replied as he was completely caught off guard.

"My ass," She turned her head and smiled at him. "It's real."

"What? Girl, wasn't nobody thinking 'bout ya ass," he lied.

"Umm hmm." She stated sarcastically, and then used her key to open the front door.

When they entered the house the first thing that grabbed his attention was the glossy hardwood floors. There were four bedrooms, three bathrooms, a laundry room, and a finished basement. She led him out back to the extended patio, and showed him the in ground pool.

"So," she turned to face him, "how do you like the house?"

He shrugged his shoulders in a nonchalant manner. "It's a'ight. I can fuck wit' it."

"Alright, well I already talked to Mook, so I know your situation. For $20,000, my connect at the bank is gonna approve the loan that you're gonna need to buy the house."

"Loan?" He looked at her like she was crazy. "I don't need a loan. You said that the house was going for $240,000 right? Yo, I got that in the car right now."

She looked at him and laughed. "Boy, you can't just drop a quarter of a million dollars down on a house. Especially when it's drug mone. The feds will be on ya ass faster than you can blink. That's why I got my connect at the bank. She's the manager. The bank is gonna buy the house, and then charge you a monthly mortgage. That way everything will appear to be legit, and you won't have to worry about the feds being all up in your shit. All you gotta do is pay me $10,000 for my services, give me the $20,000 for my girl at the bank, and then the house is basically yours. Well, providing that you keep up wit' ya mortgage payments."

"A'ight, ma, I got you. There is only on one condition, and that is that you gotta let me take you out to lunch."

"Yeah, we can do that." She smiled. "But that's only because you're cute."

"More or less."

*****

A Half An Hour Later...

They were at the Applebee's restaurant on Old York Road, and seated at a table that provided them with a clear view of the entrance.

"Are you guys ready to order?" asked the young waitress who was assigned to their table.

Sonny looked at the chubby white girl and smiled. "Yeah, we'll both be having turkey burgers and French fries."

The waitress wrote down their orders, then asked, "And would y'all like anything to drink?"

"Yeah," Daphney interjected, then looked at Sonny with a fake attitude. "We'll *both* be having cranberry juice."

As the waitress walked away from their table, Sonny looked at Daphney, and smiled. "Tic for tac, huh?"

"What's good for the goose is good for the gander." She smiled back.

"So, Miss Daphney, where you from?"

"I'm originally from Southwest, but now I'm living in Mt. Airy. I've been out there for the past two years."

"So, how you know my man Mook?" He tested the waters, wondering if she had ever fucked his man.

"I've known Mook my whole life. He used to work for my daddy back in the day."

"Your dad?" Sonny asked in disbelief. "Hold up, you mean to tell me that Alvin Rines is ya pops?"

"Yep, that's my daddy."

"Yo, ya pops is a fuckin' legend in Philly. They say he was one of the first niggas to move crack in the city."

"Yeah, and they gave him a life sentence behind that shit too," she sadly replied, and then looked down at the table.

Sonny placed his hand on her chin and lifted her head back up. "Yo, don't let that shit get you down ma. I can't exactly say that I know how you feel, but trust me, I understand ya struggle."

She took a deep breath. "Can we please change the subject? So what are you planning on doin' wit' that big ass house?" She asked, wondering why someone so young would be interested in a house of that magnitude.

"My girl's about to have our first baby, so to show her that I'm ready to step up to the plate and handle my business, I'm gettin' us a new house."

She smiled and nodded her head. "Yo, that's a good look. I hope that she's appreciative. My nut ass baby's daddy ain't shit. All he wants to do is waist his life doin' county bids, and whenever he's outta jail, all he wants to do is chase pussy. His trifling ass doesn't even take care of his son."

"Damn, I ain't no hater or nothin', but if whatchu sayin' is true, then main man outta pocket. He supposed to be playin' his part, especially wit' a chick like you. You're beautiful. You out here makin' moves *and* you keep it hood at the same time. Yo, that nigga trippin'."

"Humph, who you tellin'? Niggas are so grimy."

"Nizzaw," he shook his head from side to side. "Every nigga ain't like that. If you was my girl, it's nothin' that I wouldn't do for you. You got ya head on straight, you beautiful, and it seems like you on top of ya game. Any nigga would be lucky to have a lady like you by his side. Real shit."

She looked at him and sighed. "I wish I woulda met you a few years ago, Sontino."

"Yo, why you say that?"

"Because you're everything that I've ever wanted in a man. You're a cutie, you're focused, and you're not one of these broke ass niggas that be runnin' around the city frontin'. Actually, in a lot of ways, you remind me of my father."

"So you're basically sayin' that you could see yourself fuckin' wit' a nigga like me?"

"In a heartbeat."

"So what's stoppin' you?"

She screwed up her face and snapped her neck *sista girl* style.

"Hold up, didn't you just tell me that you had a girl, and that she was about to have your baby? See, that's the shit that I be talking 'bout. Y'all niggas are so grimy."

"A'ight, now what if I told you that even though I love my girl she's not everything that I need in a woman?"

"Well, what is it that you need in a woman?"

"I need a woman that I can relate to. It's like, my girl, she ain't really 'bout nothin'. Don't get me wrong, I love shorty to death, but at the same time it's like, she doesn't complete me."

"Well, what does she do?"

"She looks pretty and lies around waitin' for me to bust her ass."

"Does she work or go to school?"

"Nizzaw, she doesn't do none of that."

"So, if she's not everything that you need in a woman, then why are you still wit' her?"

"To be honest wit' you, I don't even know. I guess you could say that it's love," he shrugged his shoulders, "or maybe I'm just used to her."

"A'ight." She nodded her head. "Well, what is it that you love about her?"

He smiled. "I love the way she make a nigga feel. She's always encouraging me to do better, but at the same time, she's not really doin' nothin' to better herself."

"Well, do you encourage her to do better?"

"Naw, now that I think about it, I don't."

"Well, if you truly love her and you wanna make y'all relationship work, then you need to motivate her to do somethin' wit' her life. As a woman, I know that if my man was handlin' his business, and constantly encouragin' me to do the same, that would be enough to motivate me."

"Damn, Daphney, that's some real ass shit."

"Well, I'm a real ass woman. What else would you expect?"

Sonny just looked at her and smiled. "Yo, you a tight lil' piece of work. You know that, right?"

She giggled.

"On some real shit though, you got a nigga feelin' you. At the same time, I got a girl. So the only thing I can really offer you is my friendship."

"I know," she quickly responded, "and I can respect that. All I ask is that you stay in touch because I really think you're a good dude, and I enjoy your conversation."

He nodded his head and smiled. "I enjoy your's too."

Chapter Thirteen

"Sontino, wake up!" Riana shouted, while nudging his shoulder.

"Damn, Riri, I'm try'na to sleep man. What the fuck."

"Boo, it's nine o'clock in the morning and Erika is downstairs waitin' on us. We gotta go to the jail to pick up Breeze."

He instantly remembered that today was Breeze's release date, and a huge smile spread across his face. He climbed out the bed and hopped in the shower. After getting dressed, and grabbing the money that he set aside for Breeze he descended the stairs, and found Riana and Erika sitting on his mother's couch.

"Finally," Erika stated in a sarcastic manner. "It's been about two years since the last time I've been wit' my baby, and now that he's finally comin' home you wanna take all day to wake up and get dressed."

"A'ight Erika, we're leavin' damn." Sonny shot back, and then threw her the keys to his Tahoe. "Here, you take the truck. Me and Riri gon' ride in the Benz."

When they arrived at the Camp Hill Correctional Facility, Breeze was standing out front in the Polo sweat suit and Polo snorkel that Erika had dropped off for him during their last visit.

"What's poppin', Scrap?" Sonny greeted, and then embraced him with a brotherly hug.

"That Five," Breeze shot back, and then threw up his Brim set with both hands.

At 6'1" and 215 pounds, Breeze was husky as shit. He had short, dark, wavy hair, and a darkbrown complexion. His face was usually set into a serious expression, but today he was all smiles.

Erika hopped out the Tahoe, ran up to him, and leaped in his arms. "I missed you so much!" She shouted and smothered his face with kisses. "I can't believe that you're finally outta there."

"Yeah, I know right." He put her down and examined her from head to toe. "But, look at you though. You're lookin' good as shit! You know a nigga gonna tear that pussy up, right."

"Umm hmm," she purred. "My shit is super duper extra tight too."

"Eeewwww! Y'all are so nasty." Riri laughed as she approached Breeze and embraced him with a warm hug.

Breeze smiled at her. "What Riri? I know ya lil' pregnant ass ain't out here callin' nobody nasty."

"Boy, shut up," she continued laughing, and then playfully punched him in the arm.

"Hey Breeze, lemme show you somethin' real quick," Sonny interrupted, and then led him toward the back of the Tahoe.

He opened the back doors and showed him the two duffle bags that were lying in front of his speaker box. He opened the first bag and showed him the bulletproof vest, the AK-47, and the Glock .40 that was stashed inside. He then opened the second bag and showed him the $100,000 that he stacked up for him.

"All this shit is for you my nigga. Welcome home."

"Damn," Breeze shook his head in disbelief. "Niggas was sayin' that you turned it up out here, but I didn't know you was doin' it like this." He nodded toward the two duffle bags and the SL 550.

"This shit ain't 'bout nothin'. It's a $100,000 in there." He pointed at the bag. "Use that to get you a new spot and a new whip. Tomorrow, I'm a take you clothes shoppin', and after you get settled in. I'm a start hittin' you off wit' these bricks." He gestured toward the bag of guns. "You gon' need them because shit a lil' shaky out here right now."

"Yeah, I know." Breeze nodded his head. "I heard y'all had beef wit' the ol' head Grip. You already know what time I'm on so all you gotta do is bring me up to speed, son. Word."

"Yo, don't even worry about that right now. All I want you to do is focus on gettin' ya money right." Sonny said, while zipping up the duffle bags and closing the back doors. "I'ma let Erika hold the truck so y'all can do y'all thing for the day. But tomorrow, make sure you get wit' me so we can do what we do."

Breeze nodded his head. "That's gangsta. I'ma definitely need a lil' time to get my bread back up, but as soon as I do you know what time it is."

"So, what do you plan on doin'? You stayin' in PA., or is you movin' back to New York?"

"I'ma stay in Pennsylvania, between Philly and Allentown. While I was booked, I met the homies, R.O. and Evil. Yo, them niggas is official, son. They originally from up top, but be doin' they thing in Allentown. So I'ma go out there and fuck wit' them niggas."

"Well, whatever you wanna do, just know I got you nigga."

They hugged one another, and then went to their separate vehicles. Breeze climbed in the Tahoe with Erika, and Sonny hopped in the Benz with Riana.

*****

An Hour Later...

Sonny and Riana were sitting in her doctor's office waiting to be seen for her monthly check up. Riana had her nose buried in a baby magazine, and Sonny was thinking about the conversation that he had with Daphney the day before.

He closed the magazine that she was reading and said, "Boo, did you figure out whatchu wanna do after you have the baby?"

"I'ma be a good mother, silly. What do you think?"

"Naw, that's not what I'm talking 'bout. I'm sayin' like, what is it that you wanna do wit' ya life?"

She shrugged her shoulders. "I don't know. Right now, I'm just focused on havin' the baby. Whatchu think we're gonna have, a boy or a girl?"

"I don't even care. I just want the baby to be healthy," he responded in a somber voice.

While they were caught up in their conversation, Daphney entered the doctor's office. She was holding the hand of her four year old son. When she spotted Sonny sitting with Riana her heart skipped a beat, and she became momentarily jealous. Although she didn't really know him, to her the time that they'd spent together was like a breath of fresh air. She was so sick and tired of the games that her son's father played, and ever since she met Sonny she wished that he was the man in her life.

She looked at Riana and sized her up. *Humph, she's cute and all that, but she ain't got nothin' on Alvin's daughter,* she thought to herself. She put an extra pep in her step, and her voluptuous ass to jiggle with every movement.

As Riana was talking to Sonny, she noticed that the dark skinned woman with the little boy was staring at her. Sonny noticed that Riana was looking across the room so he looked over to see what she was staring at. When he saw Daphney sitting at the other end of the waiting room, he smiled at her.

"What's up, Daph? That ya lil'' man right there?"

"Yeah, this is my son Dayshon." She returned his smile, and then looked at the little boy. "Say hi, Day Day."

"Hi," the little boy smiled, and then waved at Sonny and Riana.

Riana scowled at Daphney, and then directed her attention to Sonny. "Daphney? Who the fuck is Daphney?"

"Yo," he looked at her like she was crazy. "Fall back, Riri. That's just my homie."

"Ya homie. I don't know that bitch," Riana spat as she stood to her feet.

"Excuse me, but who do you think you're talkin' to?" Daphney spoke up.

"*Bitch*, I'm talkin' to you!" Riana pointed at her, and then began walking in her direction.

Sonny grabbed her by the arm and made her sit back down. "Yo Riri, you outta pocket. Didn't I just tell you that she was my peoples."

"Pussy, I ain't got no male friends, so how the fuck you gon' have a female friend? Especially some *bitch* that I don't even fuckin' know! Ahn ahn, I ain't goin' for it," she shot back, and then folded her arms across her chest.

Sonny shook his head, and then looked over at Daphney. "Yo, I'm sorry about that. I see you over there wit' ya lil' man, and y'all ain't deserve to be disrespected like that. I apologize."

"What?" Riana snapped. "You really gon' stand here and apologize to *this bitch*. You know what Sontino..."

She cocked back, and smacked him in the face.

Whack!

A red hand print appeared on his left cheek as she broke down crying, and then ran out of the doctor's office.

He followed her outside. "Riri, what the fuck is wrong wit' you? You buggin' out for nothin'."

"Fuck you, Sontino! I wanna go home! Take me home!"

Without another word, he did as she asked. When they pulled up in front of her house, she hopped out the car and slammed the door.

"Pussy, I'm done wit' you! And get ya shit outta my fuckin' house!"

He entered the house behind her, and found her mother sitting on the couch, looking confused. "Sontino, what happened?"

"I don't know, Ms. Mary. We was at the doctor's office, and a female friend of mines was there wit' her son. All I did was speak to her, and Riri started trippin'."

"Pussy, stop lyin'!" Riana shouted from the top of the steps, and then threw down the gym bag that was holding his last six keys. "I saw the way that she was lookin at you. Y'all think I'm stupid."

"Riri, what the fuck is you talking 'bout?"

"Don't act dumb, bitch! You was lookin' at her the same fuckin' way!"

"Yo, what the fuck is you talking 'bout? How was I

lookin' at her?" He yelled back because his frustration growing immensely.

"You was looking at her the way that you used to look at me!" She burst out crying, and then ran to her room and slammed the door.

He began to follow her, but her mother stopped him. "Baby, just give her a little time to calm down. She's going through her emotions right now. Believe me, I know what it's like to be pregnant. She's feeling insecure about her weight, and she thinks that you would rather be with a woman who she feels is more attractive than she is."

He took a deep breath. "A'ight, Ms. Mary, if you say so. Can you please just tell her that I love her, and that I'll call her later?"

"I will baby. Just give her some time to get her emotions in check. I'm sure that everything will work itself out."

When he got back to his car, he stashed the Nike gym inside of the trunk, and then pulled out his iPhone and called Daphney.

Ring! Ring! Ring!

"Hello," she answered.

"Daph, it's Sontino. Can you meet me somewhere?"

*****

In Lebanon, Pennsylvania...

Tommy was sitting in Larry Santiguida's waiting room with the heel of his foot tapping a hole into the carpet. *Damn man, I hope this mu'fucka can get me outta this shit.* He was still nervous and afraid from the phone call that he received from his grandmother earlier that morning. According to her, when she left the house for work and opened the front door, her porch was covered with lit candles, flowers and Teddy Bears.

Initially, she didn't know what to think, but when she took a closer look and noticed that one of the Teddy Bears was holding an obituary with Tommy's picture on the front page she called him to make sure he was safe. Now, here he was sitting in his lawyers waiting room bitching! *How did they know I was tellin? Do they know where I'm at? Are my peoples safe?* All of these questions ran through his mind as he sat there nervously biting his fingernails.

The phone rang at the receptionist desk, and Santiguida's secretary answered it immediately. She nodded her head up and down, and looked at Tommy. After a couple of seconds, she placed the phone back on the receiver.

"Mr. Santiguida is ready to see you, Mr. Wilson."

When Tommy entered the office, he paced back and forth with the facial expression of a doomed man. "Yo Larry, you gotta help me man!"

"Whoa Tommy, just calm down and tell me what's going on."

Tommy told him all about his encounter with Detective Smith and how he planted the gun in his car, and then pressured him into setting up Mook. He then told him about the phone call that he received from his grandmother earlier that morning. Santiguida wrote down everything he said, then picked up his phone and called Detective Smith.

Ring! Ring!

"Hello, you've reached Detective Smith. How can I help you?" The detective answered.

"Good morning, detective. My name is Lawrence Santiguida, and I'm Tommy Wilson's attorney. It's been brought to my attention that you illegally searched my client's vehicle and discovered a firearm." He stated but still somewhat asking a question.

"I illegally searched your client's vehicle? I didn't illegally search shit." The detective snapped through the phone. After a brief pause, he calmed himself and chose his next words carefully. "Your client was speeding on a public street, and I pulled him over for a routine traffic stop. When I approached his vehicle, I smelled the distinct aroma of marijuana, and based on a reasonable suspicion that drugs were inside of the vehicle, I conducted a search and ultimately discovered an unregistered firearm."

"Well, based on my client's version of the events, you egregiously violated his rights to privacy under the 4th and 14th Amendments to the United States Constitution, and under Article I, Section 8 of the Pennsylvania Constitution. Moreover, according to my client, you're using the illegally obtained evidence to force him to cooperate in the investigation of," he looked down at his notes. "Michael Brooks."

"Well, did your client happen to tell you that he sold a kilogram of cocaine to my confidential informant, and that lab results confirmed that his fingerprints were all over the packaging?"

"No, I was not aware of that fact."

"Listen, Mr. Santa, ah, whatever your name is. The only reason your client is a free man at the present time is because of me. I could've easily charged him with the possession of a stolen firearm and a direct sale, but I didn't. I gave him the opportunity to do the right thing. Now," he paused for a couple of seconds, "either he cooperates or his drug dealing ass is going to jail."

Click!

Santiguida placed the phone back on the receiver, and then looked at Tommy. "I'm sorry to tell you this, but he's got you by the balls. He's claiming that you sold a kilogram of cocaine to his confidential informant, and that lab reports confirm the presence of your fingerprints on the packaging. Did this really happen?"

"Fuck no. That pussy's lyin'. I didn't sell a brick to a confidential informant. I *gave* the brick to him so he could use it to build a case against Mook! I didn't sell to a confidential informant! I *am* the confidential informant!" He continued shouting.

Santiguida remained silent and just sat there tapping his

pen against his note pad.

"Damn, man, don't just sit there. I need you to get me outta this shit!" Tommy cried. "I can't testify against Mook! If I do, they'll kill me!"

"Well, I've gotta be honest with you Tommy. From what Detective Smith just told me, I'd say that your best bet is to cooperate."

"Man, they're gonna fuckin' kill me! They already know that I told. I'll never even make it to the witness stand." Tommy retorted. "Yo, it's gotta be somethin' you can do for me."

Santiguida shrugged his shoulders. "Look man, I don't know what else to tell you. If you take your chances at trial, then there's a strong possibility that you're gonna lose. In cases like this, where it comes down to the word of a detective against the word of the defendant, more than likely the jury is gonna believe the detective."

Tommy gathered his composure. "Fuck it. I guess I gotta do what I gotta do."

After leaving Santiguida's office, he went to his house, grabbed a brick of raw and headed back to Philly. When he pulled up in front of police headquarters at 8th and Race, he sat behind the steering wheel of his Benz, and broke down crying. The last thing he ever wanted to do in his life was carry the burden of being a rat, but unfortunately, this was a line that he had already crossed. *Fuck it, man. It is what it is,* he rationalized to himself.

He entered the building and headed straight for Detective Smith's office. Without knocking on the door, he barged inside of the small room, and sat the brick on the desk.

"Here man, damn."

"What the fuck is that?" Detective Smith shouted. "And who in the hell do you think you are, storming into my goddamn office?"

"Man, fuck ya office!" Tommy shouted. "You said that you wanted Mook, well now you got him! It's a key of coke in that bag, and he just sold it to me on 10th and Susquehanna. Is that good enough for you?"

Detective Smith looked at the bag and smiled. "Yeah, that's good enough." He laughed and stood up from behind the desk. "Now, turn around and place your hands behind your goddamned back. You're rat ass is under arrest."

"Under arrest?" Tommy looked him, refusing to believe what he had just heard. "What the fuck you mean I'm under arrest? I did everything that you asked me to do."

"Let's just say I need a little insurance. So therefore, you're rat ass is gonna sit in the county jail until you testify, and after that maybe you can go home. Now for the last time, turn around and place your hands behind your fuckin' back."

Chapter Fourteen

The Following Morning...

It was 4:59 a.m. and Detectives Smith and Sullivan, accompanied by the Dover Task Force, were standing outside of Mook's estate, preparing to execute their warrant. The five security guards who worked the gated community were standing off to the side, and approximately thirty Swat Team members were positioning themselves around his mansion.

Detective Smith looked around and smiled. "As soon as my watch hits five o'clock, we're going in fellas. Our suspect is known for carrying a firearm so be extremely cautious." He glanced at his G Shock. "Alright, in Five, Four, Three, Two, One."

Boom!

Inside of the house, Mook and his wife Saleena were awakened by the sound of their front door being kicked off the hinges. Initially, he thought that the invasion was an attempt on his life, but when he heard the intruders identify themselves as police officers, he knew that he was facing something far worse. *Damn, these pussies caught me slippin',* he said to himself as he thought about the 200 keys of cocaine that was stashed in the vault behind his bed.

He looked at Saleena. "Baby, put ya hands up and don't move. These jealous ass crackers will shoot us at the drop of a dime," he instructed in a calm voice. "And remember, whatever they ask you, just tell 'em you don't know nothin'."

"I got you, daddy. I know the drill," she responded with tears in her eyes and fear in her voice.

Their bedroom door flew open and two members of the Dover Task Force stormed inside with their guns drawn, aimed, and ready to fire.

"Get on the fucking ground!"

*****

When Mook arrived at the police headquarters on the corner of 8th and Race all he could think about was whether or not the police had searched his house. If they did, he wondered if they found the cocaine that was stashed inside of his vault. After being processed, he was taken upstairs to the Narcotics Division, and placed inside of an interrogation room. A few minutes later, Detective Smith entered the small room with a huge smile spread across his face.

"So, Mr. Brooks, we meet again."

"Fuck you, pussy. I ain't got no mu'fuckin' rap. Call my lawyer down here. You know his name, *Mario Savino*. It seems like every time you drag me down here, Savino drags his ass to the courtroom and I drag my black ass home." Mook laughed, and then spat on the floor.

"Oh, so Mr. Big Shot wants his grease ball attorney huh?" The detective taunted him. "Sorry to tell you this dickhead, but that whop attorney of your's can't get you outta this one. I've gotta surprise for you. Can you guess what it is?" Detective Smith laughed.

"Fuck you, Smitty! I want my fuckin' lawyer!" Mook demanded.

"Alright, alright. I'm gonna let you call him. Just be sure to tell him that I've got a witness who is willing to testify that on the fifth of December, you sold him a kilogram of cocaine. To make things more interesting, his testimony is gonna be corroborated with the fingerprints that you left on the duct tape that you used to package it," Detective Smith stated in a cocky voice.

After hearing all of the evidence that the detective had against him, Mook felt relieved. He knew they didn't find the 200 keys, because if they did, Detective Smith would have surely threw it in his face.

"Yo, I ain't try'na here that shit you kickin'. Whatever it

is gotta say, tell that shit to my fuckin' lawyer."

The detective chuckled. "Well, unless you can bring Mr. Cochran back from the dead, I'd pretty much say that you're fucked."

He shook his head from side to side, and then left the room. Next door, Detective Sullivan was watching Mook through a two way mirror. Smitty entered the room and gave him a high five.

"We finally got him, Sully."

Detective Sullivan smiled. "You got that right partner. When the D.A. is done with him, he's gonna look like Al Sharpton's hairdo...fried, died, and laid to the friggin' side."

*****

An Hour Later...

Mook was transported to the Curran From Correctional Facility, also known as CFCF. After spending the remainder of the day going through the intake process, he was placed on A Block for quarantine. The Philadelphia County Jail was a city within the city. Everybody knew everybody, and for the most part, everybody rolled with the niggas from their section of the city.

There was nothing on the streets that you couldn't get in the county jail. If a nigga wanted some pussy, he could get it. If he wanted drugs, he could get it. If he wanted a cell phone, a DVD player, or an iPod, for the right price, he could get it. To say that these items were a good thing to have in the county jail would be an understatement, but at the same time, they were the last thing on a nigga's mind. The most important and first order of business was getting their hands on a whack!

As soon as Mook stepped on the cell block in his orange jumpsuit, damn near everybody on the block knew who he was. Some loved him, some envied him, but at the end of the day, they all respected his gangsta. When he went to his cell, he saw that his man Reon from Southwest Philly was lying on the bottom bunk, and rapping the lyrics to Beanie Siegel's, *What Ya Life Like.*

Niggas wanna know if Beanie Siegel's life is real/ Nigga, twenty-five to life is real/ I catch a body, send me right to jail...

Reon was arguably one of the craziest niggas from Southwest. He had just beaten a double homicide back in September, and not even three months later, here he was back in the county, fighting another body. When the cell door popped open, he jumped off the bed with a whack in each hand, and his war face on full display.

Mook just stood there smiling at him. "Nigga you crazy, but ya crazy ass ain't stupid," he laughed.

Reon looked him in the face, and then placed both of the whacks back in his waistline. "Man, I didn't even recognize ya big ass." He smiled back. "What the fuck is you doin' in here, dawg? Rich niggas don't go to jail."

Mook stepped inside of the small cell and gave Reon some dap. "Rich niggas don't go to jail, huh? Try tellin' that shit to Big Meech." He continued smiling, and then sat his linen package down on the desk. "But, what's up wit' you though? What they try'na book you for?"

Reon shrugged his shoulders as if he didn't have a care in the world. "Another body, but it ain't really 'bout shit. I'ma spank this jawn, just like I spanked my last two jawns." He sat back down on the bed, and lit up a Newport. "So, what's ya situation?"

"Awww, man, these pussies talking 'bout I sold a brick to a confidential informant. Now, you know that's some bullshit! I ain't served a nigga just one brick in over ten years."

"Damn, my nigga, you know whatchu gotta do right?"

"Come on man, you know a nigga on point. I just gotta get word to my young buls. Them niggas don't even know I'm locked up. But trust me, as soon as them niggas know what's good, they gon' move."

"What's up wit' a bail? Did they give you one?" Reon

asked, while exhaling a cloud of smoke.

"Yo, they got my shit at $1,000,000 wit' no ten percent."

"*Dizzamn!* Even if you pay that jawn, all they gonna do is sic the feds on you."

"Shit, who you tellin'? I'm try'na get in touch wit' my lawyer though. He should be able to get me a bail reduction, and if he does, I'm a have my lil' homie put up a property and get me the fuck outta here."

"Yeah, I feel you my nigga. Oh, yeah, you know ya young bul, Tommy, on D24?"

At the mention of Tommy's name, Mook's blood pressure began to boil. "Nizzaw, I ain't know he was here. What's up wit' him? He good?"

"I don't know." Reon shrugged his shoulders. "I never got a chance to holla at the nigga. When they brought me on the block for quarantine, they was movin' him to D24."

*****

The Following Morning...

Mook's attorney, Mario Savino, came to see him for an official visit. When he entered the segregated cubical, and saw Mario sitting at the desk in a navy blue, Louis Vuitton dress suit, a wave of relief washed over him.

"Mario, what's up man?" He shook the Italian man's hand, and then took a seat at the desk. "Yo, they got my bail set at a $1,000,000. I need you to get that mu'fucka reduced so I can get outta here."

"I'm two steps ahead of you. I already filed a bail motion, and if it's granted, I'll have you outta here by Thursday."

"That's good shit," Mook smiled. "What's up wit' Saleena? Is she home yet?"

"As of right now, she hasn't been released. My guess is that they're playing hardball, and trying to get her to flip on you."

"Man, you know Saleena's gon' hold it down. My baby's

a rida. Them pussies ain't doin' nothin' but wastin' their time. If I woulda knew she was still locked up, I woulda told you to get her out before you came to see me."

"Alright, I'm on top of it. Before we get to that, I need you to clear something up for me. I spoke to the District Attorney about an hour ago, and he's claiming that he has a witness that's willing to testify that on the fifth of December you sold him a kilo of cocaine."

"Yo Mario, that's some straight up bullshit." Mook protested. "I haven't sold just one kilo in years."

"Well, according to the District Attorney you did, and they're further claiming that your fingerprints were all over the packaging. Now," he leaned back in his chair. "I do have some good news. A buddy of mine works in the district attorney's office, and he provided me with the name of the confidential informant. Does the name Tommy Wilson mean anything to you?"

Mook nodded his head. "Yeah, I know that nigga, but I haven't seen him in over three months. There's no way I could've sold him a brick a couple of days ago."

"Well, how in the hell did they get your fingerprints on the packaging?" Savino asked with a confused look on his face.

"Back in August, I fronted the nigga thirty keys, and then he skipped town on me. That's the only way they coulda got my fingerprints."

"Alright, well at least they don't have any wiretaps or video surveillance. If this thing makes it to trial, I'm pretty sure that I can establish reasonable doubt, but then again why risk it?"

Mook took the hint. In so many words, Savino was telling him no witness, no case.

Savino smiled. "Without Mr. Wilson, I can beat this shit in my sleep."

Mook nodded his head. "A'ight, write down this number, 215-555— that's my young bul, Sonny. When you leave, I need you to call him and tell him to send somebody up here to see me, preferably a female that's not connected to our situation."

Savino wrote down everything that Mook said, and then laid his pen on the notepad.

"I'll handle that as soon as I get back to my car. Is there anything else that you need me to do?"

"Naw, just make sure that you get me called down for the bail hearing. I wanna see the look on Smitty's face when I slide up out that mu'fucka."

*****

When Mook returned to his cell, he confided in Reon, and told him about the situation with Tommy.

"Well dig dis," Reon said. "I should be transferred to D24 by tomorrow. All you gotta do is have one of ya young buls drop $50,000 off to my mom and I'll murda that nigga 'fore the week is over."

Mook studied Reon's face, and then silently weighed his options. He'd always known Reon to be a stand up nigga, but at the same time, he used to think the same thing about Tommy. He thought about his man Kabani, and how he was stuck in the feds behind some shit that he said in his cell. He began searching their cell looking for a listening device. He searched the toilet, the vent, the light, the door, underneath the bunks, and underneath the desk.

Reon looked at him like he was crazy. "Hey, yo, Mook, what the fuck is you doin', dawg?"

Mook held his index finger up to his lips, "Shhh!"

He then proceeded to search Reon's body. Reon wanted to protest, but the look in Mook's eyes made it clear that he didn't want to challenge the 6'5", 265 pound beast. After he was satisfied that the authorities weren't listening, he straightened out Reon's shirt.

"It ain't nothin' personal, homie. It's just that these mu'fuckas is on my top, and I gotta be extra cautious of everything and everybody."

"I'm sayin, though." Reon held out his arms for emphasis. "Have you ever known me to be on some rat shit?"

"Never." Mook shook his head from side to side. "And that's why you gon' call ya mom tomorrow night, and she gon' tell you that my young buls dropped that bread off."

*****

Later That Day...

Tommy entered the visiting room in his orange jumpsuit. He looked around the room full of detainees who were charged with everything from DUIs to Murder. Despite their charges, all of them, at least for the moment were enjoying themselves as they appreciated their hour long visit with their loved ones.

He handed his pass to the corrections officer at the front desk, and then received a bunch of, "What's up, Tom Toms?" He cautiously walked down the aisle and took a seat on the fourth row of benches. Apparently, his treacherous actions had yet to spread throughout the jail, and unfortunately he was receiving the respect and love that was only designated for real niggas.

After a few minutes of sitting there lusting over the female visitors, a huge smile spread across his face when Nahfisah entered the room looking like a superstar. Her hair was professionally done, and her soft yellow Dolce & Gabbana sweat suit allowed her voluptuous booty to jiggle freely. It was eliciting the attention of every man in the room. She handed her visitor's ticket to the officer at the front desk, and then sashayed over to Tommy. He stood up to give her a hug and a kiss, but to his surprise she gave him the cold shoulder.

"Damn, Fis, what's ya fuckin' problem?"

"Nigga, *you're* my fuckin' problem." She snapped, causing unwanted attention.

Tommy looked around nervously, and then lowered his voice a few octaves. "Listen, can you just calm down and let me explain the situation? Here," he gestured toward the seat that was next to him. "Sit down."

She sucked her teeth, and then sat down beside him. "All I know is that you better have a good fuckin' reason as to why I'm out here all alone and takin' care of our daughter."

"Listen, Fis, the cops pulled me over and told me that they had wiretaps between Mook and Sonny, and that them niggas was plottin' to kill me," he lied.

"What? Why would Mook and Sonny wanna kill you? I thought they was ya peoples? And Sonny," she shook her head in disbelief, "he's like my brother, and he's Imani's godfather. He would never do some shit like that," she fired back.

"Fis, I'm tellin' you, them niggas was plottin' to kill me *and* you. Because the cops knew about it, the second they saw me, they locked me up for my own protection."

"They was plottin' to kill you *and* me?" She shook her head and refused to believe her ears. "Tommy, stop lyin' and tell me what's really goin' on."

"A'ight man, damn!" He took a deep breath and lowered his head. "They had me caught up." He said just above a whisper.

"Who, Sonny and Mook? What do you mean they had you caught up?"

"Naw, not them. The detective bul Smitty. He pulled me over a few months ago, and planted a gun in my car. Then, he took me down 8th and Race, and told me that if I didn't tell on Mook he was gonna turn the gun over to the feds and get me a mandatory minimum of fifteen years."

Nahfisah scrunched up her face. "Hold up nigga, you ratted!"

"Yo, lower ya voice. You drawin' attention like a mu'fucka." Tommy whispered, and then glanced around the room to see if anybody was listening to their conversation. "Nizzaw, it wasn't even like that. This pussy ain't leave me no choice. It was either be loyal to you and Imani, or be loyal to Mook. What the fuck was I 'posed to do? I couldn't keep it hood and do fifteen years in jail, locked away from you and the baby." He explained with tears in his eyes.

"Well, what about Sontino? Did you tell on him too?"

"Nizzaw, but by me tellin' on Mook, that's just like tellin' on Sonny. That's why them niggas was on the wiretaps talking 'bout killin' us," he continued to lie. "And that's the real reason why I moved us to Lebanon."

Nahfisah was crushed. *How could Sonny do something like this?* They'd been best friends since the second grade, and they had never even had an argument. Now, he was plotting to kill not only Tommy, but her as well. Tears began pouring down her beautiful face as she weighed her options. She knew that if Sonny wanted those dead it would only be a matter of time before he accomplished his mission.

"Boo, this is *Sonny* that we talking 'bout! This can't be right. I gotta call him because I know that if I talk to him, I can fix this shit."

"Fis, you're not listenin' to what I'm tellin' you," he shook his head in frustration. "Mook gave him orders to kill us, and now that's what he *has* to do. Fuck all that he's my brother shit. We can't trust him or nobody else. All we got is us right now." He counted off his fingers. "Not Sheed, not Riri, not Erika, not Saleena, not Flo, not nobody."

Nahfisah broke down crying. She knew that ratting was a crime that was unforgivable, but she couldn't understand why her closest friends would turn their backs on her. Especially when she didn't do anything wrong.

Tommy held her hand and caressed her smooth skin. "Baby, look at me." She complied. "I'm tellin' you, we won't be safe until I testify against Mook. After that, the cops are gonna put us in the witness protection program."

"Witness protection," she whined. "Yo, this some bullshit! Why the fuck did you do this to us?"

A tear slid down Tommy's left cheek, and he quickly wiped it away. "Look, I did what I felt was necessary to keep my family together. Just promise me that no matter what happens, you're gonna stay by my side." She didn't respond. "Fis, you gotta promise me."

She took a deep breath, and then wiped away her tears. "I promise."

"Promise that you're not gonna leave me."

"I promise."

"And promise me," he paused for a second, "that under no circumstances will you reach out to Sonny."

She bit her fingernails and lowered her head like a child.

"*Fis*!"

Against her better judgement, she looked him in the eyes, and said, "I promise."

Chapter Fifteen

When Sonny left Riana's house, he met Daphney at the King Of Prussia Mall in Montgomery County, and they spent the rest of the day shopping. The thing that he liked about her the most was her listening skills. He told her all about his argument with Riana, and she attentively listened to every single word. Moreover, instead of her using their argument as a means of hating on Riana, Daphney was supportive of their relationship and gave him sincere advice on how to make things right.

Today, she invited him over to her house, and he accepted the invitation. When he entered her living room, he was impressed by the earth tone colors of her cocoa brown walls, eggshell white ceiling, and her French vanilla sectional and matching ottoman. A marble fireplace with a glass door and gold trimming occupied a corner of the room, and directly in front of it, an off white polar bear rug was elegantly laid on the hardwood floor. A 62 inch plasma was positioned on the wall adjacent to the sectional and ottoman, and directly underneath a state of the art sound system was stationed on a rectangle mahogany shelf.

He removed his Gucci snorkel and handed it to her. "Damn, Daph, you got this jawn decked out."

"Thank you," she smiled, and then hung his coat in the closet. "I did all of the decorating myself."

"Yo, I like ya style. You should help me decorate my shit."

"Say no more. Just let me know when you want me to start, and make sure that you got a check for me," she stated with her hands on her hips. "Ain't nothin' for free." She turned around and headed toward the kitchen. "Are you thirsty?"

"Yeah, lemme get some Kool-Aid. I want the red kind if you got some." He walked over to the sound system and pressed the on button. Ironically, the sounds of Fabolous and Lil' Mo's, *Can't Leave You Alone,* eased through the speakers...

You're the one I want in my life/ And I already got a wife/

But I can't leave you alooonnnne/ And I know I'm living wrooonnnng/ But I can't let you goooo...

He walked into the kitchen, and the sight of her standing at the sink in her cream and brown, zebra striped Versace pants made his dick hard. *Damn, she got a fat ass,* he thought to himself. Although they had never engaged in any sexual activity, their level of comfort was beginning to produce a heavy sexual tension. He approached her from behind and placed his hands on her hips.

"Yo, where lil' man at?"

"He's at my mom's house," she responded in a sensual voice. "And just what in the world do you think you're doing?"

"Somethin' that you want me to do," he answered, and then gently rubbed the tip of his nose along the nape of her neck. "Damn, you smell good," he stated in reference to her Chanel #5 perfume.

He spun her around to face him, and for the first time he realized the full extent of her beauty. Her rich chocolate skin had a natural glow, and her silky hair coupled with her African features gave her an exotic look. Her long eyelashes complimented her hazel eyes, and the lip gloss on her juicy lips made him want to scream.

"Sontino, don't start nothin' you can't finish," she moaned.

"Trust me ma, it ain't nothin' in this world that a nigga like me can't finish."

"But what about ya girl?"

"That's the thing, she's my *girl* and I need a woman in my life."

When he said that her pussy erupted like a volcano and her juices dripped down her fat pussy lips like molten lava. She placed her hands behind his broad neck and kissed him with a passion that he'd never felt before. He palmed her ass with both hands as he pulled her closer to his body. After a couple of minutes of tongue wrestling, he broke their kiss and began licking and softly sucking on her neck. The feeling of his tongue was so intense that she closed her eyes and moaned his name. He opened her Versace blouse one button at a time, and then unfastened her Victoria's Secret bra. One by one, he gently sucked her chocolate nipples, causing her legs to vibrate and her eyes to roll in the back of her head.

"Yeah, daddy! Ummmmm!"

He unbuttoned her zebrastriped pants, and then knelt down in front of her. After pulling them to the floor, and moving her Victoria Secret thongs to the side, he inhaled the sweet scent of her pussy, then expertly flicked his tongue against her clitoris. Simultaneously, he slid his index and middle fingers inside of her and swirled them in a circular motion. After two minutes, her knees began to wobble and she almost fell to the floor. He stood to his feet and lifted her body on the edge of the sink. After dropping his boxers and pants, he placed both of her legs on his shoulders, then grabbed his dick and buried it deep inside of her sloppy wet pussy. Her box was so tight and creamy that he struggled to keep his composure.

"Damn. Daph, ya pussy is good as *shit*." He groaned, while stroking her box at a moderate pace. Her walls were so strong that every time his 9 inches filled her up she would squeeze her walls around his shaft and attempt to keep him in side of her.

"Ahhhh! Fuck me, Sonny! Fuck me, daddy!" She cried out in ecstasy.

Instead of pounding her out, he took his time. Not because he didn't want to, but because her pussy was so good that he didn't have any other choice. It was either run at a steady pace or finish the race ahead of schedule. He chose the former. Slowly, he used his pelvis to massage her clitoris.

"You like that, ma?"

"I love it, daddy! I swear to God I love this dick! Ahhhh!"

After releasing her juices, she ordered him to lie on the floor. She then removed her pants from around her right ankle, and hopped off the sink.

As he lay on the kitchen floor with his dick standing at attention, she squatted over him reverse cowgirl style, and guided his hammer back inside of her. She dropped her ass on his pelvis, squeezed her walls around his pipe, and then slowly lifted her pussy up the length of his dick while maintaining her squeeze. When she finally reached the head, she released her squeeze, creating a popping sound.

Pop!

Then dropped her ass back on his pelvis, and repeated the process. The pressure of her walls, coupled with the sight of her fat pussy swallowing his dick drove him over the edge, and he couldn't take it anymore. When she felt his dick convulsing inside of her, she used her pussy lips to wrap around the head, and then spun around to face him. She then dropped her pussy against his pelvis, and slowly twirled her hips in a circular motion.

"Oh, shit! What the fuck!" He groaned, and then squeezed off inside of her.

The feeling of his hot cum splashing against her insides made her body jerk, and she came for the second time.

"Damn, boy. I did *not* know ya shot was like that. Whew." She giggled, while slowing her pace to a stop.

"Shit, you got a crazy ass shot ya'self!" Sonny shot back, wondering what nigga taught her how to work her pussy so well.

Before they could get started on round two, his iPhone vibrated in his pants pocket. "Daph, can you grab my phone for me? It's in my pocket."

After handing him the phone, she got up from the floor and left the kitchen to give him some privacy. As she walked away, all he could do was admire the way that her ass swallowing her thong. *Dizzamn! I gotta hit that jawn from the bizzack!* His iPhone continued vibrating, snapping him out of his lust filled trance.

"Yo," he answered.

“Good afternoon. My name is Mario Savino, and I’m Mook’s attorney. May I speak to Sonny, please?”

“This is Sonny. What’s up wit’ Mook? He a’ight?”

“Mook was arrested yesterday, and he’s being charged with manufacturing and distributing a controlled substance.”

Sonny got up from the floor. “Is it state or federal?”

“So far it’s a state case, but I wouldn’t be surprised if the feds came knocking.”

“Does he have bail?”

“Yeah, but it’s a $1,000,000. No ten percent.”

“Damn, that’s crazy.” He shook his head. “So, where they holdin' him? Philly or Delaware?"

“He was arrested in Delaware, but the alleged crime happened in Philly."

"So, they got him on State Road?"

"Yeah. They're holding him at the CFCF. I just left him a few minutes ago, and he instructed me to tell you to send someone to visit him. He said preferably a female, and one that’s not connected to the family. He also made it clear that he needs her to visit him tonight.”

“Say no more. I’m on it,” Sonny confirmed, and then disconnected the call.

Daphney reentered the kitchen in a pink Chanel bathrobe. She noticed the look of distress on his face, and asked him what happened. He told her about the conversation that he just had with Mook’s attorney, and she decided that she was the perfect person to visit him. She took a quick shower, got dressed, and then headed for the county jail. Sonny stayed behind because he didn't know if the cops were looking for him too. He sent a text message to Sheed to tell him what happened, and advised him to get low until they figured out all of the details. He then, sent a text message to Easy, telling him the same thing.

*****

When Mook entered the visiting room, he was pleased to see Daphney sitting in the front row. She was definitely someone that he trusted, and he was comfortable relating his message through her. He handed his visitor's pass to the correction's officer at the front desk, and then walked over to Daphney. He embraced her with a warm hug.

"Come on Daph, let's sit in the last row. I don't wanna be too close to this ear hustlin' ass C.O." He nodded at the middle aged black woman who was sitting at the desk, and watching everybody like a hawk.

When they chose a couple of seats in the last row, Daphney got straight to business. "Mook, what the fuck is goin' on? Sonny told me what ya lawyer said, but I'm still confused about the whole situation," she stated, while staring him square in the eyes.

He looked around the visiting room to see if anybody was watching or listening, and then he spoke to her in a hushed tone.

"Tell Sonny that I need him to take $50,000 to my man Reon's house. He should know exactly who I'm talking 'bout, and if he doesn't, tell him 'The Southwest Reaper'. Also, I need you to tell him that I just holla'd at my man from Miami, and that I got a fresh one at the house. It's in the vault that's behind my bed, and tell him that the combination number is east to the west."

"A'ight." She nodded her head. "Is that everything?"

"Yeah, that's everything. I gotta bail hearing on Thursday morning, and if everything goes according to plan, I should be outta here that night. Oh, yeah, tell him that we're goin' against all odds."

*****

Daphney returned to her house a little after eight o'clock, and when she walked through the front door, she found Sonny sound asleep on her leather sectional. She woke him with a soft kiss on his lips, and then relayed Mook's message. As soon as he heard the words, *Against All Odds*, he knew that the rest of the team was safe, and that Tommy was the reason that Mook was in jail. He wiped the sleep out of his eyes, and then hopped up from the sectional.

"Yo, I gotta go handle this shit for the big homie, but I'm a hit you up as soon as I get a chance," he said, while grabbing his Gucci snorkel from the closet.

"A'ight, but before you leave, can you answer something for me?"

"No doubt. Tell me what's on ya mind."

She folded her arms across her chest and shifted her weight to her left hip. "I'm sayin' though, after everything that happened earlier, where do we go from here?"

He thought about her question and couldn't come up with an answer. "Truthfully, I don't know." He kissed her on the forehead, and then zipped up his snorkel. "Just gimme a lil' time to figure things out."

*****

Later That Night...

Inside of his warehouse on Delaware Avenue, Grip and his henchmen were sitting around his conference table discussing their strategies of war. A Philadelphia Daily Newspaper was lying on the table in front of him, and a picture of Mook's mug shot was plastered on the front page. In bold capital letters, the caption read: *Alleged Drug Kingpin, Mcheal Brooks Was Arrested In Sting Operation!*

Grip looked at his captains and lieutenants with a smile on his face. "Y'all know what this means, right?"

"Hell yeah," Monster answered. "That nigga's vulnerable right now. The newspaper said that they were holdin' him at the F, therefore he's a sittin' duck, literately!" He joked, and everybody else in the room laughed.

"Absolutely," Grip agreed. "They said his bail was set at a

$1,000,000 so we gotta move fast. I spoke to a friend of ours, and he told me that he's gotta a bail hearing on Thursday morning." He looked at his two capos. "Smack and Monster, y'all know what to do."

Chapter Sixteen

The Following Morning...

After dropping off the $50,000 to Reon's mom, Sonny and Sheed rented a U Haul truck, and drove to Mook's mansion in Delaware. Upon their arrival, Saleena opened the front door and ushered them inside.

"Saleena, what's up big sis? You good?" Sonny asked in a compassionate voice.

"Yeah, I'm good. I'm just busy try'na get Mook outta jail. Savino got me out yesterday, and this morning, he called to tell me that y'all was comin' to get this work outta the house. The vault is upstairs in the bedroom behind the bed," she stated, while leading them to the second floor.

When they reached the master bedroom, and pulled the bed away from the wall, just like she said there was a four foot high, stainless steel vault built into the wall. Sonny examined the touch screen combination pad, and then punched in the numbers: 69-93.

Zzzzz! Click!

He opened the door, and the sight of the 200 bricks sent chills down his spine. They were neatly piled on top of one another, and each brick was 9 inches long, 3 inches wide and 2 inches thick. He pulled a trash bag from his back pocket, and began filling it with the cocaine.

"So, Saleena, did you hear anything new about his bail?" Sheed asked.

She nodded her head. "Yeah, Savino said that he's gonna get it reduced to a reasonable price, and that he should be home Thursday night."

After loading the keys in four separate trash bags, Sonny stood to his feet and looked at Saleena.

"The next time you talk to Mook, tell him that everything's in order, and to kick his feet up. We got him."

*****

Back In The County Jail...

Mook and Reon were sitting in their cell, smoking a Vanilla Dutch, and plotting Tommy's murder. Reon was scheduled to be transported to D-Block later that day so Mook wanted to use their short window of time to make sure that everything was good.

"Yo, that bread is gonna be there today so when you get to D-Block, make sure you call ya miz and verify it. Another thing, I should be outta here tomorrow night, but make sure I'm outta the building before you put ya thing down," Mook said, while exhaling a thick cloud of Kush smoke.

"I got you, my nigga. Just fall back and let me do what I do best. I ain't gonna move on the nigga 'til the third shift anyway, so you good. Plus, you gotta remember, I just left this mu'fucka a couple of months ago, and before that, I was here for over two years, fightin' my last two bodies. My lil' C.O. bitch, Johnson, she works the night shift on D24. So this is what I'ma do, shorty already knows I'm back in the buildin', and she the one that's gettin' me transferred to her block. As soon as she makes her first round, I'ma pull her over and tell her to check and see if you're still here. If she tell me that you gone, I'm a have her pop my door, and then pop the nigga Tommy's door. Trust me Mook," he threw on his war face, "this shit ain't 'bout *nothin'*! I'm a slide in his cell, twist him out, slide back to my cell, and them kick my mu'fuckin' feet up. They ain't gonna find that pussy 'til the mornin', and when they do, all the heat is gonna fall on the nigga's celly. Trust me big homie, I got you."

*****

The Following Night...

The block officer came to Mook's cell to tell him that he

made bail. After going through the discharge process, he was escorted from the jail, and for the first time in a long time, he cherished the feeling of being a free man.

As soon as he emerged from the gray building, he saw that Saleena was parked out front in his Bentley. He climbed into the passenger's side, and then leaned over the center console to give her a kiss.

"You a'ight, babe?"

She smiled. "Yeah, I'm good, daddy. I'm just worried about you and this fuckin' case. Savino told me that if you get convicted, they can give you up to twenty years."

The look of concern written on her face made his heart melt. After assuring her that everything would be okay, they pulled out of the parking lot and drove up State Road. When they reached the corner of State Road and Cottman Avenue, a red traffic light caused Saleena to bring the Bentley to a halt. As they sat there waiting for the traffic light to turn green, a navy blue Ford Excursion pulled up behind them. When the traffic light turned green, the blue and red lights on the Excursion's front grill came to life signaling Saleena to pull over on the side of the road.

"Oh, my God! Why are they fuckin' wit' us?" Saleena complained. "We didn't even do shit."

When Mook looked out the back window and saw the navy blue Ford Excursion, he figured that the occupants of the SUV were the last people that he wanted to see. The feds! He looked at Saleena, who was pulling over to the curb.

"Just calm down. They probably just fuckin' wit' us," he lied, knowing in his heart of hearts that the feds had more than likely claimed jurisdiction over his case.

As they sat in the car waiting to be confronted by the authorities, the driver and passenger of the Excursion exited the SUV. Both men were dressed in navy blue jackets, and the letters *DEA* were printed across their chest in bright yellow caption. The driver approached Saleena's side with his gun drawn, and the passenger approached Mook's side in the same exact manner.

"Michael Brooks?" The agent on the passenger side asked.

"Yeah, I'm Michael Brooks."

"Step out the vehicle, and place your hands behind your back. You're under arrest."

Mook complied with the agent's order and exited the Bentley with his hands raised in the air. While the agent placed a pair of handcuffs on him, he looked at the agent that was standing on the other side of the car. *Damn, dude look familiar as shit,* he thought to himself. He tried to figure out where he'd previously seen the tall, brown skinned man, but couldn't come up with the answer.

As the agent ordered Saleena out of the Bentley and made her put her hands on top of her head, a light bulb flashed inside of Mook's brain. He remembered where he knew the agent. He was one of the niggas that was with Grip when they had the sit down at T.G.I.Fridays. Unfortunately, before he had the chance to protest, Smack raised his Glock .19 to the back of Saleena's head and squeezed the trigger.

Boc!

"Noooo!" Mook screamed as the bullet, followed by a mist of warm blood, burst through her forehead, and she slumped over the hood of the car.

He struggled to free himself, but the handcuffs wouldn't allow it. He rocked back and forth as he tried to create enough space for him to run away, but before he could, Monster smacked him in the back of the head with the butt of his gun, and everything went black.

*****

When he regained consciousness, his hands and feet were tied together, and his naked body was strapped to a workshop table. His head was throbbing, and the blood from the laceration on the back of his head had formed a small puddle that was beginning to drip off of the table. The image of Saleena's murder flashed inside of his mind, and he let out a cry of rage that was more akin to the cries of a wounded animal.

He struggled to free himself, but quickly realized that he couldn't move. His mind kicked into survival mode, and he calmed down. He knew that his chances of surviving were slim to none, but at the same time, he had to come up with something. He glanced around the large room and realized that they had him inside of a warehouse. He heard a growling noise, and then he looked to his right where a black and white pitbull was chained to a forklift. When he locked eyes with the muscular dog, it began barking and desperately tried to reach him. A second later, the door to the loading dock slid open, and Grip, followed by Murder and Malice, entered the large storage room, and walked toward him. At the sight of the light skinned old man, Mook lost his cool, and struggled to get free.

"Grip, I'ma kill you! I swear to *God* I'ma murder ya nut ass!" He shouted at the top of his lungs. When he discovered that his attempts to free himself were futile, his rage became immense, and with tears pouring from his eyes, he released his frustration. "Aaaggghhhh! I'ma fuckin' kill you, pussy!"

Grip laughed at him as he approached the workshop table. "You's a stupid mutha'fucka."

"Nigga, fuck you!" Mook shouted, and then spat in his face.

Grip wiped away the saliva with the back of his hand, then hammer punched Mook in the nose with the side of his fist.

Whack!

"Don't get mad at me, nigga. You brought this on ya mutha'fuckin' self. Didn't nobody tell ya lil' dirtyass to overstep your boundaries, and try to lock down the city wit' them cheap ass prices. You don't run this shit, I do! Gervin 'Mutha'fuckin' Moreno! I'm the one!" He shouted, then karate chopped Mook in the neck.

Whack!

Mook shook away the dizziness and struggled to remain conscious. "Nigga, I tried to bring you on board and you shitted on me," he whispered, exasperated from the mental and physical torment. "How you gon' knock a nigga for feedin' my family? Especially, when I went outta my way to offer you a plate?"

"See, that's the problem right there," Grip replied while circling the workshop table. "I'm the only mutha'fucka handing out plates in this goddamned city! *Not you*!"

Whack!

Grip hammer punched him in the stomach, and vomit shot out of Mook's mouth.

"How the fuck you gonna try to change the way I've been runnin' this shit for so many goddamned years? I'm the king of Philly mutha'fucka! And now you got these lil' dirty mutha'fuckas runnin' around the city on this Blood shit! This ain't Compton, bitch! And it damn sure ain't New York! This is Phila! *Whack!* Mutha'fuckin'! *Whack!* Delphia! *Whack!*

The three karate chops to Mook's chest and torso left him depleted. He coughed uncontrollably and his head lollied to the side. He gathered up the little bit of energy that he had left, and whispered, "My niggas gon' come at you wit' everything they got."

Grip smiled. "Who? Them lil' dirtyass *Block Boy* niggas? Yeah, I'm sure they'll be mad at first, but when those hunger pains start kicking in, and they realize that I'm the only one who can feed 'em, they'll come around."

"Not my young bul. Sonny. He gon' knock ya mu'fuckin' head off," Mook responded in a hushed tone.

"Sonny?" He cocked his head to the side, and then started laughing. "Oh, you mean my grandson, Sontino Moreno. Humph, he'll be the first one to embrace me." He walked to edge of the table and positioned himself at Mook's head. "Now, before you leave this world, tell me where I can find all these keys that you've been telling me about."

Mook blinked his eyes and took a deep breath. "Take it in

blood!"

Grip shrugged his shoulders. "Your wish is my command." He looked at Malice and said, "Kill this mutha'fucka."

Malice pulled out a meat cleaver, raised it in the air, and then buried the blade deep in Mook's neck.

Chop!

His body convulsed and his eyes blinked rapidly.

Satisfied, Grip gestured for Malice to step aside. He then pulled the cleaver from Mook's neck and his decapitated head rolled off of the table.

*****

Back In The County Jail...

Tommy was on the top bunk sound asleep when his cell door popped open, and a dark shadowy figure slipped inside. As quiet as a church mouse, Reon crept toward him with a sinister look on his face. So far, everything was going according to plan. When C.O. Johnson conducted her first security round, she stopped at Reon's cell and handed him a Black & Decker box cutter. She also promised to open his cell when she returned to her station. Now, here he was, creeping toward Tommy with the blade on the box cutter fully extended. When he reached the bunk beds, he looked down at the bottom bunk where Tommy's celly was in a deep *coma like* sleep. The 600 milligrams of Seroquel that he gave him a few hours ago had done their job.

He directed his attention to Tommy, and shook his head in disappointment. *Rat ass nigga!* He thought to himself as he anxiously bit his bottom lip. He reached out and snatched Tommy off the top bunk.

"Yo, what the…"

"Pussy, shut the fuck up!" Reon snarled, and then viciously attacked him with the box cutter.

*****

The Following Morning...

Tommy's celly awoke from his Seroquel induced sleep and took a deep breath. *Damn, them pills that Reon gave me wasn't no mu'fuckin' joke. I need some more of them jawns*, he thought to himself as he wiped the sleep out of his eyes. Seemingly, out of nowhere, a pungent odor invaded his nostrils, and he figured that Tommy was on the toilet taking an early morning shit. He was facing the back wall, and was therefore oblivious to the fact that a mutilated corpse was right behind him.

"Damn celly, you takin' a shit? Put some water on that mu'fucka," he complained, while covering his nose and mouth with his nylon blanket.

Silence.

After Tommy failed to respond, he snapped out, "Hey, yo celly, like what the fuck is up wit' you, fam? Flush the fuckin' toilet."

Silence.

Frustrated and feeling disrespected, he turned around to confront him, but the sight of Tommy's mutilated body shook him to the core. He was butt ass naked, and hanging from the air vent that was positioned above the toilet. Whatever it was that had his neck tied to the vent had cut so deep that his head was nearly decapitated. His face was covered in blood and had swelled to the size of a pumpkin, and a stream of dried up diarrhea was stuck to his legs, and covering the toilet seat. To make matters worse, his chest and stomach appeared as though Freddy Kruger had used his index finger to carve a gory message. That message was, *Death to all rats!*

Chapter Seventeen

Back In North Philly...

When Egypt and Zaire arrived on the block, the first thing that they noticed was Mook's Bentley parked in front of the trap house. "Yo, I love this fuckin' Bentley Zai," Egypt stated to his twin brother. "When we come up, we coppin' twin Bentleys."

Zaire nodded his head, and then knocked on the front door. A second later, the door swung open and Nasty was standing there in a wife beater and boxer shorts. Before he had the chance to even greet them, the twins bombarded him with questions about Mook.

"Yo, where he at?"

Nasty wiped the sleep from his eyes, and shrugged his shoulders. "I don't know. Whatchu askin' me for?"

Egypt pointed at the red Bentley. "Ain't that his car?"

The second Nasty laid eyes on the Bentley, he knew something was wrong. For one, it had been months since the last time Mook came to the block. Secondly, why would he leave his car parked out front, and not come in the house to at least tell him he was in the hood?

The twins noticed the look of confusion on Nasty's face, and on instinct, they both took a step backwards. "Hey Nast, somethin' ain't right Blood," Zaire stated the obvious.

"I was just thinkin' the same thing," Nasty admitted. "He was supposed to have made bail last night. But my thing is this, I've been chillin' in the spot all night, and I know for a fact that Mook wasn't over here. It wouldn't make sense for him to make bail, drive all the way to the block, and then leave his car outside without ever comin' in the house to holla at me."

"Well, maybe he went somewhere wit' Sonny," Zaire suggested.

"Yeah, that's a possibility," Nasty nodded his head. "I'm a call Sonny and find out." He disappeared inside of the house, and then returned with his cell phone. He called Sonny, and then held the phone to his ear.

Ring! Ring!

"Yo," Sonny answered.

"Big homie, what's poppin'? It's Nasty. Did you see or hear from Mook yet?"

"Naw, I ain't heard from the nigga. Why? What's up?"

"His Bentley is in front of the spot, but I was here all last night, and I know for a fact that he didn't come through here."

"Yo, don't even sweat that shit, scrap. He probably left it out there for a reason. I'ma call him and see what's up, and then I'ma come around there."

Click!

An hour later, Sonny arrived on the block with a look of concern on his face. After talking to Nasty, he called Mook, but didn't get an answer. He knew that Mook had made bail yesterday because he was with Daphney when she put up one of her properties to cover the $100,000 bond. He called Savino to verify if Mook was ever released, and that's when he heard the news about Saleena.

According to Savino, Mook was released from the county jail around seven o'clock last night, and a couple of hours later, Saleena's body was found on the side of the road with a single gunshot wound to the back of her head.

When he approached Nasty and the twins, he told them about his conversation with Savino. They walked over to the Bentley and looked through the tinted driver's side window. A black trash bag was sitting on the driver's seat and there was something inside of it that resembled the shape of a bowling ball. Sonny tried the door handle, and was surprised to find that the door was unlocked. When he opened the door and a strong, copper like smell permeated his nostrils and caused him to gag.

What the fuck is this? He asked himself as he picked up the bag. When he peaked inside and laid eyes on Mook's decapitated head, he just stood there in a state of shock.

Nasty could see the disturbed look on his face. "Sonny, what's in the bag?" When he didn't reply, Nasty grabbed the trash bag from his hands and looked inside of it. "Oh, shit!" He shouted, and then dropped the bag on the ground.

It rolled over and a pool of blood spilled out and onto the sidewalk. Zaire opened the bag with his the tip of his Timberland boot, and was surprised to see Mook's head covered in blood. His eyes were swollen shut, and there appeared to be something stuffed inside of his mouth. Zaire pulled out his pocket knife, and then used it to extract the dark object.

"Nizzaw, yo this shit *can't* be real," he stated in disbelief. They all crowded around the bloody object, and instantly recognized that piece of flesh was Mook's dick.

*****

In Allentown, Pennsylvania...

Breeze and Erika were sound asleep in their new apartment when they were awakened by the sound of his iPhone vibrating on the nightstand.

Vrrrrrm! Vrrrrrm!

Breeze looked at his alarm clock and saw that it was a little after nine o'clock in the morning. Initially he was pissed, but when he picked up the phone and saw that the caller was Sonny, he calmed down.

"Sonny Money, what's poppin' bro?" He answered in a groggy voice.

"Yo Breeze, I need you to come to the city a.s.a.p."

"A.s.a.p.? Nigga, it's early as shit."

"Listen, I can't say too much over the jack, but it's Mook. We found him this mornin'," Sonny replied in a somber tone.

"Y'all found him? Whatchu mean y'all found him?"

"We *found* him."

"Ohhhh." He sat up in the bed, and used his free hand to massage his chin. "Damn son, what happened?"

"I'ma put you on when you get here."
Click!

*****

An Hour Later...

When Breeze arrived on the corner of Fairhill and York, he could clearly see that Sonny was preparing for war. There were approximately twenty men whom he'd never seen before positioned throughout the strip, and judging from the bulges in their hoodies and coats, they were heavily armed. The cold December weather had them rocking back and forth to keep warm, and the second they spotted him pulling up in front of Sonny's trap house, he was the center of their attention. Zaire peeped game and immediately let it be known that Breeze was family.

"Naw, he's good. That's the homie Breeze," he informed them, and then embraced Breeze with their Blood handshake. "What's poppin', bro?"

"Them Maybachs and them Phantoms," Breeze replied, while looking at the men who just a few moments ago could have easily murdered him by mistake. He returned his gaze to Zaire. "Yo, where Sonny at?"

"He's in the house. The door ain't locked, so just go inside."

When Breeze entered the house, it looked like the U.S. Army had come to town. Assault weapons of all kinds were scattered around the living room floor, and a slew of bulletproof vest were piled on the couch. Damu, Sonny's pitbull, ran up to him and began sniffing his leg.

"Hey yo Sonny, where are you at?" He announced his presence, while patting Damu on the head.

"I'm upstairs!" Sonny shouted from the second floor. "I'll be down in a minute!"

A couple of minutes later, Sonny, followed by Sheed and

Nasty, descended the stairs and greeted him. They went over to the dining room table, and after rolling up a Backwood, Sonny got down to business.

"I hope y'all niggas is ready for war 'cause this shit about to get real fuckin' ugly," he informed them with a murderous rage in his eyes. "These niggas violated the big homie and his wife. Then, they had the nerve to send us his head wit' his dick stuffed in his mouth."

"Well, where these niggas at?" Breeze asked. "I'm ready to get it poppin' right now."

"Oh, we definitely gon' get it poppin'," Sheed proclaimed with tears in his eyes. "I'm a park every one of them niggas, and that's word to Blood."

"Calm down," Sonny checked him. "We gotta be thinkers before doers. These niggas is definitely food, but we gotta be strategic in the way we move. We all know that Grip's got three captains down in South Philly; Biggs, Monster, and Smack. The only way we gon' get to Grip is by goin' through them niggas first. We already killed Biggs, so now we gotta focus on Monster and Smack. The nigga, Smack, is the captain for his 22nd and McKean crew, and Monster is the captain for his 5th and Washington crew."

"But Sonny," Nasty interjected, "them niggas is probably layin' low right now. It ain't no way in the world they gonna be runnin' the streets after what they just did."

"You're right," Sonny nodded his head. "But just in case them niggas take the aggressive approach," He gestured toward the weapons in the living room. "We gonna stay on point. And if they *do* lay low, we gon' fall back and make them niggas think shit sweet. They'll pop back up eventually, and when they do, we goin' straight at 'em."

Sheed was pissed. Everything inside of him wanted to go down to South Philly and put his murder game down, but now under Sonny's orders he had to fall back.

"So how long do you want us to chill? For a week or

two?" asked Sheed.

"Nizzaw," Sonny shook his head. "More like a month or two."

Sheed shook his head and looked away. *Yo, lemme find out this nigga bitchin',* he thought to himself.

Nasty was also concerned about the two month hiatus, but his concerns were centered around money. "I'm sayin' though, what exactly do you mean by fallin' back? That's not including the block is it?"

"Yeah, that goes for the block too. I want them niggas to think they got us shook. That's the only way we gonna catch 'em slippin'."

"A'ight, I can dig it, but at the same time, me and the twins ain't got money like you and Sheed. How we 'posed to live for two months without any money comin' in?"

"I already thought about that, and I'ma give y'all $20,000 a piece to hold y'all down. In the meantime, I want y'all go outta town and stay at the apartment in Trenton. This shit ain't a game, and that's why I got everybody posted outside like that."

"On another note, I holla'd at Sunshine and Rah about an hour ago to let 'em know what's going on. They offered to send us some soldiers from Brooklyn, but I told 'em we were good. They bumped me up to Mook's status as the Triple OG of the hood, and I'm movin' Sheed up to the double spot. Nasty," he looked him square in the eyes, "I'm moving you up to OG and the twins," he looked at Egypt and Zaire. "Y'all gettin' bumped up to fivestar generals."

He reached inside of his back pocket and pulled out a red bandana.

"This flag represents the Blood of our ancestors and the homies who lost their lives at the hands of oppression. This is what holds us together as a set and as a nation. This is the creed that we live and die by. Big Bizness!"

"Bizness as usual!" Sheed and Nasty replied in unison.

Sonny nodded his head assuredly. "A'ight," he looked at

Nasty and Breeze, "I need y'all step outside for a minute, so I can holla at Sheed."

After they left the house and closed the door behind them, Sonny directed his attention to Sheed. "After the funeral, we're gonna break down the bricks that we got from Mook's house. We're both gonna keep 75, and the remaining 50, we're gonna split amongst the team."

Instead of responding, Sheed just nodded his head.

*****

A Week Later…

On the morning of Mook and Saleena's funeral, Sonny drove to the Baker's Funeral Home on Broad Street to drop off the $30,000 that he owed the funeral director. As he sat in his Chevy Tahoe, discreetly behind the tinted windows, he took slow pulls on his Backwood and nodded his head to the soulful sounds of Tupac Shakur's, *Life Goes On...*

How many niggas fell victim to the streets?/ Rest in peace young nigga, it's a heaven for a gee/ I'd be a liar if I told ya that I never thought of death/ My niggas, we the last one's left/ And life goes on.

Soft raindrops pelted against his windshield, and the only thing he could think about was the day that he'd first crossed paths with his big homie and mentor...

Feburary 2, 1996

He was walking down 5th Street, heading to school when a cranberry 1996 Lexus GS 300 sitting on 20" rims drove past him. The tinted windows were rolled up, but yet and still the trunkrattling sounds of the Notorious B.I.G.'s, Who Shot Ya?, could be heard from blocks away. He was walking in between Susquehanna Avenue and Diamond Street when the Lexus cruised by, sending vibrations throughout his entire body. The bandage on his left hand was beginning to itch and he was pissed off due to the fact that instead of rocking the new Air Jordan's that his dad stole from him, he was wearing a tattered pair of Bo Jackson's.

As he continued walking, the cranberry Lexus stopped at the corner of 5th and Susquehanna, and then rode in reverse until it was cruising beside him. The tinted passenger's side window rolled down and the music went mute.

"Hey, yo, lil' man!" The driver called out, catching him off guard. "Come here for a minute!"

His instincts told him to run, but something deep inside of him told him to remain calm. He threw on his mean mug and ice-grilled the dark skinned man with the short, wavy hair. "What's up?"

A twenty-five year old Mook smiled at the skinny young man. "Yo, you're Lil' Easy right?"

"Fuck no. My name's Sonny," he barked back, trying his best to look hard when he said it.

Mook chuckled at the young man's body language. "Yo, let's try this again. Is Easy ya pop?"

Instead of a verbal response, Sonny just nodded his head.

"A'ight, well I got somethin' for you," Mook replied as he climbed out the Lex with a pair of black and red Jordan's in his hand.

His 6'4" frame gave him the appearance of an NBA player. At the time, he was tallest man that Sonny had ever seen. He was wearing a red Coogie sweater, a pair of dark blue Guess jeans with the pencil pockets, and a fresh pair of black chuckas or low top Timberlands. A gold Cuban link with an iced-out Jesus piece hung from his neck, and a gold Movado with a diamond bezel was wrapped around his left wrist.

He held up the black and red Jordan's and said, "Are these yours, lil' homie?"

"Yeah," He looked up at the 6'4" giant. "My pops stole

'em from me."

Mook nodded his head. "I figured that. Here," he handed him the sneakers, and then reached inside of his pants pocket and pulled out a wad of Ben Franklins. "And take this too." He peeled off two of the bills and handed them to Sonny.

"What's this for?"

"That's for you," Mook stated, while placing the money back in his pocket. He then pulled out a white business card and handed it to him. "That's my number. I want you to call me whenever you need something. I don't give a fuck what it is, just call me."

"Man, I don't even know you. Why you doin' all of this for me?"

"Let's just say that I'm doin' for you what my ol' head Alvin did for me back in the day. From here on out, you my lil' homie and I got ya back. All you gotta do is get good grades in school, stay out of trouble, and you gotta stay true."

Sonny scrunched up his face. "Stay true? Whatchu mean by that?"

"That means you gotta always keep it real wit' me, and whenever you gimme ya word, you gotta keep it."

Sonny nodded his head and smiled. "A'ight, big homie, but you never even told me ya name!"

"Mook."

"A'ight Mook. I got ya back too."

"Humph," Mook smiled. "We'll see lil' homie. We'll see."

He hopped back in the Lex, turned up his DJ Clue mixtape, and sped off.

Back To 2012

Sonny killed the ignition, climbed out the truck, and then walked into the funeral home. After handing the director an envelope full of money, he was led to a redwood casket with gold trimming.

"Here he is," said the funeral director. "As you already know, we never received the rest of his body so there was no possible way for an open casket." He gestured toward the casket that was positioned across the room. "Now, the woman on the other hand, our makeup artist and hair dresser did a wonderful job. If you want, we can have an open casket for her."

"Naw, that ain't necessary," Sonny replied in a somber voice. "Their havin' a joint funeral so it won't make sense for one of 'em to have an open casket, and the other one to have a closed casket." He looked at his Breitling. "My home girl, Daphney should be here within the next hour or so and she's gonna drop off some 10X12 pictures of them. The flower shop's bringin' the floral arrangements, so just place their pictures on top of their caskets, and surround them wit' the flowers."

"Yes, sir, Mr. Moreno," the funeral director confirmed, while placing the money filled envelope inside of his suit jacket. "Is there anything else?"

"Yeah," he nodded his head. "I need a couple of minutes alone wit' my big homie."

As the funeral director left the sanctuary, Sonny took a deep breath, and then approached Mook's casket. His heart was heavy, his chest was tight, and his stomach was tied into a knot. For the past sixteen years, the man who was lying in that wooden box had become his everything. He was his father, his mentor, his brother, his big homie, and most importantly his best friend.

He desperately tried to keep it together, but when a picture of Mook appeared in his head, he became completely unglued. He broke down crying and bear hugged the wooden casket.

"I promise you bro, I'ma murder them niggas. The only thing that can stop me is death."

*****

Later That Night...

After the funeral, Easy was in a state of deep depression. The pain and grief that surrounded him at the funeral was immeasurable, and the second he returned to his Center City loft, he went straight to his stash. He opened a brick and extracted a small rock. He then, grabbed a plate, a razor blade, a straw, and a bottle of Moet from the refrigerator. He took the items to the living room, laid them on the coffee table, and then plopped down on his suede sofa. His desire to ingest the cocaine was immense, but there was something in the back of his mind that was telling him to refrain. His palms were sweating and tears were falling from his eyes.

"What the fuck am I doin'?" He questioned himself. "How the fuck did this shit become the center of my life?"

The answer to his question was the day that he linked up with the Medellin Drug Cartel.

December 31, 1985

Before the crack wave smothered the streets of Philadelphia, Easy was a twenty year old stick-up kid who robbed everything from drug dealers to jewelry stores. His profession had provided him with a lavish lifestyle, and earned him a bankroll that peaked at $200,000. However, it wasn't until New Years Eve of 1985 that he met a man by the name of Juan Nunez, and his life changed forever.

Juan was a captain in the Medellin Cartel, and he was sent from Columbia to the Unites States to expand the distribution of the cocaine that was manufactured by the cartel. He was stationed in Miami, and upon his arrival, he instantly fell in love with the tropical weather, the beautiful beaches, and most importantly, the beautiful women.

It was New Year's Eve, and Juan was partying at a Miami nightclub when he noticed a young black man who stood out from the rest of the crowd. He was dipped in a tailor made MCM sweat suit, and a gold rope with a diamond encrusted Mercedes Benz emblem decorated his neck. A gold Rolex was wrapped around his left wrist, and his iced-out four finger ring spelled 'Easy' in cursive.

Being that Juan was from Columbia where his culture taught him to never flaunt his wealth, he was intrigued by the young man's flashy appearance.

He turned toward the bartender and said, "Gimme a double shot of rum, and send a bottle of ju finest champagne to de guy over dere," he pointed at Easy. "Tell him it's from a friend." He reached inside of his slacks and pulled out a wad of hundred dollar bills. He peeled away ten of them, and then laid them on the counter.

"Whatever you say buddy." The bartender replied as his eyes feasted on the money that he was now holding in his chubby hands.

After pouring Juan's drink, he reached behind the counter and grabbed a bottle of Dom and a tin bucket. He placed the champagne inside of the bucket, and then filled the bucket with crushed ice. As Easy and Annie were enjoying themselves in the V.I.P. area, they were approached by an overweight white man.

"Excuse me sir, but that guy over there," he pointed at Juan who was watching them from the bar. "He told me to bring you a bottle of Dom." Easy looked at the bartender, and then fixed his gaze on the small Spanish man.

He was dressed in cream slacks and a white button up. The top three buttons were unfastened, which revealed his curly chest hair and a small crucifix that was connected to a thin gold chain.

"Yo, why did he send this to me?" Easy asked. "I don't know that nigga."

"I don't have the slightest idea," the bartender shrugged his shoulders. "All I know is that he handed me a $1,000, and told me to bring you a bottle of our finest champagne. Oh, yeah, he also told me to tell you that it was from a friend."

Easy stared at the bartender with a skeptical look on his

face. He then looked at Annie who shrugged her shoulders as if to say "I don't know." He grabbed the bucket of champagne, and then headed toward the bar to confront Juan. "Hey, yo poppy, do you know me from somewhere?"

"No, I don't know ju," Juan replied in a nonchalant manner. "But I know ju type, and I like ju style," he continued in a thick Spanish accent.

Easy screwed up his face. "My type? What do you mean by that?"

Juan scanned him from head to toe. "Ju got de gold chain, de diamoans, and de beautiful girl on ju arm. In dis country, only de pushers move like ju, so I figured dat ju was a pusher, no?"

At the sounds of Juan's rationalizing, Easy assumed that he was being targeted for a robbery so he casually reached for the 9mm that was tucked in his waistband. Juan noticed his movements, and quickly waved him off.

"Whoa, take it easy poppy. Ju know wanna do that dat, trust me. I am heavily guarded and my men will shoot ju down faster den ju eyes can blink."

Easy glanced around the club looking for the bodyguards that the little man spoke of, but he couldn't see them. Confused, he asked, "Yo, what's up wit' you poppy? Whatchu want from me?"

Juan smiled. "I'm Juan Nunez, and I come from Columbia." He extended his right hand, and Easy accepted the gesture.

"My name is Easy, and I'm from North Philly," he replied, while taking a seat at the bar. "So, you're from Columbia, huh poppy? Whatchu doin' all the way in America?"

"I'm here on business," Juan answered, while sipping his drink. "I work for a very important man back in my country, and he sent me here to expand his distribution network."

"Distribution network? Hey, yo poppy, what the fuck you talking 'bout?"

Juan chuckled. "Ju know somethin' 'bout cocaine?"

"Yeah," Easy lied, knowing damn well that his only connection to the white powder was the hustlers that he terrorized and extorted.

Juan nodded his head. "Ju know how to move cocaine?"

"Yeah, I know how to move that shit."

"Well, I tell ju what, I can make ju richer than ju ever dreamed of."

"Oh, yeah," Easy chuckled. "And how do you plan on doin' that?"

Juan gulped down the rest of his drink, then pulled out a cigar and held it between his thumb and index finger. "Ju say ju was from North Philly, and it just so happens dat my brother, Poncho is in North Philly. He owns a bodega on de corner of Marshall and Tioga. Do ju know where dat is?"

"Yeah." Easy nodded his head. "That's Poppy Land."

"When ju go back to North Philly, ju go see him, and he's gonna take good care of ju."

"A'ight poppy, I think I just might do that."

"Sure ju will. Ju look like a smart man." Juan smiled, and then rested his hand on Easy's shoulder. "Dere is one thing dat I must tell ju about me. De country where I come from, loyalty is de foundation for everything. Dis is de only thing I know, poppy. Ju show me ju loyalty, and I'll show ju my love. But if ju show me disloyalty," he shrugged his shoulders. "Well then, I'll have to show ju my hate, and trust me poppy, ju no wanna see my hate, lemme tell ju."

"Say no more poppy. I can dig it."

When Easy returned to North Philly, he paid a visit to Poncho, and the rest was history. Poncho fronted him 5 kilos of pure Columbian raw at the price of $14,000 a piece, and he taught him something that would change the streets of Philadelphia forever. He taught him how to cook crack!

Back To 2012

Now, almost three decades later, here he was sitting on his couch, struggling with the white faced demon that surrounded his life.

"Man, fuck this shit." He flipped over the coffee table and jumped to his feet. "I'm takin' my black ass home."

Chapter Eighteen

Two Weeks Later...

It was Christmas Eve, and Sonny was at a car dealership in Cherry Hill, New Jersey finishing the paperwork on his new truck. The owner of the dealership reminded him of Tony Soprano. He was a connected, middle aged Italian man, and he didn't blink twice when Sonny waltzed into his office and dropped a $75,000 on his desk.

In addition to the money, Sonny also gave him a brick of cocaine. This assured that the paperwork on his new truck would appear to be legit. Specifically, the owner of the dealership would doctor up the paperwork, making it appear as though he made a $7,500 down payment and would be paying a monthly car note.

An hour later, he drove off the lot in a brand new black on black 2013 Cadillac Escalade.

When he returned to Philly, he drove downtown to Jeweler's Row, and paid a visit to his jeweler. He dropped $50,000 on a five carat, emerald cut engagement ring, and another $40,000 on three iced-out tennis bracelets. Altogether, he spent a total of $190,000, but couldn't have cared less. He still had close to a $1,000,000 in the vault at is new house, and 80 keys of raw.

An hour later, he pulled up in front of Daphney's house and honked the horn. When she peaked her head out the front door and saw him sitting in his new truck, she came out the house and climbed in the passenger's side.

"What's up, Daph? You good?"

"Yeah, I'm okay," she sighed. "I'm still try'na get over what happened to Mook and Saleena. Their funeral was so sad."

"I feel you, but at the same time, I know they're in a better place. The only thing we can do at this point is move on."

"I know, but it's still hard for me to get over what happened. Mook was like my brother."

Attempting to change the subject, he reached inside of his center console and pulled out a gift wrapped box. "Here," he handed her the rectangleshaped box. "Merry Christmas."

When she opened her gift and laid eyes on the tennis bracelet her heart melted. "Awwww, thank you Sonny. This is so pretty."

"Here," he grabbed the bracelet. "Lemme help you put it on."

Once the bracelet was clamped around her wrist, she opened the visor and examined the clarity of the diamonds in the small mirror.

"This is the nicest thing that anybody has done for me in a long time. Thanks boo."

He nodded his head. "No doubt. But dig though, I'ma keep it a hunnid wit' you, It's more of a goin' away gift."

She looked at him with a confused expression. "A goin' away gift? What's that supposed to mean?"

"Look, I ain't try'na hurt ya feelins' or nothin' like that, but I can't do this no more."

"Why?" She held out her hands for emphasis. "We were just startin' to get close, and I was seriously considering whether or not I was gonna start bringin' my son around you. I just don't get it. I thought we were gonna take a chance and follow our hearts."

He took a deep breath. "That's what I'm doin', Daph, I'm followin' my heart. Right now, my heart's wit' Riri and the baby."

She stared out the passenger's side window and a warm tear fell from her left eye. Every fiber of her being wanted her to be selfish and fight for the man that she so desperately wanted in her life, but she knew that if she truly loved him then she had to let him go. *If it's meant to be, it'll be,* she thought to herself as she turned her head to face him. "I can respect it. I just need you to know that you have my heart, and if you ever need me, I'm here for you."

*****

Christmas Morning...

It was 10:30 a.m. when Sonny woke up in his new house. He climbed out of bed and went over to his bedroom window. He peaked outside and noticed that it snowed the night before. *Damn, I gotta remember to put the Benz in the garage 'fore I leave*, he thought to himself.

After getting dressed and eating breakfast, he picked up his iPhone and called his mom.

Ring! Ring! Ring!

"Hello," Easy answered.

"Pops? Man, whatchu doin' over there?"

"Come on, Sontino. Don't be askin' me no dumbass questions," Easy chuckled. "I'm spendin' quality time wit' my wife."

Sonny chuckled. "That's what's up. Where mommy at?"

"She's downstairs cookin' breakfast."

"Put her on the phone for me."

A couple of minutes later, Annie's voice eased through the receiver. "Hey, baby. Merry Christmas."

"The same to you," he quickly replied. "A'ight, now what's my pops doin' over there?"

"Humph, don't be questioning me because I'm grown."

"Yeah, whatever," he laughed. He was happy that his mom and dad were working things out. "Did you get the gift that I left for you under the Christmas tree?"

"Yeah, baby, I got it this morning. Thank you."

"Aww man, that ain't 'bout nothin'. You deserve that and a whole lot more. On another note, did you do what I asked you to do for me?"

"Yeah, and I just got off the phone with your grandmom, Jeanette. She was up all last night cooking for the occasion, so don't worry."

"A'ight, well we should be there by six o'clock, so make sure that everybody's ready."

"Boy, stop worrying so much. Me and your grandmother are on the job, and we got it covered. Now, stop bugging me."

He laughed. "A'ight mom, I love you and I'll see you later."

"I love you too, baby."

Click!

*****

Later That Day...

Sonny pulled up in front of Riana's house, hopped out the Escalade and knocked on the front door. It had been a little over two weeks since their argument at the doctor's office, and he missed her like crazy. When she opened the door, she looked so beautiful that all he could do was smile. She was wearing a softpink Polo sweat suit, and her baby bulge looked like a miniature sized basketball underneath her jacket. As he stood there admiring her almond shaped eyes and her juicy pink lips, he fell in love all over again.

"Merry Christmas, Ri." He embraced her with a warm hug, and then kissed her passionately. He reached inside of his waist length mink coat and pulled out a gift wrapped jewelry box. "Here, this is for you."

Instead of responding, she looked at him and broke down crying.

"Yo, what's wrong? What are you cryin' for?"

"Because I'm stupid. I was buggin' out for no reason, and you didn't deserve it."

He wrapped his arms around her and kissed her tears away. "Yo, don't even sweat that shit. We gonna keep that in the past, and focus on the here and now."

She nodded her head and wiped her face. "Okay," she said in a baby's voice, and then bear hugged him. "I got you a present too. It's upstairs in my room. Wait here while I get it for you."

As she went upstairs to her room, he took a seat on the couch and made himself comfortable. A couple of minutes later, she descended the stairs with a Rottweiler puppy clutched in her arms. "Here," she smiled as she handed him the puppy. "I named him Rocko."

He held the little black and brown dog in the air and smiled. "Thanks, Ri. He's definitely official. Good lookin', babe."

"I got a little cage for him too," she giggled. "It's upstairs in my mom's room. Ever since I got him last week, she's been treating him like a little baby."

"A'ight, I got my gift, but you still haven't opened yours."

She retrieved the gift wrapped jewelry box from her pocket and peeled away the wrapping paper. When she opened the box, she was excited to see the iced-out hearts that were fashioned into a tennis bracelet. "Awwww, thank you Sontino. It matches the necklace you gave me."

"Here, lemme help you put it on."

She handed him the bracelet, and after he clamped it on her wrist, she waved it back and forth and admired the bling of the diamonds.

'A'ight, I see you ballin' and all dat." He laughed, and then tapped her on the ass. "Now, go get ya necklace, so we can see how they go together. As a matter of fact, grab ya coat while you at it. One of the homies is havin' a lil' Christmas party at his house, and we're invited."

"Alright, just let me put Rocko in his cage before we leave."

"Nizzaw, we gon' take him wit' us, and I'll just drop him off at my mom's house."

*****

About Fifteen Minutes Later...

They pulled up in front of their new house, and just as Sonny anticipated, the cars of their family and friends were lined up and down the block. He pulled into the driveway, and parked beside Easy's Range Rover. Inside of the house, all of the lights were on, and through the curtains, they could see the silhouettes of everybody inside.

"Sontino, whose house is this?'

"This my bestfriend's house."

"But what about Rocko? We can't just leave him in the car?"

"I know, that's why we're takin' him wit' us," he replied as exited the truck, and then walked around to the passenger's side to help her do the same.

He then reached in the backseat and grabbed Rocko. As they walked up the driveway, Riana spotted a black Nissan Maxima and said, "That looks like my mom's car."

He ignored her statement and continued walking toward the front door. When he slid his key in the door knob, she immediately became suspicious. "Sontino, what are you doin' wit' a key to the front door? I thought you said this was your friend's house?"

"Wrong. I said this was my *bestfriend's* house."

"And who's your bestfriend?"

He kissed her on the forehead. "You."

"Huh?" she asked, completely dumbfounded.

He opened the front door, and everybody inside of the house shouted, "*Surprise.*"

"Ahn ahn, boo, you didn't?"

"I definitely did," he continued smiling and nodded his head up and down. "This is for you, me, and the baby."

When they entered the house, she was ambushed by her mom, his grand mom, Annie and Erika. They each took turns hugging her and rubbing on her belly.

"Hold up, you mean to tell me that all of y'all knew about this, and didn't none of y'all tell me?" She whined like a baby.

Erika smiled at her. “Girl, Sontino woulda had a heart attack if one of us woulda said somethin’. That nigga has been plannin’ this for about two weeks now.”

Annie grabbed Riana by the arm and along with Sontino they gave her a tour of the house. When they finally reached the nursery, she bear hugged Sonny and cried on his shoulder. “I love you so much, Sontino.”

“Yeah," he smiled at her, then got down on one knee. He reached iside of his pocket and pulled and out an engagement ring. "Well, do you love me enough to marry me?”

“Huh?” She replied, not believing what he’d just asked her.

“I *said*, do you love me enough to be my wife?”

She looked at the huge emerald cut diamond set in white gold, and continued crying. “Yes, baby! Yes, I’ll marry you!”

He placed the ring on her finger, and then stood to his feet and wrapped his arms around her. As their family and friends congratulated them, Sheed raised his bottle of Spades in the air and proposed a toast.

“To the big homie and his new fiancé. I wish y’all all the happiness in the world, and I pray that y’all have a healthy baby, and that it doesn’t have a big ass head like Sonny.”

Everybody in the house erupted with laughter.

*****

In The City’s Logan Section...

Nahfisah was sitting behind the steering wheel of Tommy’s Benz. She was snorting cocaine from a matchbook, and nodding her head to the sounds of Nicki Manaj’s, *Super Base*. Ever since the day she heard about Tommy’s murder, her desire for the white powder grew stronger and stronger. She and Imani were now living with her grandmother, and after a hectic Christmas Day, she was ready to hook up with the smoothtalking dude that she met at a party a few nights ago. After ingesting the last bit of cocaine, she wiped her nose, and then pulled away from the curb.

About fifteen minutes later, she pulled up in front of a shabby row house on 12th and York, and honked the European horn.

Beep! Beep!

A couple of seconds later, the front door opened and Teddy *Beaver Bushnut* Reynolds, a washed up hustler and pimp, emerged from the house with a Newport dangling from his lips. He was dressed in a black leather jacket, a crisp pair of jeans and a fresh pair of black chuckas. Although he was twenty years her senior, his lightskin, green eyes, curly hair and slim build screamed sex appeal. He climbed in the passenger's side, and then leaned over the center console to give her a sloppy, wet kiss.

"What's shakin, sweet thang? You ready to party?"

"Now, you know I'm ready to party," she smiled, and then adjusted her Fendi shades.

"A'ight," he nodded his head, and then reached inside of his jacket pocket. He pulled out an eight ball of crack. "Whatchu know about this, though?"

She examined the small rock, and then looked at him skeptically. "What's that, crack?"

A devious smile spread across his face, and he nodded his head up and down. "Yeah, baby. This is that shit right here! I thought you knew!"

"I'm sayin', though. Does it make you feel like regular coke?"

"Baby, this shit right here," he held the rock in front of her beautiful face. "This is the shit that stars are made of."

She shrugged her shoulders. "Well, fuck it! I'm down."

He licked his lips, and then settled into the passenger's seat. "Now, that's what I'm talking 'bout." He lowered his voice a few octaves, and then held up his index finger. He gestured for her to come close. "Give daddy a kiss."

Chapter Nineteen

A Week Later...
New Year's Eve...

Sonny and Riana were lying in bed and watching the movie, *Friday After Next*, when his iPhone vibrated in his sweatpants pocket.

Vrrrrrm! Vrrrrrm!

Riana heard the humming noise and pulled the phone from his pocket. After examining the screen, she said, "Here boo, it's Sheed." She handed him the phone, and then climbed off the bed. "I'm goin' downstairs to get somethin' to drink. Do you want somethin'?"

"Naw, I'm good."

As she left the room, he accepted the call. "Sheed, what's poppin' homie?"

"Yo, I just left the barbershop and while I was in there I heard niggas talkin' about the bul, Smack. They said he was havin' a New Year's Eve party at Plush. I know we agreed to fall back and all dat, but these niggas is still doin' they thing. Instead of layin' low, these pussies are hoggin' up the spotlight."

"Say no more," Sonny nodded his head and contemplated his next move. "Since these niggas wanna be out here partying and shit, we gonna show 'em how to have a gangsta party, you dig?"

"Like a mu'fuckin' shovel," Sheed shot back. He was happy to hear that Sonny was finally ready to ride on their adversaries. "But, dig though, do remember them lil' Spanish bitches from Camden?"

Sonny nodded his head. "Yeah, I remember them bitches. Why?"

"Well, I was thinking 'bout using them bitches to line this pussy up."

"Nizzaw, we don't even know them bitches. As far as we

know, them bitches could be rats."

"Fuck it. We can kill them, too."

"Nizzaw, that's too extra. We gotta be sharper than that. I tell you what though, I got the perfect chick."

"Who?"

Sonny smiled and said, "I'ma put you on later."

'A'ight scrap, I'm get wit' you later then. Soowoo*!*"

"Bang! Bang!"

After disconnecting the call, Sonny dialed Daphney's number, and she answered on the second ring.

"Hello."

"Daph, it's Sonny. Whatchu you doin' later on tonight?"

"Nothin', why?"

"I need you to handle somethin' for me."

*****

Later That Night...

Smack's New Year's Eve party was in full swing. The D.J. was playing all of the latest hits, and everybody was having a good time. In the V.I.P. area, Smack and the 'Grip Boys' were having the time of their lives. The champagne was flowing, Kush smoke filled the air, and some of the baddest women in the city were showing them love and affection. Smack was feeling like a boss. He was dressed in a pair of white Prada's, white Prada slacks, a fresh wife beater, and a white full length mink. Huge diamonds decorated his ear lobes and if anybody in the vicinity didn't know his name, then they must've been blind because the 40 carat charm that hung from his platinum chain spelled, *Smack*. He walked over to one of his bodyguards and told him to go to the bar to get another case of Spades.

When the bodyguard left the V.I.P. area and approached the bar, he spotted a thick dark skinned woman talking to the bartender. Her white Gucci dress hugged her body like a glove, and the way she was leaned over the bar with her ass tooted in the air made his dick hard. He slid up beside her, and then pulled out a wad of money.

"What's up, beautiful? Whatchu sippin' on?"

Daphney looked him up and down, and then licked her lips. "Well, if you're buyin', I'm sippin' on that Ciroc."

"A'ight, if that's the case then you're sippin' on me tonight." He turned his attention to the bartender. "Hey, yo' my man, lemme get a case of Spades and a bucket of ice. And umm, lemme get a bottle of Ciroc for the beautiful young lady right here."

As the bartender prepared his order, he counted out $5,000 and laid the money on the counter. "So, what's ya name, sweetheart?"

"My name's Dee, and yours is?"

"Rome."

"Well, a'ight Rome. Thanks for the drink."

"Don't even mention it." He looked around the club to see if anybody was watching him. "But, um, where's ya man at?"

"Well first of all, I don't have a man. Secondly, I'm here by myself. I didn't have nothin' else to do so I figured I'd hang out, and possibly find me some new *dick*," she shot back flirtatiously.

"Oh, is that right?" He smiled, and then licked his lips. "Well check it out, me and my niggas got the V.I.P. on lock. You should come over and party wit' us."

"Yeah, I can do that," she smiled, and then reached in between his legs to measure his dick size.He looked down to see her hand massaging his crouch, and a huge smile spread across his face.

The second they entered the V.I.P., Smack approached them with a bottle of champagne in his hand. "Yo Rome, who's dis?"

"Her name's Dee," he responded with an attitude because he knew full well that Smack was about to take her for himself. "I just met her at the bar."

Daphney looked at him from head to toe, and then smiled when she read the name on his iced-out charm. *Jackpot*! She leaned up against him and whispered in his ear. “So you the bul Smack, huh?”

*****

The Following Morning...

She was lying in Smack’s bed butt ass naked, and regretting her actions from the night before. *I cannot believe I let this lil’ dickass nigga fuck me,* she thought to herself. *‘But fuck it, if this was the only way that Sonny could get close to him, then it is what it is. At least he won't live to talk about it.* She looked at him and shook her head in contempt. He was balled up under the covers, and dead to the world. She climbed out the bed, got dressed, and then tip toed out of the door.

When she stepped into the hallway, she could hear Rome downstairs watching T.V. so she crept to the bathroom as quiet as possible. After locking the door behind her and turning on the water faucet, she reached inside of her Birkin bag and grabbed her cell phone. She called Sonny and he answered immediately.

“What’s up, Daph? Is everything good?”

“It’s even sweeter than we thought. This nigga Smack was drinkin’ champagne and poppin’ Xanax all last night. He’s out for the count. And to make it even sweeter, there’s only one bodyguard in the house. He’s downstairs watching T.V.”

“A’ight, well, how much more time you need?”

“Just gimme a couple of minutes to handle the nigga downstairs.”

After disconnecting the call, she placed a straight razor in her mouth, and turned off the faucet. She opened the door, and was surprised to find Rome standing on the other side.

“What were you doin’ in the bathroom?” He asked in a suspicious voice.

“I was washing out my panties.” She reached inside of her

Birkin bag and pulled out a white Gstring. "See."

Rome just stared at her. "Yo, why you was frontin' on me last night?"

"Boy, I don't *even* know what you're talking 'bout. Wasn't nobody front on you," she replied in a sexual tone.

"I'm sayin' though, how you gonna fuck my man when I was the one who holla'd at you?"

"Humph, that's a question you need to be askin' ya man. I was plannin' on fuckin' both of y'all, but ya man was hatin' on you."

"Oh, yeah, well what's up now? You know a nigga try'na see how that coochie work."

She smiled at him. "A'ight, come downstairs and I'ma show you."

When they reached the living room, she kissed him and massaged his dick through his boxer shorts. Aroused, he returned her kiss, palmed her ass and pulled her close. Her tongue slid from his mouth to his neck, and at a slow pace, she continued stroking his dick. After a couple of seconds, she spit the straight razor from her mouth and grabbed it with her right thumb and index finger.

"Ummm baby, you got me wet as shit!" She licked his neck one more time, and then without warning she stopped.

Rome was caught up in the moment. He was breathing heavy and his dick was so hard that it was beginning to hurt.

"Damn Dee, why did you stop?"

"I stopped because I gotta gift for you," she whispered in his ear.

"A gift?"

"Yeah, it's from my brother."

"Ya *brother*? Who the fuck is ya brother?"

"Mook!"

"What the fu…"

Before he had the chance to finish his statement, she slid the razor across his throat. He reached out to grab her, but she kicked him in the nuts and he fell to the floor. He desperately tried to breathe, but he couldn't. He grabbed his throat with both hands and attempted to stop the bleeding, but it was useless. She stepped over him and unlocked the door for Sonny. When he entered the house and saw Rome lying on the floor and fighting for his life, he looked at her and smiled.

"Damn, lil' mama, you did ya thing, huh?"

She kissed him on the cheek. "Only for you, daddy!"

He nodded his head, and then tapped her on the ass. "Go outside and wait for me in the car. It's the black Tahoe that's parked at the top of the block."

When she left the house, he opened his Gucci snorkel and pulled out a sawed off shotgun. He glanced around the living room, and then quietly crept to the second floor. After searching the first two bedrooms, he finally approached the room where Smack was sleeping.

He pushed the door open with the barrel of the shotgun, and then slid inside of the room. He aimed the shotgun at the ceiling right above the bed, and then squeezed the trigger.

Boom!

Broken dry wall fell from the ceiling and crashed down on Smack.

"Yo, what the fuck?" He slurred. He was so high from the Xanax that he could hardly move. He spotted Sonny standing in the doorway, and sluggishly hopped off the bed, and backed into the corner. Sonny aimed the shotgun at his head.

"What the fuck is you lookin' so surprised for? You had to know I was comin' for you!"

"Hey, yo Sonny, it wasn't me! I swear to God it wasn't me!"

"Nigga, die like a man and stop bitchin'!"

Smack held up his hands in a defenseless posture, and continued begging for his life.

"Don't kill me Sonny! Please!"

"Pussy didn't I just tell you to stop bitchin'?"

"I'm sayin' though, it wasn't even me! I didn't ki…"

Boom! Click! Click! Boom!

The top half of Smack's head splattered against the wall, and he collapsed to the floor. His body convulsed, and then slowly came to a stop as his soul eased from his body. Sonny removed a red bandana from his back pocket, balled it up, and then tossed it on Smack's decapitated body.

*****

The Next Day...

The corner of 22nd and McKean was flooded with lit candles, flowers, balloons, and members of the *Grip Boys* who came to pay respects to their fallen comrades. Unknowingly, Nasty was up the block sitting behind the steering wheel of his tinted out Toyota Tundra. The sounds of the Notorious B.I.G.'s, *Life After Death* album was thumping from the speakers and his Kushfilled Backwood had him high as a kite.

Niggas bleed just like us/ Picture me being scared of a nigga that breathe the same air as me/ Niggas bleed just like us/ Picture me being shook, we can both pull burners, and make the muthafuckin' beef cook/ Niggas bleed just like us/ Picture a nigga hiding, ya' life in that man's hands while he's just deciding/ Niggas bleed just like us/ I'd rather go toe to toe wit' all of y'all, running ain't in my protocol.

He reached inside of the glove compartment and grabbed the eighth of syrup that he had purchased from Thompson Street an hour earlier. He twisted the top off, and then took a huge swig of the thick yellow liquid. He then turned the sound system up to the max, and cruised down the block at a calm 5 m.p.h.

The crowd of *Grip Boys* stopped talking and wondered why the black pickup truck was stopped at the corner with the music blasting. One of them felt as though the driver of the truck was being disrespectful, and he became angry. He yelled for the driver to keep it moving, but Nasty just sat there nodding his head to the music and puffing on his Backwood. Again, the man yelled for Nasty to keep it moving, but instead he cut off the music and rolled down the passenger's side window. He looked at the man with an expressionless face, and then at the top of his lungs he shouted, *"Soowoo!"*

Egypt and Zaire hopped up from their positions in the bed of the truck. Both of them were strapped with a Mack 11 and red bandanas were tied aound their faces. They aimed at the crowd and fired.

Bddddoc! Bddddoc! Bddddoc! Bddddoc!

As soon as the first wave of bullets sprayed the corner everyone attempted to flee, but the majority of them were gunned down. The man who was yelling at Nasty got it the worst. He suffered thirteen gunshot wounds to his face and chest, and was dead before he hit the ground.

At the sight of all the bodies sprawled out on the corner, Nasty was satisfied that they conveyed their message: *The Block Boys Were Not to Be Fucked With!* He grabbed the red bandana that was hanging from his rear view mirror, tossed it out the passenger's side window, and then sped away from the scene.

Chapter Twenty

The Following Morning...

Sonny drove his Escalade to the Frankford section of the city to bring Diamondz his January shipment. As a precaution, he had Nasty and the twins behind him in a tinted out minivan. When they arrived at Diamondz's apartment building on Bridge Street, Sonny called him to let him know that he was outside. A few minutes later, Diamondz and a light skinned man that Sonny had never seen before emerged from the building and approached his truck.

"Sonny, what's good, fam?" Diamondz greeted him, while extending his right hand.

Instead of shaking his hand, Sonny just scowled at him. "That nigga that's standin' next to you, that's what's good!"

Diamondz looked at his companion, and then returned his gaze to Sonny.

"Naw, this my man Kev. He's from Pittsburgh. I told him to come to the city so he could holla at you."

Before Sonny had the chance to respond, Kev spoke up on his own behalf.

"Yo, I don't want no trouble, Ike. I just came out here to see if you could hit me off wit' some work. Me and my squad is getting crazy money out my way, and I was hopin' that you could hold us down the same way that you been holdin' down Diamondz."

Sonny ignored him and spoke directly to Diamondz.

"Didn't I tell you I wasn't try'na to meet none of ya peoples?"

Diamondz nodded his head. "I know, dawg, but I ain't have enough work to hold the nigga down. I hit him off wit' 5 bricks a couple of weeks ago, and he called me back three days later for 5 more. I'm only coppin' 25 at a time so obviously I couldn't cover his order, and still have enough work to break down with the coop. I know whatchu told me about introducin' you to niggas, but wit' the type of bread this nigga try'na spend, I was hopin' you would hit me off wit' a finder's fee," Diamondz explained.

After hearing Diamondz's position, Sonny directed his attention to Kev.

"Normally, I wouldn't fuck wit' you, but on the strength of Dia I'ma make an exception."

"Now, that's what I'm talking 'bout." Kev smiled. "And hopefully, you can bless me wit' the same deal that you be givin' Diamondz."

Sonny nodded his head. "I can do that for you, but you gotta give me a couple of weeks to put shit together."

"That's a bet." Kev continued smiling. "Shit, I wish you woulda holla'd at me the *last* time. We coulda been put this shit in motion."

"The *last* time?" Sonny scrunched up his face. "Whatchu mean the last time? Nigga, I ain't never seen you before."

"Nah Ike, I saw you a couple of months ago at the party that Diamondz had for Shiz. I was try'na holla at you back then, but I overheard you tellin' Diamondz that you wasn't try'na meet nobody."

Sonny thought back to the night of the party and he remembered the light skinned nigga that was at the bar staring at him.

"Yo, I *do* remember you. You was the nigga that was starin' at me when I was leavin' the club. What the fuck was up wit' all dat?"

"Nothin' Ike, you had a nigga mad as hell," Kev laughed it off. "I drove all the way out here 'cause my man told me that you was movin' them chickens for the low, but when you came through the spot, you wouldn't give a nigga the time of day."

Sonny shrugged his shoulders. "That wasn't nothin' personal fam, that's just the way I move."

"A'ight Kev," Diamondz interjected. "Me and Sonny got

business to handle."

Sonny grabbed the gym bag from his passenger's seat, and then hopped out the Escalade. After shaking Kev's hand and giving his young buls a look that said, *be on point*, he followed Diamondz up to his apartment.

An hour later, he emerged from the building with a book bag on his left shoulder and his right hand wrapped around the gun that was tucked in his hoodie pocket. He glanced up and down Bridge Street looking for any suspicious activity, and then casually strolled across the street toward his Escalade. When he opened the driver's side door, he saw that Zaire was sitting in the passenger's seat smoking a Vanilla Dutch, and playing Madden on his PS3. He looked at Sonny and asked him if everything was good.

"Yeah, everything's straight," he replied while hopping in the truck.

He tossed the book bag in the backseat, and then started the ignition and pulled off with the black minivan close behind.

*****

In The City's Logan Section...

Nahfisah was sitting on her bed, sky high from the crack she'd just finished smoking. Unfortunately, ever since the day Beaver Bushnut introduced her to the white chunky substance, she'd been hooked like a fish.

"Nahfisah!" Her grandmother called from the first floor.

"Yes, granny!" She nervously replied. She was paranoid from the crack.

"I need you to drive to the drug store and pick up my heart medicine."

"Damn. Why the fuck is her old ass always askin' for somethin'?" She said to herself. "This bitch be killin' my vibe!"

"Nahfisah, did you hear what I said?" Her grandmother continued shouting from the living room. "I need you to pick up my medicine!'

"Yeah, granny, I heard you. Damn!"

*****

At the A Plus gas station on Broad and Windrem, Sheed was sitting behind the steering wheel of his new 2013 Chevy Corvette. He was puffing on a Backwood and counting the $10,000 that he'd just made from his last sale. As he sat there waiting for a local crack head to finish pumping his gas, his cell phone vibrated in his lap. He looked at the screen and saw that it was his older brother, Pooky calling from SCI Graterford.

"Yo, bro!"

"Sheed, what's up baby boy? Did you take that money to the lawyer?"

"Yeah," Sheed nodded his head and smiled. "He said that the DNA test came back negative, and that he's in the process of puttin' together ya new appeal."

"Awwww man!" Pooky snapped. "I knew it. I knew that DNA test was gonna get us outta here, bro! It's been seventeen years, and all over some shit we didn't have nothin' to do wit'! I told you that wasn't our blood that they found in that mu'fuckin' house," Pooky continued, referring to the blood evidence that convicted him and their cousin, Rahman sixteen years ago. "So, did he say how long it's gonna take for him to get us outta here?"

"He said it's gon' take at least a year before the entire process is completed. It's cool, though, because he said the after discover evidence will establish actual innocence and that the judge ain't gonna have no other choice but to let y'all go," Sheed smiled. He was happy that his brother and cousin were finally coming home after all those years.

"Hey, yo, you know when I come home it's on right?"

"I already know, big bro," Sheed continued smiling. "Make sure you tell Rahman that I send my love, and I'll be up there to see y'all next week."

“A’ight, lil’ bro. I love you, dawg.”

“I love you more.”

Click!

After disconnecting the call, a pearl white SL 550 drove pass and pulled into the drugstore across the street. Initially, he thought the driver was either Sonny or Riana, but when a curvy, light skinned woman with long, silky black hair hopped out the car, he realized that the driver was Nahfishah, and that the Benz was Tommy’s.

Approximately ten minutes later, she emerged from the drugstore, hopped back in the Benz, and pulled out of the parking lot. As she drove up Old York Road, nodding her head to Nicki Manaj’s latest mixtape, she failed to notice the cherry red Corvette that was following her.

She made a left turn on Wyoming Avenue, and continued driving until she reached 10th Street. She parked the Benz in front of her grandmother’s house, hopped out and headed toward the front door. When she placed the key in the door knob, Sheed slid up behind her and placed the barrel of his Desert Eagle to the side of her neck.

“What’s poppin’ Nahfisah?”

She tried to turn around, but he mashed her face into the door. “Bitch, where the fuck is them bricks at?”

She looked out the corner of her eye and saw that it was Sheed. “Oh, my God! Sheed, I didn’t have nothin’ to do wit’ Tommy tellin’ on y’all!”

“Bitch, shut the fuck up. That rat ass nigga stole them bricks from us, and I *know* you got ‘em, so where they at?”

“I don’t know whatchu talking ‘bout,” she lied. “Tommy never told me nothin’ about no bricks.”

He glanced from left to right, looking for any possible witnesses. He saw none.

“Yo, open the door. We gon’ go inside and get to the bottom of this shit.”

“I ain’t openin’ nothin’. Fuck you.”

Again, he bashed her face against the wooden door.

"If I gotta tell ya stupid ass one more time, I'ma fuckin' kill you."

"A'ight, damn! I'ma open the door." She cried as she nervously unlocked the door.

When they entered the house, her grandmother was sitting in her wheelchair, and Imani was lying on the carpet watching cartoons. He punched Nahfisah in the back of her head, and she crashed to the carpet.

"Oh, my God!" Her grandmother cried out. "Nigga, whatchu you doin' in my goddamn house? You better get yo ass outta here 'fore I call the poe-lice!"

"Bitch, I ain't goin' no fuckin' where 'til this stankinass bitch gimme my shit!" He snapped, while aiming the gun at Nahfisah.

Imani hopped up from the carpet and ran over to her mother. She wrapped her little arms around Nahfisah's neck, and then looked at Sheed with hate in her eyes. "Leave my mommy alone!"

Her grandmother looked around for the house phone, but couldn't find it. "Nahfisah!" She shouted. "If you have something that belongs to this black heathen, you need to give it to him 'fore somebody gets hurt!"

"Granny, he's lyin'! I ain't got nothin' that belongs to him!" Nahfisah screamed as she lay on the carpet hugging Imani.

Sheed kicked her in the ribs with the tip of his boot.

"Bitch, you better stop playin' and gimme my shit! As a matter of fact," he reached down and grabbed Imani by her hair. "Get ya ass over here."

"Noooo!" Nahfisah screamed. "Don't hurt her!"

He ignored her pleas and dragged the little girl over to her great grandmother. In a fit of rage, he clunked the grandmother upside the head with the side of his pistol, and then pushed her out of the wheelchair.

He then aimed the .50 caliber at Nahfisah's face and

snarled, “Get ya ass upstairs! I need to show you somethin’.” He dragged Imani up the stairs and led her to the bathroom.

“Please don’t hurt my baby, Sheed. She didn’t do anything.”

“Well, gimme them bricks and I won’t.”

“Sheed, I’m tellin’ you the truth. I don’t know nothin’ about no bricks,” she continued crying.

He scowled at her and shook his head in disbelief. He ordered her to remove her shirt, and when she declined he fired a shot into the bathroom wall.

Doom!

“Okay! Okay!” She complied and quickly removed her shirt.

He shoved Imani toward her. “Now, tie her hands behind her fuckin’ back! And if you try some slick shit, I’m killin’ both of y’all.”

Reluctantly, she followed his orders and tied Imani’s hands behind her back.

“Please don’t hurt her. Whatever happened between you and Tommy, that was between y’all,” she sobbed. “Me and Imani ain’t got nothin’ to do wit’ this shit.”

“I ain’t try’na hear that,” Sheed spat. “That rat ass nigga left you them bricks before he died, and now you try’na keep ‘em.”

He reached out and grabbed Imani by the front of her shirt.

“Agggghhh! Mommy make him stop!” She screamed at the top of her lungs.

He wrapped his hands around her neck and squeezed.

“Shut ya lil’ ass up ‘fore I kill you.” He looked at Nahfisah. “This is ya last mu’fuckin’ chance. Now tell me where you hidin’ that fuckin’ work.”

When she didn’t respond, his face became red with anger.

“Oh, you think I’m bluffin’, huh? You think this shit’s a game?” A sinister expression spread across his face, and he lowered his voice a few octaves. "A'ight, watch this."

He turned Imani upside down, and then dipped her head in the toilet bowl. Her little body bucked back and forth and her legs kicked wildly.

At the sight of her daughter's torment, Nahfisah begged him to stop, but Sheed just scowled at her. He lifted Imani's head out of the toilet, and she coughed and gagged. The second she regained her breath, she cried, "Mommy, make him stop!"

"Bitch, you see I ain't playin'. Now, gimme my shit or I'ma kill ya whole fuckin' family!" He looked at Imani. "And I'm startin' wit' her!"

Again, he dipped her head in the toilet bowl.

"A'ight, Sheed. Damn, I'ma give you ya shit."

He lifted the little girl's head out of the toilet, and she continued to cough and gag. He laid her fragile body on the tiled floor, and then looked at Nahfisah.

"Well, what the fuck is you waitin' for? Where they at?"

"I got 'em in my bedroom closet," she finally admitted.

He nodded his head, and then followed her to her bedroom. When she pulled the pillow case from her closet and dumped the keys on her bed, he immediately began counting them.

"Hold the fuck up. It's only 24 bricks right here. It's supposed to be 30, so where's the rest of 'em?"

"I don't know," she shrugged her shoulders, and wiped the tears from her face. "Tommy must've sold 'em."

"Well, how much money you got?"

She lowered her head. "A little over $5,000."

He shook his head from side to side, and for the first time he felt sorry for her. He remembered a time when he considered her his sister, and would've done anything for her. *Damn, this rat ass nigga got me in here terrorizing this girl and her family,* he thought to himself, feeling slightly ashamed.

"Hey, yo Fisah, I didn't mean for shit to go this far, but Tommy stole this work, and I ain't have no other choice."

“Whatever, Sheed. You got whatchu came for, now can you please leave my house?”

“A’ight, and you can keep the money,” he replied, while stuffing the bricks back into the pillow case. “Oh, yeah,” he looked her square in the eyes, “you know if you tell anybody about this I’ma kill you right?”

“Whatever, Sheed. Just take ya shit and get the fuck out.”

Chapter Twenty-One

Two Weeks Later...

After wiping out the 22nd and McKean crew, the *Block Boys* laid low. They were waiting for Grip and his soldiers to strike back, but so far they hadn't. In Trenton, New Jersey, Nasty and the twins were becoming impatient. They were yearning for action. They were yearning for the block. The game's funny like that. The same way a crack head was addicted to crack, the hustler was addicted to the hustle. It wasn't even about the money. It was all about the intoxicating feeling of making the money. They needed to hustle. They needed Sonny to reopen the block.

"Yo Zai, call Sonny and ask him to meet us at the spot," said Egypt.

"Nizzaw, you call him," Zaire shot back.

Nasty entered the living room and said, "Here, gimme ya phone, I'll call him."

Zaire handed him his Samsung, and then slouched back in the leather recliner. Nasty dialed Sonny's number, and then held the phone to his ear.

Ring! Ring! Ring!

"Yo," Sonny answered.

"Peace, big homie! What's poppin'?"

"Nasty, what's bangin'?" He replied, immediately recognizing the voice of his favorite young bul.

"Aye, me and the twins need to holla at you."

"A'ight, where y'all at?"

"We at the Trenton spot."

"Say no more. I'll be there in an hour."

"Well actually, we was hopin' you could meet us on the block."

"On the block? For what?"

"Yo, I ain't gon' hold you scrap, niggas is tired of layin' low. We try'na get back on them streets."

Sonny sighed. "You know what, meet me on the block in an hour."

Click!

After disconnecting the call, he went downstairs to the basement and opened his vault. He looked at the $1,800,000 that was stashed inside, and shook his head in disbelief. *Damn, if wasn't for Mook, I wouldn't have none of this shit*, he thought to himself.

As he stood there staring at the pyramids of money, his iPhone vibrated in his pants pocket. He grabbed it and looked at the screen.

"Pops, what's good?"

"Hey Sonny, we need to talk," Easy stated in a somber voice.

"What's wrong pops? Everything good?"

"Yeah, everything's good. I just need to talk to you about the block."

"Damn, you too. First Nasty and the twins, and now here you come wit' the same shit. Don't y'all realize we in the trenches right now?"

"I understand all that, but at the same time, we still gotta eat," Easy responded.

"A'ight man. I'ma be on the block in an hour, so come through and holla at me."

"I'll be there," Easy assured him.

"Hey, pops, before you hang up, I need to ask you somethin'."

"A'ight, just keep in mind that we're on the phone," Easy warned him.

"When you was doin' ya thing back in the day, did you ever get the feelin' that enough was enough?"

"Without a doubt. Me and every other nigga in the game."

"Well, what did you do about it?"

"I ignored the feelin' and kept on pushin'," he replied, full of regret. "I went full speed ahead and ended up crashing into a brick wall."

"Hey, yo pops, I ain't gonna hold you man, but I'm really startin' to feel like it's time for me to fold my hand. It's like, I done came up so fast that it's kinda scary. Me and Riri got the baby comin', and I'm afraid that if I keep on movin' the way I'm movin', this shit gonna fuck around and get the best of me."

"Well, if you're feelin' like that, then you need to follow ya instincts. It seems like you've already got whatchu came for, so you might as well walk away while you still can. Don't make the same mistake that I made when I had my run. You's a smart mutha'fucka, and deep down you know whatchu need to do."

"I'm sayin' though, what about my niggas?"

"What about 'em? If they truly love you the way they say they do, then they'll have no other choice but to respect ya decision."

"But what if they don't?"

"Then you keep it pushin' and don't look back."

"A'ight, pops, I'm a holla at you some more when I get to the block."

Click!

After disconnecting the call, he picked up the manila envelope that was lying on the floor in his vault, and then called upstairs to Riana. A few seconds later, she descended the stairs with Rocko cradled in her arms.

"What's that?" She nodded at the envelope.

"College applications. After you have the baby, I want you to go back to school and get a degree in somethin'."

She handed him Rocko, and then grabbed the envelope. She opened it and pulled out applications for Temple, Drexel, Lincoln, and West Chester.

"A'ight, I'll make you a deal. Since you want me to go back to school so bad, I'm a do it, but only if you stop hustlin'."

He smiled at her. "I'm two steps ahead of you. As soon as I run through these last 55 joints, I'ma do whatchu said and open up my own business."

A huge smile spread across her face and she wrapped her arms around him.

"A'ight Riri, damn. You're gonna fuck around and smother me," he laughed.

"Shut up." She released her bear hug and punched him in the shoulder. "So, do you have any ideas about what kind of business you wanna open?"

"Yeah," he nodded his head. "I'ma open a sports bar and call it Donkees."

"Donkees? What the hell kinda name is that?" She teased.

"A'ight, well you know how Hooters got pretty waitresses wit' big titties?" She nodded her head. "Well, Donkees is gonna have pretty waitresses wit' fat asses."

She burst out laughing. "Boo, you're crazy as shit, but you know what, that's a good idea. The way y'all niggas love a cute face and a fat ass, that shit could be a goldmine. Especially if you throw some of my cookin' up in the mix 'cause you know a bitch can burn," she bragged.

"Damn yo, now that I really think about it that shit could definitely be a gold mine. I'ma call my real estate agent and see if she can find me a nice location. In the meantime," he smacked her on the ass. "You need to fill out these applications so we can get ya lil' sexy pregnant self back in school."

*****

An Hour Later...

When Sonny pulled up on the block and spotted Nasty and the twins sitting on milk crates, he shook his head in disbelief.

"These niggas really think shit's sweet," he said to himself as he parked the Escalade in front of his trap house.

After turning off the ignition, he hopped out with a duffle bag strapped to each shoulder. He grinded them up about not being on point, and then led them inside of the house. He laid the duffle bags on the dining room table, then twisted up a

Backwood. Breeze and Sheed walked through the front door and joined them at the table.

Sonny sparked up his Backwood and took a long pull. He coughed a couple of times, and then exhaled a cloud of smoke. He glanced around the dining room table, then began talking. "First of all, I want y'all to know that I love y'all, and that I honor y'all loyalty. Secondly, I want y'all to know that whatever y'all chose to do when it comes down to gettin' money, I'ma support y'all movement. As of right now, well at least when I knock off this last lil' bit of work, I'm officially out the game."

"Out the game?" Sheed looked at him like he was crazy. "What the fuck do you mean you gettin' out the game? We're in the middle of a mu'fuckin' war!"

Sonny looked at him and gritted his teeth. He wanted to snap on him, but instead he held his composure. "Listen, as far as this hustlin' shit, I'm done, dawg. But when it comes to this beef," he pulled out a nickel plated .45 and laid it on the table. "I'm locked and loaded, and I'm ridin' 'til the day we kill every last one of them niggas. But the second we do, and this war is over, I'm fallin' all the way back."

"But what about us?" Egypt asked. "Me, Zai, and Nasty ain't got nothin' but the block. If you leavin' the game, then how we supposed to eat? You the one that's feedin' us."

"Yeah," Nasty concurred. "How you just gon' turn ya back on the family? We all we got," he continued in a disappointed tone of voice.

"I'm not turnin' my back on the family!" Sonny shouted with frustration in his voice. "I've gotta worry about Riana and the baby. I already got what I came for, so now y'all gotta get what y'all came for!"

Easy walked through the front door and waved his hands in the air. "Yo, what the fuck is y'all in here screamin' for? I could hear y'all halfway down the block."

"Pops, I was telling 'em that I'm done wit' the game, and that it's time for me to move forward," Sonny explained.

Easy glanced around and took an assessment of everyone's facial expressions. "So, how y'all feel about that?"

Egypt spoke up and said, "On some all the way gee shit, I tip my hat to the big homie. I just don't know how we supposed to eat without him. It's like damn, what the fuck is we supposed to do now?"

"What is y'all supposed to do?" Sonny snapped, then reached inside one of the duffle bags and pulled out a brick. "This is what the fuck y'all are supposed to do, get money." He tossed the brick to Egypt, and then reached inside of the other duffle bag and pulled out a brick of money. "I'm givin' all of y'all 10 bricks and a $100,000 a piece! If y'all can't bubble from here, then y'all ain't got no business bein' in the mu'fuckin' game."

The room became silent as they sat there staring at him. Easy was thinking about resurrecting his glory days. Egypt and Zaire were imagining themselves driving around the city in twin Bentleys. Breeze and Nasty were fantasizing about becoming their own bosses, and Sheed was thinking that Sonny was going out like a sucka.

Sonny held out his arms. "Damn, what y'all ain't got nothin' to say?"

They all started laughing and took turns hugging him, but Sheed just sat there giving him the icegrill. Sonny noticed his demeanor and addressed him, "Damn nigga, what the fuck is up wit' you?"

"Yo, y'all niggas is buggin'!" Sheed snapped, and then pointed his index finger in Sonny's face. "Ya nut ass is sittin' here talking 'bout leavin' the game, and the rest of these niggas don't care about nothing except money. You niggas is actin' like we aIn't in the middle of a mu'fuckin' war! What, y'all think that just because we dropped couple of bodies that this shit is over? Fuck no, this shit ain't over! Them niggas is probably plottin' on us right now! Man, y'all niggas ain't geed up! Y'all niggas is pussies!"

Sonny snapped. "Hold up, nigga! First of all, you better

watch ya fuckin' mouth! Secondly," he leaned across the table and pointed his index finger back in Sheed's face, "out of all people, you think I don't know what time it is nigga? You think I don't wanna win this war and avenge the murder of my big fuckin'homie?"

Sheed jumped to his feet and stormed toward the front door. He grabbed the door knob, and then turned back around to address the niggas that he loved and would've died for.

"Yo, I can't believe y'all niggas! Y'all niggas don't care about Mook! If I gotta park these niggas by myself, then *that's* what it is!"

He stormed out the house and slammed the door behind him. Sonny got up to follow him, but Easy stopped him in his tracks.

"Let him go, Sontino. He's hurtin' right now. Just give him some time to cool off."

Sonny looked at his father, and then looked at the faces of the men sitting around the table. He fully understood where Easy was coming from, but in his heart he could feel that something bad was about to happen.

Chapter Twenty-Two

When Sonny left the block, the only thing he could think about was Sheed. He tried calling him, but all he got was his voice mail. As he cruised through the Bad Landz, he saw the hood for what it really was, an ongoing cycle of struggle and deception. He thought about the past six months of his life and how it had drastically changed. He thought about Mook and Saleena, and his eyes began to water. Although he was sitting on $1,300,000, he swore that he would give it all up just to see them breathe again. As he was caught up in his thoughts, the LCD screen on his iPhone illuminated; alerting him that he had an incoming call.

"Yo."

"What's up, boo? Can you talk right now?"

"Daph?" He questioned the identity of the caller.

"Yeah, it's me. I need to talk to you."

He sighed. "Damn, Daph, you know I can't be fuckin' wit' you like that."

"I know, but I really need to see you. Can you meet me somewhere?"

"Yeah, I can do that. Where are you at?"

"I'm on 25th and Master."

"A'ight." He took a deep breath and sighed. "You know the halal restaurant on Ridge Ave?"

"You talking 'bout Mom and Me's?"

"Yeah, meet me there in fifteen minutes."

*****

Two Cars Behind...

Detective Smith was following Sonny's Escalade, and talking to Grip on his cell phone. "Mr. Moreno, I'm two cars behind him. Should I pull him over, or do you want me to keep following him?"

"No Smitty, don't pull him over. Just keep following him,

and see where he takes you. The second he stops give me a call, and I'll tell you what to do from there," Grip instructed from the back seat of his pearl white Mercedes Maybach.

"Whatever you say, Mr. Moreno. You're the boss!"

"That's right, Smitty. I am the boss, and you better never forget that!"

*****

When Sonny pulled up in front of the halal restaurant, he spotted Daphney's Porsche Panamara, and parked directly behind it. He turned off the engine, and stepped out into the cold January weather. As soon as he walked through the front door of the restaurant, the aroma of fried catfish made his stomach do cartwheels. He looked to his left and smiled when he saw her sitting by the wall sipping on a bottle of Akbar juice. They locked eyes and he walked toward her.

"What's up, beautiful? You good?"

"I'm a'ight," she answered in a soft voice. "I'm not gon' beat around the bush, so I'ma come right out and tell you. I'm pregnant."

Her words caught him off guard. He immediately thought about the times that they had unprotected sex, and then shook his head in disappointment.

"Well, I guess you're tellin' me this because it's my baby, huh?"

She didn't respond.

"Yo', you know I'm 'bout to get married, right? How the fuck I'm 'posed to tell my wife I got another chick pregnant at the same time that she's pregnant?"

"I don't know, boo boo, but whether you like it or not, I'm keepin' my baby. I would love for you to be there for us, but if not," she shrugged her shoulders, "fuck it. I've got my own money."

"Hold up, ma, pump ya breaks! I ain't said nothin' about

not bein' there for y'all. At the same time, it ain't like you was my girl, so how do I know if the baby's even mine?"

"Pussy, whatchu callin' me a hoe?"

"Naw, I ain't callin' you nothin'. I'm just sayin'."

"Fuck you, Sontino!" She started crying. "Nigga, I fell in love wit' you! I did shit for you that I woulda never done for another nigga, and you really gonna sit here and try to play me?"

She got up from the table and started to leave, but he reached out and gently grabbed her by the arm. "Hold up Daph, I'm sorry. Can you please sit back down?"

She did as he asked, and with tears pouring from her eyes, she asked him, "Why would you disrespect me like that?"

"My bad." He slowly shook his head from side to side. "I know you're a good girl, and I shoulda never said no shit like that," he responded while wiping the tears from her face.

"Sontino, do you love me?"

"If I said that I didn't, I'd be lyin' to you. You're everything that I ever wanted in a woman, and between you and Riri," he paused for a moment. "I don't know what I'ma do."

She looked at him, and her facial expression was beyond serious. "Listen, I knew you had a girl from the rip, so I'm not gon' do nothin' to come in between that. All I want is a part of your heart that's exclusively for me. I mean damn, at the end of the day, is that too much to ask for?"

"Naw, that not too much, but at the same time I need you to understand that I gotta do everything I can to protect Riana's feelings. Shorty been down for a nigga since day one, and to keep it real wit' you, I can't see myself livin' without her."

As they continued their conversation, Riana and Erika walked through the front door. "Girl, I can't believe I'm havin' a boy!" Riana beamed as they approached the counter. "Sontino's gonna be happy as shit!"

"I know that's right," Erika replied, while examining the large menu that hung from the ceiling. "So, what are you try'na order? I think I'ma get me some roasted lamb and wild rice."

Riana looked up at the menu, and selected fish fried rice and cornbread.

After a ten minute wait, the slim Muslim sister who worked at the register handed them their food on two separate trays. They walked toward the other side of the restaurant where the tables and booths were situated, and the first thing that caught their attention was the site of Sonny and Daphney sitting in the far corner. Daphney was smiling at him from ear to ear, and he was caressing her hand. Riana was livid. She stormed toward the table and threw her hot tray of food at Sonny's head.

"Yo, what the fuck?" He snapped, while leaping from the table. He turned to look at the culprit, and when he saw Riana standing there crying, his heart damn near jumped out of his chest.

"Pussy, I knew you was fuckin' this bitch!" Riana screamed as she got up in his face. She mugged him, and then turned her attention to Daphney. "Bitch, if I wasn't pregnant, I'd fuck you up!"

Daphney got up to confront Riana, but Sonny held her back. "You better calm the fuck down! You know y'all can't be fighting!"

Erika sat her tray on the table and quickly removed her diamondstudded earrings. "Ahn ahn Sonny let her go! I'm a trash the shit out this bitch," she shouted, and then swung a wild punch, missing Daphney's face by inches.

Daphney swung back, but because Sonny was holding her, she missed her target. Riana threw a punch of her own, but she missed Daphney and hit Sonny on his right shoulder.

"Hey, yo, Riri, calm the fuck down!" He shouted. "It's not whatchu think. She's Mook's cousin."

She folded her arms across her chest, and shifted her weight to her right hip. "Now, what the fuck that gotta do wit' you sittin' here holdin' this bitch's hand? Pussy, you must think I'm stupid."

"I'm sayin', though, she's Mook's cousin and my real

estate agent. She's the one that helped us get the house, and we was talkin' about findin' a location for my sport's bar," he lied.

After hearing Sonny's excuse, Daphney grabbed her Marc Jacobs bag off of the floor, and stormed out of the restaurant. He looked at her through the window and shook his head as she climbed in her Panamara.

Riana slapped him back to attention.

Whack!

"Pussy, look at me when I'm talkin' to you! As a matter of fact, fuck this shit! Come on, Erika, let's go!"

As he attempted to follower her out of the restaurant a, short middle aged Muslim brother approached him, and said, "I don't know what's goin' on, ahk, but you need to leave my establishment."

"Damn, my bad, ol' head." He reached inside of his pocket and pulled out a thick wad of bills. After counting out $300, he handed over the money. "Here, take this for ya trouble, and if it ain't too much to ask, can I use ya bathroom real quick so I can clean myself up?"

The Muslim brother nodded his head. "Yeah, but make it quick." He then ordered one of his employees to clean up the mess.

As he headed toward the men's room, Detective Smith entered the restaurant and followed him.

"Yo, this shit is crazy," he said to himself, while looking in the mirror and wiping the fish fried rice off of his cream colored Chanel For Men's sweater.

As he turned on the water faucet, an older white man entered the bathroom with a cell phone clutched in his left hand. He looked out the corner of his eye and noticed that a badge was hanging from the man's neck, so he quickly adjusted his sweater to conceal the ACP that was tucked in the small of his back.

Detective Smith positioned himself by the door and smiled at him. "Well, if it isn't the *prince of the friggin' city!*"

"Excuse me," Sonny replied. "I think you got me

confused wit' somebody else."

Detective Smith continued smiling. "I don't think so, Sontino. I know exactly who you are. Actually, I know everything about you," he stated while walking toward him.

"Oh, yeah! So what, I'm under arrest or somethin'?" He asked in a cocky voice.

"No, you're not under arrest, well at least not yet."

"Not yet? What the fuck is that supposed to mean?"

Detective Smith stopped smiling and his face became serious. "Damn, that's right. You're grandfather told me you were an arrogant sonofabitch!"

In the blink of an eye, Sonny pulled the .45 ACP from the small of his back and aimed it at Smitty's face. "What the fuck you just say?"

"Whoa, wait a minute. You can't kill a cop!" Smitty protested with his hands raised in a defenseless posture.

Sonny gritted his teeth, and then cocked back the top of his pistol.

Click! Clack!

"What, you're workin' for Grip?"

"Listen, Sontino, just calm down. There's a gang of witnesses on the other side of this door, and if you shoot me, you'll spend the rest of your life on death row. Don't be stupid. Just take it easy and put the friggin' gun down."

"Yo, what the fuck do you want from me, dawg?"

"Here," Detective Smith held out the cell phone. "You're grandfather wants to talk to you."

Sonny snatched the phone and held it to his ear. "Nigga, what the fuck you want?"

"I want my grandson to take his rightful position at the head of my family," Grip's deep raspy voice eased through the phone. "So far, you haven't disappointed me, and I must say, throughout our minor misunderstanding, the ruthless approach that you've taken has me extremely proud. I'm more than confident that you have enough of my blood running through you're veins to not only maintain the status of my family, but to take it to the next level. All you have to do is make the right decision, and I can guarantee you that you'll receive everything that your hand calls for."

As Sonny listened to Grip's logic, all he could do was shake his head in disbelief. *This nigga killed my big homie. He chopped his head off and sent it to me. Now he's got the nerve to ask me to take over his so called family.*

Grip continued, "I heard the news about your father, and it didn't surprise me. I mean, after all, just like you, he *is* a Moreno. I knew it would only be a matter of time before he got his shit together, and now that he does, it's time for the three of us to come together as a family. Just think about it Sontino, that's three generations of greatness. Three generations of gangsters. Three generations of Morenos!"

Sonny laughed. "Hey, yo' dig this, I know what this is about. This is about me puttin' that pressure on ya ol' ass, and now you try'na wave the peace flag, talkin' this grandpop/grandson shit. Yo, you's a funny mu'fucka."

"Are you serious? That's whatchu call pressure? Killing Biggs, Smack, and a couple of nobodies that I've never even seen before. The only reason that you and your little dirtyass crew is alive right now is because I allow it. Now, since you wanna talk about pressure, I'm a show your little ass the meaning of pressure!" Grip shouted through the phone.

"Oh, yeah, well I'll tell you what, nigga, suck my *dick*!" Sonny yelled through the receiver, and then threw the phone against the bathroom wall. He looked at Detective Smith with a menacing stare, holstered his .45, and left the bathroom.

Chapter Twenty-Three

When Sonny returned to his house in Cheltenham, Pennsylvania, the garage doors were open, and he could see that Riana's Tahoe was gone. He walked inside of the house, and headed straight for their bedroom. "Damn," he said to himself. The room was ransacked as if the house had been burglarized. Ironically, all of the items that appeared to be missing belonged to Riana. The only thing in the room that was still in place was their kingsized bed. He looked closely and saw a single sheet of paper lying on her pillow. He picked it up and saw that it was a letter addressed to him.

Sontino,

I can't believe that after everything we've been through, you would lie to me and disrespect me like that. I fuckin' trusted you. I loved you and was always there for you, and this is how you do me? I'm carrying your fuckin' child, and you're out here runnin' around with the next bitch. I'm done! I left your engagement ring on the top shelf in the closet, and I'm movin' to Atlanta to live with my dad. Don't call me, and don't bother try'na find me. It's over!

P.S. I went to my doctor's appointment this morning, and he told me that I'm having a boy. As a woman, I know that I can't raise a man, but I'm a bad bitch. I'm pretty sure I can get one of them Atlanta niggas to put a ring on it, and be the man that I need him to be. Fuck you!!!

He crumbled the paper in his hand and regretfully shook his head. "Damn, I fucked up!" He loved Riana with all of his heart, but now she was gone and there was nothing he could do about it. He walked over to her walk-in closet, and grabbed the velvet box from the top shelf. He opened it, and the bling of her engagement ring made his heart flutter. "Damn," he sighed. "I think I really might've lost her this time. What the fuck was I thinking?"

*****

Back In North Philly...

Nasty was sitting behind the steering wheel of his Toyota Tundra, smoking a Vanilla Dutch, and watching the latest *Smack* DVD. He was parked at the gas station on Broad and York, and was waiting for his man, Goon to pull up, so he could serve him the brick that was sitting on his passenger's seat. A dirty homeless man approached his truck with a squeegee in one hand and a spray bottle in the other.

"Hey, young buck, lemme wash ya windows for ya, young buck."

Nasty reached inside of his pants pocket and pulled out a wad of money. After peeling off a twenty dollar bill, he rolled down the window, and extended the money.

"My windows is already clean ol' head, but you can have this dub though."

The homeless man smiled at him. "Good lookin', young buck." He took the money from Nasty's hand, but didn't walk away from the truck.

Nasty became annoyed by his awkward presence. "A'ight ol' head, I gave you twenty dollars, so what the fuck is you standin' here for?"

The homeless man didn't budge. Instead, he just stood there staring at him.

"Ol' head, if I gotta get out this truck, I'ma throw a foot in ya ass," Nasty warned with a serious expression on his face. "Now, roll the fuck out."

The homeless man just stood there smiling at him. When Nasty reached for the door handle, the dingy looking man dropped his spray bottle, and then pulled the .44 Bulldog that was tucked on his waist. He aimed the barrel at Nasty's face and squeezed the trigger.

Boom! Boom!

The bullets ripped through the left side of Nasty's head, sizzled out the right side, shattered the passenger's side window, and lodged into the gas station wall. Nasty slumped over the center console and the homeless man took off running down York Street. He headed toward the money green Escalade that was parked under the 12th Street Bridge. When he reached the SUV, he tried to open the back door, but it was locked.

"What the fuck?" He stated in disbelief, still trying to open the door. He tapped the passenger's side window. "Mr. Moreno it's me. Open the door."

Grip rolled down his tinted window and stared at the disguised young man, who just two hours ago was promised the capo position of the 24th and Berks Street crew. "Antonio, did you get the job done?"

"Yeah," the young man nodded his head as he was still trying to catch his breath. "I blew—I blew his brains out. Just—just like you told me to."

"Good." Grip pulled out a Glock 19 and shot him in the forehead.

Pow!

A bloody mist of brains and skull fragments burst out the back of his head, and he crumbled to the ground. Grip rolled up the passenger's side window, and then looked to his left where Muhammad was sitting behind the steering wheel with a confused look on his face. He'd known Grip for over thirty years, but he'd never known him to kill his own soldiers for no apparent reason. Grip shrugged his shoulders, already knowing what his driver and personal bodyguard was thinking.

"What?" He screwed up his face. "His granddaddy was a rat. His daddy was a rat and his ass was bound to rat sooner or later, so I just said fuck it."

They fell out laughing as Muhammad pulled away from the curb.

*****

Fifteen Minutes Later...

When Grip and Muhammad pulled into the parking lot of his warehouse, they spotted Detective Smith, Monster, and Lil' Buggy standing around talking. Grip climbed out the Escalade and got up in Smitty's face. "What the fuck are y'all standin' around for? Didn't I tell you mutha'fuckas to turn the heat up around this bitch?"

"Calm down Mr. Moreno, everything's under control," Detective Smith stated, attempting to ameliorate Grip's hostility. "As we speak, some of your soldier's are patrolling their neighborhood, and your guy right here," he nodded at Monster. "He gave 'em specific orders to shoot on sight."

Grip reached inside of his trench coat and pulled out an envelope full of money. "Here," he handed the envelope to Smitty, "this is the bread that I owe you for tracking down Sontino. Now, that friend of his, the tall brown skinned kid, what's his name?"

"Who, you talking 'bout the bul Sheed?" Monster asked.

"Yeah," Grip nodded his head, "that's his name. I want him dead by the morning. The same goes for those twins."

"A'ight, but what about Sonny?" Lil' Buggy asked. "Whatchu want us to do wit' him?"

"Well, I doubt you'll catch him slippin', but if you do," he pointed his index finger in Lil' Buggy's face, "you throw his little arrogant ass in a trunk, and bring him straight to me. I wanna make this extremely clear," he paused for a second and looked each of them in the face. "Do not, and I repeat, do not bring any devastating harm to my grandson."

"Alright, Mr. Moreno, we've got it covered," Detective Smith assured him, while placing the money filled envelope in his jacket pocket. He headed toward his Crown Victoria, and Grip and Muhammad disappeared inside of the warehouse.

As Smitty drove away from the parking lot, and the

warehouse door closed behind Grip and Muhammad, Lil' Buggy looked at Monster. "Unc, I don't trust that detective."

Monster folded his arms across his chest. "I don't trust that cracker either."

"Oh, yeah, Unc, I forgot to tell you about the latest word that I got from my man in the Bad Landz. He was tellin' me about some ol' head named Easy that's supposed to be the bul Sonny's pop. You ever heard of him?"

"Yeah, I've heard of the nigga. He's Mr. Moreno's son. The nigga was gettin' money back in the day, but now he ain't nothin' but a dirtyass crack head."

"Nizzaw," Lil' Buggy shook his head from side to side, "My man in the Bad Landz told me that the bul Easy is in his bag right now, and that he's runnin' Fairhill and York."

"Man, fuck that nigga," Monster replied. His words were full of contempt. "That niggas a bitch! Me and Black kidnapped his ass back in the day when he refused to get down wit' the movement, and the only reason we let him live is because Mr. Moreno told us he was his son."

"So whatchu think?" Lil' Buggy scratched his chin. "You got the ol' head Easy bein' a problem?"

"I doubt it. I guess we gonna have to wait and see. But on some real shit, it don't even matter 'cause at the end of the day, you and me gon' be the ones runnin' this shit"

"What?" Lil' Buggy looked at him skeptically. He didn't understand his uncle's logic. "How do you figure that?"

"Cause I'ma kill Sonny. And if Mr. Moreno feels some type of way, then fuck it, I'ma kill his ass too."

"You're losin' me, Unc. Even if we kill Sonny, Mr. Moreno's still gonna be the boss."

"Naw, Lil' Buggy, that's where you're wrong. Think about it, Mr. Moreno's old as shit. He's been trying to leave the game for years, but up until he found out about Sonny, he didn't have anybody that was actually a blood related Moreno that could take over the family. In the late eighties he was groomin' Alvin for the position, but even then it wasn't a quote on quote *Moreno Family* situation," he used his fingers as quotation marks, "but more of a *Black Mafia* situation which is basically a myth. Mr. Moreno never sanctioned a so called *Black Mafia*. It was always *The Moreno Crime Family*, but the media was the ones who labeled us the *Black Mafia*. And now that he knows about Sonny, he wants to hand the whole shit over to him. At the same time, he's usin' us as pawns to see what the lil' nigga's cut like. I mean, think about," he shrugged his shoulders and used his hands for emphasis, "how the fuck he gon' tell us to take a nigga to war, and at the same time tell us not to kill him? Fuck that! I've been ridin' for this family for too mutha'fuckin' long. If anybody's gonna be the next boss, it's gonna be me."

*****

Across the street, in the parking lot of an abandoned warehouse, Detective Sullivan was sitting in a black Grand Cherokee looking at the pictures that he'd just stored into his digital camera. The pictures depicted Detective Smith fraternizing with the city's most violent crime syndicate, and they further depicted him receiving a pay off from the infamous Gervin Moreno. When he was first transferred to the Philadelphia Police Department he'd heard all of the rumors about his new partner being a dirty cop, but it wasn't until a week ago that he discovered how true the rumors actually were.

They were patrolling the Bad Landz in an unmarked vehicle when they approached the corner of 7th and Clearfield. As they cruised by the corner they realized that an intense dice game was in progress. A crowd of approximately six men were huddled in front of the Chinese store, and there was a large pile of money on the ground. A tall, fat, light skinned man who the both of them knew as *Doe Boy* was in the middle of the crowd rolling a pair of dice against the stoop, while the rest of the men were eagerly awaiting the outcome. Unfortunately, they were too busy clocking the strawberry red dice to see the two detectives creeping up behind them.

Both of them had their guns drawn when they ordered the men to get up against the wall. After a thorough search they found large amounts of cash and approximately twenty-five bundles of PCP. When Detective Sullivan attempted to call for back up, Detective Smith stopped him and told him that they were giving the guys a break. He then stuffed his pockets with the drugs and money and led a confused Detective Sullivan back to their unmarked vehicle. He drove them to the corner of Germantown and Allegheny and parked in front of the Carmen's Skating Rink. After counting the confiscated money, he broke down half and handed it to Detective Sullivan. Initially, Sullivan declined because he didn't approve of Smitty's unlawful conduct, but after five minutes of listening to his partner's persuadable tactics, he finally conceded.

Unfortunately for Detective Smith, at the end of their shift, Detective Sullivan went straight to his supervisor and spilled the beans about Smitty's egregious and unethical actions. In turn, he was given the green light to conduct an investigation, and now, just eight days later, he had enough evidence for Internal Affairs to give Smitty everything that a dirty cop deserved.

Chapter Twenty-Four

In Cheltenham, Pennsylvania...

After calling Riana's cell phone for the twentieth time and leaving messages on her voice mail, Sonny went to his basement and released his frustrations on his weight bench. He placed two 45 pound weights on both sides of the bar, and began lifting reps of fifteen. After completing his fourth set, his iPhone vibrated on the concrete slab that he used as a weight pad.

Vrrrrrm! Vrrrrrm!

He wiped the sweat from his forehead with his wife beater, picked up the phone and accepted the call.

"Sonny, they killed Nasty!" Egypt cried through the receiver. "They fuckin' killed him!"

"What?"

"The cops got his truck taped off, and he's still slumped behind the steering wheel."

"How? Where?"

"At the gas station on Broad and York. We across the street watchin' the whole thing! They caught him slippin', and left him slumped behind the wheel."

"Fuck!" Sonny snapped as he hopped up from the weight bench.

He ran upstairs to his bedroom and went straight to the closet. He strapped on his bulletproof vest, threw on a black one piece Dickies suit, and grabbed the AK-47 that was lying on the closet floor. Strapped for war and eager to get busy, he darted out the front door and hopped in his Escalade.

*****

A Half Hour Later...

He pulled up in front of his trap house and hopped out the Escalade with the AK-47 clutched in his left hand. "What the fuck is y'all just standin' around lookin' stupid for?" He snapped on Easy, Breeze, and the twins. "Y'all mu'fuckas better suit the fuck up!"

"Sontino, you need to calm down," Easy suggested. "And put that gun away 'fore the cops ride by and start some dumb shit."

"Naw, fuck that! These niggas wanna get it poppin' so I'ma show 'em how we get it the fuckin' poppin'!" He continued his rant, and then pulled back the lever on his assault rifle.

"Sontino, it's not that simple!" Easy retorted. "This wasn't no ordinary shit! They found the body of some young bul that was disguised as a homeless man, and he was holdin' the gun that probably killed Nasty. That was one of Grip's people, and they killed his ass too! This ain't no playground, everyday beef. Grip is the real deal, and if you think for onemutha'fuckinsecond you just gon' run down on him like he's the average nigga, then you got the game fucked up!" Easy continued shouting, trying to get his son to realize and respect the caliber of a gangster that they were dealing with.

Before Sonny had the chance to respond, a black Crown Victoria and a gray Chevy Caprice turned the corner with their tires screeching.

Sccccrrrrrrr!

By the time they realized what was happening, Grip's soldiers under the order of Monster, hopped out of both vehicles with guns blazing.

Boc! Boc! Boc! Pop! Pop! Pop! Pop! Pop! Pop! Boom! Boom! Boom! Boom!

Sonny pushed Easy out of the way, and then raised his AK-47, and returned fire.

Boc! Boc! Brrrroc! Boc! Brrrroc!

As he continued his counter attack a devastating force crashed into his chest, slamming him against the side of Easy's Range Rover. He tried to breathe, but the wind was knocked out of him and his ribcage felt as though it was cracked in half.

"Sonny, get on the ground! I've got you covered!" Easy shouted as he crept around the back of his SUV with a .357 Desert Eagle in each hand. He raised the guns and blasted.

Doom! Doom! Doom! Doom! Doom! Doom!

The bullets hit the passenger of the Crown Victoria, spinning him around before he crashed to the pavement. He aimed at the man who was standing in front of the Chevy Caprice, but before he could let off a clean shot, a bullet shattered the back window on his Range Rover, and broken glass rained on the back of his neck. Still determined to hit his target, he readjusted his aim and fired.

Doom! Doom! Doom!

Instantly, the bullets danced up the man's chest, and left him hunched over the back, passenger side door. Egypt ran toward the trap house front door to grab the sawed off shotgun that was underneath the couch in the living room, but two bullets struck him down, one ripping through his left leg and the other through his right shoulder. At the sight of his twin brother being gunned down, Zaire shielded his face with his left arm and returned fire with the Glock .40 that was clutched in his right hand.

Moc! Moc! Moc! Moc! Moc! Moc!

The driver of the Chevy Caprice turned his gun on Zaire, but lost his life when Easy sent a succession of bullets that blew his brains out the back of his biscuit. The driver of the Crown Victoria hopped back in the car and attempted to pull off, but before he could put the transmission in drive, Breeze ran up on him with a chrome 12 gauge and decimated the left side of his face.

Boom!

The last remaining passenger of the Crown Victoria tried to run, but Easy shot him in the back, and he stumbled to the ground. As Easy walked up on him and prepared to finish the job, Sonny shouted, "Naw, pops, I got him!"

His left hand was wrapped around the handle of the AK,

and he was rubbing the burnt bullet holes on his Dickies suit with his right. The grimacing look on his face depicted his pain, but nonetheless, he limped toward his victim. He pressed the hot barrel to the back of his head and squeezed the trigger.

Boc!

*****

The emergency room at the Cooper Hospital in Camden, New Jersey was relatively empty when Zaire burst through the double doors with Egypt hunched over his right shoulder.

"Help! I need some fuckin' help! My brother got shot!" He shouted at the top of his lungs. Sonny, Easy, and Breeze were directly behind him and together they reiterated his cries for medical assistance.

"Oh my God!" The receptionist at the front desk cringed from the sight of the five men covered in blood. "What happened to him?" She pointed at Egypt. "Is he still breathing?"

"Yeah," Easy nodded his head, "but I think he went into shock. He was shot in the shoulder and leg and it looks like both of the bullets went straight through" he informed her.

Zaire laid him on the chairs in the front row, and Sonny gestured for him to follow him to the snack machine. "Listen, Zai, me, my pops, and Breeze gotta get outta here. When the cops come, just tell them that y'all was out here visiting a bitch, and that some niggas tried to rob y'all."

"A'ight," he nodded his head up and down, "but what about the Philly cops?"

"Don't even worry about 'em." He waved him off. "That's the reason we drove over the bridge in the first place. They won't even know y'all here."

"A'ight Sonny. Make sure that you find Sheed. They might be comin' for him next."

Sonny nodded his head. "I know."

*****

Later That Night...

Sheed was lounging at the Eagle Bar, drinking a double shot of Henny and smoking a Black & Mild, when his iPhone vibrated on the counter.

Vrrrrrm!

Instead of accepting the call, he placed the phone in his jacket pocket, paid his tab, and left the bar. When he stepped outside there was a group of Muslim men selling everything from scented oils to DVDs. They tried selling him some of their items too, but he respectfully declined and hopped in his Benz. When he started the ignition, the sounds of Philadelphia Freeway's, *Even Though What We Do Is Wrong,* blasted from his sound system...

"We keep the nines tucked/ Chop dimes up/ Rap about it/ Wild out, fuck niggas up, laugh about it/ I'm not try'na visit the morgue/ But Freeway move out 'til I sit wit' the Lord.

He reached in the ashtray and grabbed the stubbed out Backwood that he was smoking prior to going inside of the bar. He sparked it up, took a strong pull, and then drove away from the curb.

After a couple of minutes of driving, he approached the corner of Germantown and Lehigh and stopped at a red light. He glanced around the deserted intersection and noticed that the only thing open was the Chinese store on Lehigh Avenue. *Damn, these mu'fuckas is vicious,* he thought to himself, referring to the neighborhood Chinese store. *They'll stay open all night just to get our money, and don't ever do nothin' to give back to the hood. We the only ones who support their business, and they won't even hire a mu'fucka. You can spend ya money and do business wit' 'em yawhole life, but let you come up short one mu'fuckin' penny, and they won't even let you ride. Rotten mutha'fuckas!*

The traffic light turned green and he pulled off. As he drove through the intersection, and proceeded down Germantown

Avenue, an unmarked cop car slid up behind him with the blue light on its dashboard signaling for him to pull over.

"Damn, I ain't even do shit," he said to himself as he slowed down and pulled over to the side of the road.

Detective Smith hopped out his vehicle with his Glock 19 aimed and ready to fire. "Driver, roll down your window and put your hands where I can see 'em."

A light bulb flashed in Sheed's head, and he remembered the brick of raw that was stashed under the passenger seat. "Dizzamn. I'm slippin' like a mu'fucka." He mashed down on the gas pedal, causing the Benz to jerk forward.

"Fuck!" Detective Smith shouted. He ran back to his car, hopped inside, and then took off after the Benz.

Sheed raced down Germantown Avenue, zoomed pass Huntingdon Street, and then veered right onto 10th Street. After shooting pass Cumberland, he slowed down and made a hard left turn on Boston Street.

Detective Smith was about two blocks away, desperately trying to keep up with the Benz. When he reached the corner of 10th and Cumberland, he glanced to his left and saw Sheed creeping up Delhi Street.

As soon as Sheed made it to the corner, he spotted the unmarked cruiser and cursed himself for not getting out the car and running when he had the chance to do so. He banged a hard right on Cumberland Street, and then gunned the Benz from zero to sixty in a matter of seconds. He looked in the rearview mirror and was ecstatic to see that his V8 engine had created a good distance between himself and the unmarked cruiser.

"Now, all I gotta do is make it to 5th Street, bang a left, bang a right on Lehigh, push it to the limit, hop on the E-way, and I'm gone." He said to himself. Unfortunately, he was driving too fast when he approached the corner of 5th and Cumberland, and when he tried to make his left turn, he fishtailed into the Spanish store on the opposite corner.

Scccrrrrrrr! Crash!

The airbag ballooned from its compartment, and the white powder burned his eyes. "Aaaaggghhhh! Fuck! He shouted as he frantically wiped the powder from his face. He opened the driver's side door and staggered out the car.

Boc!

A devastating force slammed into his stomach, knocking him backwards. A burning sensation spread throughout his upper body and he was struggling to breathe. He reached for the Desert Eagle that was tucked in his shoulder holster, and again Detective Sullivan fired his weapon.

Boc! Boc!

He fell to the ground and rolled around in pain. Detective Smith stood over the top of him and aimed the barrel at his face. Just as he was about to squeeze the trigger, he heard, "Smitty, put it down!" He spun around and saw his partner, Detective Sullivan aiming a gun at his head. He smiled at him, and tried to talk some sense into him. "Sully, it's not what it looks like. He tried to shoot me."

"That's bullshit, and you know it!" Detective Sullivan shouted. "I've been tailing you all day. I saw the whole damn thing. Now, for the last time, drop the friggin' gun!"

Detective Smith looked at his young partner and continued smiling. He refused to believe that his partner would shoot him. Defiantly, he began walking toward him with his weapon by his side. "Come on Sully, you hate these sonsofbitches even more than I do. They run around this goddamned city like they own it, and make hundreds of thousands of dollars in the process. Now, guys like us, we're the good guys and the city pays us a lousy $40,000 a fuckin' year."

Detective Sullivan tightened his grasp around the pistol. "I swear to God, Smitty! You take another step and I'll shoot!'

Detective Smith ignored his warning, and continued walking toward him.

Boc!

"Aaaaggghhhh! You fucking shot me! You sonofabitch!"

Detective Smith shouted as he fell to the ground holding his right thigh.

With his gun still aimed at his partner, Detective Sullivan walked toward him. He kicked the Glock 19 out of his hand, and then knelt down and handcuffed him.

"Sully, this is bullshit. I'm telling ya man., we can really make some good money. It's not too late, Sully. We can fix this! All you gotta say that he took your gun and shot me and that I fired back in self defense."

Detective Sullivan shook his head from side to side. "Nope, I won't do it. I could never dishonor my badge and my department. It's dirty motherfuckers like you, who give cops like me a bad name, and I'm sick of it." He reached for his walkie talkie, and then ran over to Sheed who was barely breathing. "Shots fired on the corner of 5th and Cumberland! Send me an E.M.T.! I repeat shots fired! I have a man down!"

Chapter Twenty-Five

The Following Morning...

At the federal building on 6th and Arch, Detective Sullivan and DEA Agent Terry Long were sitting in a board room discussing the cases that they were building against Grip and Sonny. On the 100 inch projector screen that occupied the front wall there were two pyramid style diagrams that represented the structures of each of their organizations. The diagram on the left was titled: *The Moreno Crime Family a.k.a. The Black Mafia* and the diagram on the right was titled: *The Block Boy Bishops*. A mug shot of Grip was posted at the top of his organization and a mug shot of Sonny was posted at the top of his.

“Alright,” Agent Long began, “there’s a lot of missing pieces to this puzzle, and we’ve been entrusted with the task of finding them.” He sifted through a pile of incident reports, and then looked up at Detective Sullivan. “Do you have any suggestions?”

“Well, I was thinking that our best bet is to focus on the murders that we can tie into these organizations,” Detective Sullivan submitted, and then took a sip of coffee.

“That’s a good idea,” Agent Long nodded his head. “We’ve gotta find a way to establish that these murders are related, and as of right now we don’t have any witnesses.”

“Alright, well why don’t we focus on the evidence that we can use circumstantially?” Detective Sullivan said, and then took another sip of coffee.

Agent Long opened the file that was in front of him, and then flipped through a small stack of papers. “Here it is.” He pulled an incident report from the folder. “As far as we know, these were the first murders in this case: Officer Jason Clifford and Martin Powell. They were gunned down on the corner of 3rd and Snyder, and the incident transpired on November 10, 2012. Martin Powell, also known as *Biggs* was a captain in The Moreno

Crime Family, and it appears as though Officer Clifford just happened to be in the wrong placed at the wrong time. Now, the good thing about this incident is that the image of a white Mercedes Benz SL 550 was caught on Officer Clifford's dash cam, and we both know that Sontino Moreno and Rasheed McDaniels both drive a white Mercedes."

"The next murder was committed on December 9, 2012, and the victim was Saleena Brooks, who was the wife of Michael Brooks. Her body was discovered a few blocks away from the county jail, and apparently she was murdered after retrieving Brooks from the prison."

"The following morning, Tommy Wilson, the informant that you and Smith were using in the Brooks case, was found tortured and murdered in his jail cell. Obviously, that was Brooks' doing, and ironically, his decapitated head was discovered in his Bentley a couple of hours later on the corner of Chew and Chelten."

"A few weeks later, on January 1, 2013, our sixth and seventh victims were discovered in a South Philadelphia row house. Their names were Jerome Peters, also known as *Rome*, and Jamal Jackson, also known as *Smack*. Both were affiliated with *The Moreno Crime Family*."

He picked up another piece of paper and examined it closely. "Yep, just like I thought, the next incident transpired on the same block where Peters and Jackson were murdered, and this one in particular was a massacre. Six men and two women were killed. Apparently, they were having a vigil for Peters and Jackson when a pickup truck," he looked up at Detective Sullivan, "a Toyota Tundra, which is the same make and model that Nasir *Nasty* Lee was driving when he was murdered." He tilted his head, giving him a knowing expression, and then he went back to the incident report. "According to this report, the six men and two women were gunned down in a drive-by shooting. I'm guessing that Nasir Lee was involved, and that The *Block Boys* were avenging the murders of Brooks and his wife. Now, there were plenty of witnesses to this shooting, but none of them could make a positive identification. They all claimed that the two shooters who were positioned in the back of the truck had their faces covered with red bandanas, and we both know that this is a characteristic of the *Bloods Street Gang*. There was also a red bandana found at both crime scenes, so clearly Sontino and his men were leaving a signature on their work."

"Now," he picked up another incident report. "Back to Nasir Lee. Mr. Lee was sitting in his Toyota pickup truck when a known soldier of the Moreno's, Antonio Baker, shot him in the head at point blank range with a .44 Bulldog. As you already know, Mr. Baker's body was found on the corner of 12th and York, and the results that we received this morning from the forensic lab confirm that the gun he was carrying was in fact the murder weapon in the Lee case." He looked up and noticed the depressed look on Detective Sullivan's face. "What's up, Sully? Are you okay?"

"No, this shit is friggin' ridiculous! At the rate these son-of-a-bitches are going, if we don't hurry up and get 'em off of the street, a lot more people are gonna die! You just ran down seventeen murders, and you didn't even make it to the incident report from yesterday when we found those bodies on Fairhill Street. This shit's gotta stop!"

"Alright Sully, what do suggest we do to speed up the process?" Agent Long questioned, while folding his arms across his chest.

"I think we should use Smitty to our advantage. He was obviously connected to the Moreno organization, and there's a good chance he could shed some light on our investigation. I'm pretty sure I can get him to flip, especially with the charges that are hanging over his head."

"That sounds like a plan, and as far as Sontino Moreno and the *Block Boys*," Agent Long smiled and rubbed his hands together. "Let's just say that I'm already connected."

Chapter Twenty-Six

The Following Morning...

As Sonny looked around his family's extravagant basement, his seven year old mind couldn't decide on which video game he wanted to play. The day before, Easy surprised him with three arcade systems: *Street Fighter, Mortal Combat, and NBA Jam.* After a brief deliberation, he selected 'Street Fighter' and approached the six foot high gaming system. He pressed the start button and selected Bulrog, the fighter that resembled Mike Tyson, and began his quest to take out M. Bison. As he was beating the brains out of Chun Li, Easy descended the basement stairs and told him to go outside to play with his new dirt bike.

"Awwwww, come on Pops." He protested. "I'm playin' Street Fighter."

"So what. I need to do somethin' down here. Now, take ya lil' ass outside somewhere."

Sonny sucked his teeth, and then reluctantly made his way up the stairs. This was becoming a frequent occurrence in their household. He would be in the basement playing, and Easy would come down there and make him leave. When he reached the top of the steps, his curiosity got the best of him and he crept back down the steps hoping to find out what was so important that he couldn't stick around and finish playing his game. As he was halfway down the steps he heard a crackling noise, and an awful smell invaded his nostrils. He immediately recognized the aroma. It was the same substance that he smelled one day when he saw Easy at the stove with a cloudy liquid boiling in a Pyrex pot.

He peeked his head over the bannister and saw Easy sitting at the bar, smoking on a glass pipe. His eyes were closed and he was sweating as if he'd just completed a marathon. Automatically, Sonny thought about the scene from *New Jack City* were G Money was doing the same thing.

"Oh, snap, Pops is down here smoking crack!" He said to

himself. He spun around, and ran back up the steps. When he entered the kitchen, Grip was seated at the granite island smoking a Cuban Cigar and reading a newspaper. He handed Sonny a trash bag and told him to take it outside to the dumpster. As he exited the back door with the bag clutched in his left hand, the bag began to move and whatever it was that was inside began calling his name, "Sonny. Hey, Sonny. What's poppin', Blood?"

He opened the bag to see what it was and discovered Mook's decapitated head. "Yo, what the fuck?" He shouted as he escaped his nightmare and hopped up from the bed.

Sweat was rolling down his face and chest, and a weird feeling spread through his entire body. He frantically looked around the room. He was unfamiliar with his surroundings, but calmed down when he remembered that he'd spent the night over Daphney's house. Yesterday, after leaving the hospital In New Jersey, he called her and asked if they could get together and talk. She agreed, and after he apologized for the altercation at the restaurant, they spent night making passionate love.

The aroma of turkey bacon, cheese grits, and cheese eggs filled the room causing his stomach to do back flips. He threw on his boxer shorts then went into the bathroom to brush his teeth and wash his face.

Downstairs, Daphney could hear him moving around so she yelled up to the second floor, telling him to come downstairs and join her for breakfast.

A few minutes later, he entered the dining room, kissed her on the forehead and took a seat at the table. "Good lookin' on the breakfast Daph. I'm hungry as shit."

"Oh, that ain't all." She reached into her bathrobe pocket and pulled out a neatly rolled Dutch Master. "Here."

He grabbed the spliff from her hand, and then started laughing. "Damn, whatchu try'na spoil a nigga?"

"Nope," she smiled. "I just know how to please my man!"

He ignored her last comment and grabbed the remote control to the 50 inch plasma that hung on the wall. After surfing through the channels, the image of a white Benz crashed up on the corner of 5th and Cumberland, caught his attention. "Naw, it can't be," he said to himself as news reporter, Roland Rushin, described a high speed chase that ended in an unjustified police shooting.

"According to a spokesperson from the Philadelphia Police Department, Adam Smith, a twenty-five year veteran has been charged with attempted murder and at least one count of police corruption." The middle aged black man spoke into his microphone.

A picture of Sheed was displayed on the screen. "Oh, shit, boo! Ain't that ya man?" Daphney asked as she sat a plate of food in front of him.

"Yeah." He nodded his head. "But hold up for a minute so I can hear what's goin' on." He got up from the table and walked over to the television.

"It's being alleged that the victim, Rasheed McDaniels, lost control of his vehicle and crashed into the wall of this grocery store behind me." Roland Rushin continued. "Apparently, Mr. McDaniels was leading Detective Adam Smith on a high speed chase and according to the Internal Affairs Division, Detective Smith was the subject of a corruption scandal and was secretly being investigated by his own partner Detective Ronald Sullivan. Now, from what we've gathered here at Channel 10 News, Detective Sullivan witnessed his partner shoot Mr. McDaniels in cold blood. When he attempted to make an arrest, Detective Smith resisted and was ultimately shot in his thigh. He was treated at the Temple University Hospital and is currently in police custody. Mr. McDaniels was also taken to the Temple University Hospital, but unfortunately he's in critical condition. Reporting to you live from North Philadelphia, this is Roland Rushin, Channel 10 News."

Sonny just stood in front of the television shaking his head in disbelief. This war was getting deeper than he'd anticipated. In one day, his inner circle was nearly depleted. Nasty was dead.

Egypt was recovering from his gunshot wounds and now Sheed was laid up in the hospital fighting for his life. He realized that the only conclusion in this situation was to murder Grip once and for all.

He looked at Daphney. “I need you to go to the hospital to check on my man.”

“A’ight, I got you, daddy,” she replied with no questions asked. She kissed him on the side of his neck, and then went upstairs to get dressed.

He picked up her house phone and called Breeze.

Ring! Ring! Ring!

“Yo, who’s this?” Breeze answered because he didn’t recognize the number of the incoming call.

“It’s Sonny. Where are you at?”

“I’m on my way to the city,” Breeze answered. “Did you see the news this morning?”

“Yeah,” Sonny sighed. “This nut ass nigga got the mu’fuckin’ cops ridin’ wit’ him. Yo, this shit is crazy."

“I already know,” Breeze replied.

“But listen. I still gotta get in touch wit’ everybody so just meet me at my house in an hour.”

Click!

After disconnecting the call, he called Easy and Zaire, giving them the same message.

*****

An hour later, they were sitting in his living room discussing the war.

“Yo Sonny, I think we need to call Unique and ask him to send us some more soldiers from up top;” Breeze suggested, and then took a pull on his Backwood.

“Naw, I’m not gonna do that.” Sonny shook his head. “The last thing I need right now is Rah and Sunshine thinkin’ I can’t handle shit down here.”

"Rah and Sunshine?" Easy asked with a confused look on his face. "Who the fuck is you talking 'bout?"

"They're the big homies of their entire family on the east. The big, big homies!" Breeze informed him.

"Awwww man!" Easy threw up his hands in frustration. "Here y'all go wit' that Blood shit again! Where the fuck y'all think y'all at, South Central?"

Sonny looked at him like he wanted to smack the shit out of him. "Hey pops, that's what we *not* gon' do!" He then looked at Breeze. "Yo, we gotta find a way to get to this pussy."

"Right." Breeze nodded his head. "But at the same time, this ol' mu'fucka moves like a ghost. We don't even know where he lives, and other than you and Uncle Easy, we don't know nothin' about his family. It ain't no way in the world we gonna be able to find this nigga."

"That's not true," Easy stated. "I think I might know where we can find him."

"Where?" Sonny asked.

"Remember when I told you about the time them *YBM* niggas kidnapped me back in the day?"

"Yeah, I remember."

"A'ight, now remember when I told you about that warehouse on Delaware Ave.?"

"Yeah." Sonny nodded his head.

"I think that's still his headquarters."

"But do you remember exactly where it's at?"

"Yeah, I remember where it's at. Those stupid mutha'fuckas let me walk out the front door."

"I'm sayin' though, that was over twenty years ago. You think he'd still be there after all this time?"

"I don't know, Easy admitted. "But that's all we got."

"A'ight, well we gon' check it out tonight, and if he's there then he signed his own death warrant the day he let you leave that mu'fucka."

Sonny's iPhone vibrated on the coffee table.

Vrrrrrm! Vrrrrrm!

He picked it up and looked at the LCD screen. "Yo, pardon me for a minute." He got up from his leather sectional, and then went into the kitchen to take the call. "Diamondz, what's up nigga?"

"Everything's good on my end. I got the bul Kev wit' me and he try'na holla at you," he said before handing the phone to Kev.

"Sonny, what's good Ike? Is you ready for me?"

"Damn, dawg, you really caught me at a bad time. I ain't gon' be able to do nothin' wit' you today. It's a lot of shit goin' on right now."

"Aw, come on Ike! This the second time I drove all the way to Philly, and you stuntin' on me!" Kev complained.

"I feel you my nigga, but like I just said it's a lot of shit goin' on right now. I ain't got the time to focus on nothin' else."

"I hear you Ike, but damn, you can't do *nothin'* for me?"

Sonny sighed. "A'ight, I'll tell you what, get wit' me tomorrow mornin' and I got you."

"Yo', that's good lookin' Ike. Nephs!"

After disconnecting the call, he went back to the living room and sat back down on the sectional. "So, Zai what's up wit' Eyg? Is he a'ight?"

"Yeah, he's good. The bullet to his shoulder shattered his collar bone and the bullet to his leg was only a flesh wound so he a'ight. He's just mad that he gotta lie up in the house and can't ride on these niggas" he informed them, and then took a pull on his Dutch Master.

"Tell lil' bro not to worry about it," Sonny smiled. "By the time he's up and runnin', them niggas ain't gonna be nothin' but a mu'fuckin' memory!"

*****

At The Temple University Hospital...

When Sheed awoke from his morphine induced sleep, he noticed that Detective Sullivan was standing in the far corner of his hospital room. He tried to speak, but the tube in his mouth wouldn't allow it. Aside from the pain of the catheter tube shoved in his dick and the agony of the staples running up his torso, he felt the cold steel of the handcuff on his right wrist. *Damn!*

Detective Sullivan approached his hospital bed with a brown folder in his left hand. "Mr. McDaniels, I know that you can't speak at the present time, but in lieu of that, I was hoping that you could assist me with the with the investigation of this incident. Now, just so you know, you're under arrest for the possession of a stolen firearm and for the possession of a controlled substance. So before I continue, I need to read you your Miranda Rights..."

After informing him of his right to remain silent and his right to an attorney, Detective Sullivan continued with his interview. "When I searched you last night, I discovered a .50 caliber Desert Eagle in your shoulder holster. Upon searching your vehicle, I discovered a large quantity of cocaine under your passenger's seat."

At the sound of the detective mentioning the brick of coke, a tear fell from his left eye. He knew he was fucked.

"The stamp that was on the cocaine was the exact same stamp that was on the key of coke in the Michael Brooks' case, a five point star. Now, listen, there's been a chain of murders in the past few months that are directly connected to one another and I'm hoping that you can help me get to the bottom of things."

He opened the folder and pulled out a 10 x 12 picture of Grip. "I wanna show you a photograph of the man who I think is responsible for not only the attempt on your life, but also the murders of Michael and Saleena Brooks. Again, I understand that you're incapable of speaking right now, but if you recognize this individual just nod your head."

The second Sheed saw the picture of his arch enemy, his heart monitor began beeping at a rapid pace and he looked at

Detective Sullivan with a menacing glare.

"So, you *do* recognize him?"

Instead of nodding his head, he lifted his right hand and gave the detective his middle finger. *Get the fuck outta here!*

*****

Daphney had been sitting in the waiting room for the past two hours and she was beginning to lose her patience. She got up from her seat and approached the receptionist's desk.

"Excuse me, but I've been sitting here for close to two hours. I'm trying to find out the status of my brother, and so far, nobody's told me anything. Can somebody please let me know what's going on?" She confronted the fat white woman who was sitting behind the desk looking as though she didn't want to be bothered.

"And your brother's name is?" She asked with an attitude.

"It's the same name that I told you an hour ago, Rasheed McDaniels!" Daphney retorted, raising her voice a few octaves.

Before the receptionist had the chance to respond, a tall brown skinned man in green scrubs approached her from behind. "Excuse me, my name is Dr. Chris Lindsay. Are you the woman who's been inquiring about," he glanced at his clipboard, "Rasheed McDaniels?"

"Yeah, that's my brother," she replied. "I hope you can tell me what's goin' on." She pointed at the receptionist. "Because her fat *Honey Boo Boo* lookin' ass ain't tellin' me shit!"

The overweight white woman sucked her teeth and rolled her eyes.

"Please miss, just calm down. Here," he gestured toward a seat in the first row of chairs. "Let's have a seat and I'll gladly inform you about your brother's status."

"How's he doing? Can I see him?"

"Well, right now he's heavily sedated. He was just released from surgery this morning and he really needs his rest.

He won't be allowed to have any visitors for at least another two hours."

"Alright, but how's he doing? Is he okay?"

"Well, he suffered three gunshot wounds. One bullet shattered his left hip bone and the remaining two bullets both struck him in the abdomen, with one of them piecing his small intestines. The bullets were recovered during surgery, but unfortunately we had to remove a portion of his small intestine. Overall, I'd say that the surgery was a success. He's probably going to need some physical therapy, but after that, he should be back to himself in no time."

"Alright doc, thank you." She got up from her seat, shook his hand, and then left the hospital.

As she headed toward her Panamara, an eerie feeling washed over her. She glanced around the parking lot and noticed a white Mercedes Maybach in the far corner. She stared at the large sedan for a few seconds, and then hopped in her Porsche and pulled off.

*****

In the backseat of the Maybach, Grip took slow pulls on his Cuban Cigar and nodded his head to the soulful sounds of The Gap Band. He smiled at Daphney through the tinted window, and then ordered Muhammad to pull off.

Chapter Twenty-Seven

It was 12:30 p.m. when Riana pulled up in front of Annie's house. She climbed out the Tahoe and knocked on the front door. A couple of seconds later, the door opened and Annie was standing on the other side with a huge smile on her face.

"Hey, baby." She greeted her and gave her a warm hug. "Look at that belly of yours. Girl, you look like you about to bust any minute now." She laughed, and then ushered Riana inside of the house.

"I know," Riana smiled. "And the way this lil' boy keeps kickin' me, he's actin' like he wants to come out and see the world before he's supposed to," she laughed, and then took a seat on the couch.

"So, what brings you by? I haven't seen that son of mines in about two weeks now. When you go home, you tell his fast ass to come and visit his momma."

Riana frowned. "Ms. Annie, I ain't got nothin' to say to Sontino," she said while shaking her head from side to side. "We broke up a couple of days ago, and this time I'm not takin' him back. As a matter of fact, after I have the baby, we're movin' to Atlanta to live with my dad."

"What?" Annie asked as her heart dropped into her stomach. "What happened?"

"I caught him cheatin' again! He was at this restaurant all hugged up wit' some broad. I'm five months pregnant wit' his baby and he's got the nerve to be steppin' out wit' the next chick. Ahn ahn, I ain't goin' for it."

Annie looked at the beautiful young woman and felt sorry for her. She knew exactly how she felt because when Easy was younger, he too had a problem with keeping his dick in his pants.

"Listen to me baby because what I'm about to say is some real shit. Now, we both know what my son does for a livin', and at twenty-three years old, his stupid ass doesn't know any better. You see, this is all a part of the game. When a young bul is gettin' money, no matter how much he loves his woman, he's gonna fuck around. Not to hurt his woman, but because these skeezers out here will do any and everything to get close to a nigga who they think can financially turn their life around.

These young buls are movin' so fast and so reckless that they think with their little head instead of their big one. Now, like I said, Sontino's still young. Just give him some time to settle down and get this shit out of his system. I'ma tell you right now, all men cheat! That's just what it is! So, how can you be sure that the next nigga won't do the same or potentially do even worse?"

Riana sighed. "I hear you Ms. Annie, but I ain't goin' for it. I've never cheated on Sontino, never! He was my first, Ms. Annie! I gave him all of me, and this is how he repays me? By lying and deceiving me? Obviously, he doesn't love me the way he says he does, because if he did, he would be loyal to me. Ahn ahn, I ain't wit' it. Like you said, he gonna do him, so I'ma do me. And as soon as I have this baby, we're movin' to Atlanta."

Annie waved her off. "Hold up, stop right there because now you're being selfish. If you take that baby to Atlanta, how do you think everyone else is gonna feel about not being a part of that child's life?"

"I don't know." She shrugged her shoulders. "I guess I never thought about it that way."

"Well, what do you call yourself doing anyway, avoiding Sontino? Girl, now you know damn well that boy ain't gonna do nothin' but follow ya lil' highyellow ass down there," Annie laughed and Riana laughed with her. "I'm tellin' you, baby, just give him some time. Everything will work itself out."

"I don't know, Ms. Annie. I can't see myself sitting around and playin' a fool for nobody. If Sontino wants another chick, then he can have her. I'll just find somebody who's going to love me the way I need to be loved and give me the respect and loyalty that I deserve."

"Well, I don't know what else to say. All I know is that you and Sontino love one another and if it's meant for y'all to be together, then y'all are gonna be together."

Riana thought about what she said and took a deep breath. She loved Sonny with all of her heart, and she didn't want to lose him, especially to another woman. She gave Annie a hug, and then got up from the couch.

"Thanks for the talk, Ms. Annie. You really helped me put things into perspective. I gotta go right now, but I'll stop by to see you sometime next week."

"Alright, baby. You just learn to be more patient, and give Sontino some time to get his head together. And stop stressin' so much because I'm tellin' you right now, Riri, if that baby comes out messed up, you and Sontino gonna have to deal with me. Y'all *know* I don't play no games." Annie laughed, and then gave her another hug.

"A'ight, Ms. Annie," she continued laughing. "I don't want any trouble."

"Alright now. Make sure you call me when you get home, so I'll know that you made it there safe."

*****

For the past hour, Monster and Lil' Buggy had been driving around Sonny's neighborhood and circling his mother's block. The last time they drove past her house, the only car that was parked out front was a green minivan, but now there was a black Tahoe parked behind it.

"Ay, Buggy." Monster pointed at the SUV. "Ain't that the nigga's truck?"

"Yeah, that's his truck," Lil' Buggy confirmed with a tightly rolled Dutch Master hanging from the corner of his mouth. "It wasn't there a couple of minutes ago so he musta just pulled up."

"A'ight, circle the block and park up at the corner. We gonna lay on this pussy," Monster ordered from the passenger's seat.

Lil' Buggy did as he was instructed, and when they parked on the corner of Reese and Dauphin, the guys who were out there hustling casually strolled off.

"Damn, Unc, this tinted out Crown Vic was a good idea. You see the way them niggas scattered from the corner? Them stupid ass niggas think we the cops," Lil' Buggy laughed, and then settled back into the driver's seat.

Monster didn't respond. Instead, he just gritted his teeth and kept his eyes glued on the house.

"Yo, Unc, I'm sick of waitin'. I'd rather just run up in the mu'fucka and start blastin'!"

A second later, the front door opened and a short, petite, light skinned woman emerged from the house.

"Oh, shit! Yo, that's Sonny's bitch. I forgot my young bul told me shorty be drivin' his truck," Lil' Buggy eagerly stated.

As Monster stared at the obviously pregnant young woman, he debated his next move. *Should I give this bitch a pass, or should I send this lil' nigga a message?* he thought to himself.

"Lil' Buggy," he stated in a cold tone of voice. "Run that bitch over."

Lil' Buggy pulled away from the curb and accelerated the car's engine to sixty miles per hour.

As Riana was unlocking the driver's side door, she heard the roaring of a car's engine and an overwhelming feeling spread throughout her body. She turned her head in the direction of the speeding car, but before she had the chance to get out of the way the grill of the Crown Victoria slammed into her body with a devastating force.

Boom!

Her body rolled up on the hood of the car, and her face slammed against the windshield.

Crash!

Lil' Buggy hit the brakes and the sudden change of velocity sent her body flying through the air.

Inside of the house, Annie heard the unmistakable sounds

of a roaring engine and a loud *boom*! Her heart skipped a beat, and the only thing she could think about was Riana. She raced to the living room window, and the sight of Riana's body flying through the air and slamming against the concrete sent chills down her spine. "Ririiiiiiii!" She screamed as she opened the front door and darted out the house.

Monster and Lil' Buggy sat in silence as they watched Riana struggle to get back on her feet. The only sound in the car was the roaring of the engine as the car was in *park*, and Lil' Buggy was pressing his foot up and down on the gas pedal.

Vroooom! Vroooom! Vroooom!

Blood was pouring from Riana's nose and mouth, and the contorted position of her right leg depicted that it was broken.

As Annie ran toward her, Lil' Buggy threw the transmission in *drive* and mashed down on the gas pedal.

Scccrrrrrr!

"Oh, my God! No!" Annie screamed as she helplessly dropped to her knees.

The front grill of the sedan crashed into Riana head on.

Ba, Boom!

Her body tumbled backwards, and then slid up under the car as it sped away.

*****

Back In Cheltenham, Pennsylvania

The plot to take down Grip was finally coming together. If he was still holding court in the same warehouse that Easy remembered, then the war would end in one of two ways. Both Sonny and the *Block Boys* would win and take over the streets of Philly as Mook had envisioned, or they would die in the process.

As they sat around the living room loading their guns, Sonny's iPhone vibrated on the coffee table.

Vrrrrrm! Vrrrrrm!

"Yo," he answered.

"Boo, I just left the hospital and ya man ain't lookin' too good," Daphney said, while driving up Broad Street.

"Whatchu mean he ain't lookin' too good?"

"Well, it ain't that bad," she assured him. "The doctor told me that he's gonna make it, but they did have to remove a part of his intestines. The doctor also told me that one of the bullets shattered his hip."

Sonny didn't respond. The thought of his man lying in the hospital all shot the fuck up rubbed him the wrong way.

"Boo, are you still there?"

He sighed, "Yeah, I'm here. I'm just thinkin' about my boy." His phone beeped to alert him that he had another incoming call. He looked at the LCD screen and saw the caller was his mother. "Hey, yo, Daph, my mom's on the other line. Let me see what she wants, and I'ma hit you right back."

When he clicked over and heard the hysterical cries of his mother, his heart dropped into is stomach. "Mom, what's wrong? Are you okay?"

"Sonny, its Riri!" She screamed through the phone.

"Riri what?"

"Somebody ran her over with a car!"

"What? Yo, where are you at?"

"We're on our way to the hospital!" Annie continued to cry. "I've got her in the back of my van! And she's not lookin' good at all!"

"A'ight, I'm on my way!" He disconnected the call, and then ran toward the front door. "Come on y'all! It's Riri! We gotta get to the hospital!"

*****

Twenty Minutes Later...

They barged into the emergency room and found Annie sitting by the receptionist's desk. Her face was puffy, her eyes were red and her body was trembling.

Sonny ran over and knelt down beside her. "Mom, where's Riri? Is she a'ight? Is the baby a'ight?"

"No!" Annie cried. "They tried to kill her!"

"They tried to kill her?" Sonny scrunched up his face. "I thought you said she got hit by a car?"

Annie nodded her head up and down. "She did, but after they hit her, they backed up and ran her over again! Her body was trapped under the car until it turned the corner!"

Sonny went *ape shit*! He knew that was Grip's work, and the thought of his enemy hitting him so close to home drove him crazy. He stormed into the back of the emergency room, screaming her name. "Riri, I'm here boo! Where are you at?" He went from station to station pulling back the privacy curtains hoping to find her. The doctors, nurses, and patients were bewildered at the sight of him. "Boo, I'm here now! Where are you at?" He cried.

The fat woman at the receptionist's desk paged security. "Security to the emergency room! We have an issue down here and we need assistance! I repeat security to the emergency room!"

A white, middle aged doctor approached him, attempting to calm him down. "Excuse me, sir. Is everything okay?"

"Doc, my wife's in here and her name's Riana Smalls! Take me to her!" Sonny demanded, gripping the doctor by his shirt.

"Sir, just calm down and I'll find out what's going on," the doctor nervously replied. "Just calm down."

"Naw, fuck that!" Sonny retorted, and then wrapped his left hand around the doctor's neck. "Y'all mu'fuckas better stop playin', and take me to my mu'fuckin' wife!"

The doctor was scared to death. He frantically looked around for help, and was relieved to see Dr. Lindsay quickly approaching. "Hey, what the heck is going on here, Dr. Murray?" Dr. Lindsay asked with his face full of concern.

"Can you please tell this guy what's going on with his

wife before he snaps my neck?" Dr. Murray pleaded.

Sonny looked at the middle aged black man and said, “Her name’s Riana Smalls, and one of y’all mu’fuckas better take me to her!” He continued his rant.

Aw shit, this guy is gonna flip the hell out when I tell him about his wife, Dr. Lindsay thought to himself. He took a deep breath and chose his next words carefully. “Sir, your wife was ran over by a car. Both of her legs and arms were severely broken and she suffered from massive head trauma.”

“But is she okay?” he asked, releasing his grip from Dr. Murray's neck. “And the baby, is the baby okay?”

Dr. Lindsay took a deep breath. “Sir, I don't know how to tell you this, but your wife didn’t make it. She was pronounced dead about ten minutes ago.”

Sonny broke down crying and dropped to his knees. He cursed himself for not being there for her when she needed him the most, and the pain and guilt he felt was immeasurable. *Naw, she can’t be dead. This nigga’s lyin’.* He thought to himself. He refused to believe his first love was no longer alive. He jumped to his feet and demanded to be taken to her.

“I wish I could help you, but I’m not authorized to do so,” Dr. Lindsay explained. “Her body’s downstairs in the morgue, but because this is a murder investigation, the medical examiner and the police are the only ones authorized to see her at this time. I’m sorry.”

“Naw, fuck all dat!” Sonny snapped and grabbed him by his arm. “Pussy, you gonna take me to see her!” He yanked him toward the elevator down the hall, but when he resisted Sonny hit him with a short right hook. His limp body crumbled to the tiled floor, and Dr. Murray took off running in the opposite direction.

Four Philadelphia Police officers and two security guards burst through the double doors that seperated the back of the emergency room from the waiting area, and ran toward him.

“He’s right there!” Doctor Murray shouted from down the hallway. “He’s friggin’ crazy!”

"Get on the ground!" The first officer shouted, while running toward him. Sonny squared up and as soon as the officer came within striking distance, he threw a barrage of punches that folded him like an envelope.

The remaining three officers wrestled him to the tiled floor and placed him in handcuffs. As they led him through the waiting area and outside toward a waiting squad car, he caught a glimpse of Annie. "Mom, they killed her!" He sobbed. "They killed Riri!"

Chapter Twenty-Eight

An Hour Later...
At Police Headquarters...

Sonny was sitting in an interrogation room with his right arm handcuffed to a steel table. Warm tears ran down the sides of his face and it felt as if his heart had been ripped from his chest. "Damn ma, why you fuckin' leave me? I know you was mad at a nigga and all dat, but damn! You wasn't ever supposed to leave me Ri, not like this!" He cried out.

The brown wooden door creaked open and a middle aged black man entered the small room with a brown folder tucked under his right arm. He walked over to the table were Sonny was seated and took a seat across from him.

"Sontino, my name is Detective Ronald Sullivan, and I'm from East Detectives. I was informed by my supervisor that you've invoked your Fifth Amendment right to remain silent and that you're waiting to speak to your attorney. However, the things that I need to speak to you about have nothing to do with your pending charges, and therefore you will not be subjected to self incrimination."

Sonny wiped away his tears and ice-grilled him. "Well, if whatchu wanna talk to me about has nothin' to do wit' my charges, then why you fuckin' wit' me?"

"Let's just say that I was hoping you could give me some information on your estranged grandfather, Gervin Moreno. We both know he's the one responsible for the murder of your girlfriend and unborn child."

"What?" Sonny snapped. "Give you some information. Who the fuck I look like, Nicky Barnes?"

Enraged by Sonny's outburst, Detective Sullivan hopped up from his seat, reached across the table, and grabbed him by his shirt. "Listen, you little fuck. I'm just about fed up with your drug dealing ass. You really think this is a friggin' joke. Well, you mark my words, when this shit is over, and you realize that you're never gonna see the streets again, your stupid ass is gonna wish you cooperated."

Sonny looked at him and burst out laughing. "Yeah, nigga, suck my dick."

*****

Across the hall, just a few feet away from his own office, Detective Smith was sitting in another interrogation room. Despite the pain that he felt from the flesh wound to his leg, a huge smile was plastered on his face. He knew the tricks of the trade, and being the snake that he was, he knew just how to slither his way out of trouble.

When Agent Long entered the small room, he got right down to business. "Alright Smitty, I just finished talking to the Attorney General, and against his better judgment, he's willing to grant you immunity from prosecution."

"Oh, yeah," Smitty nodded his head up and down. "What's the catch?"

"Where gonna need you to tell us everything you know about Gervin Moreno, and *The Moreno Crime Family*."

Detective Smith continued smiling and rubbed the stubble on his chin. "Oh, yeah! Where do you want me to start?"

*****

Later That Night...

After posting a $30,000 bond, Sonny was back at his house and the only thing on his mind was murder. "Pops, did you check out the warehouse like I asked you?"

"Yeah," Easy nodded his head. "When I left the hospital, I went down to Delaware Ave., and when I rode pass the warehouse I saw his Escalade parked out front. He's got a gate surrounding the building, and two big ass Doberman Pinschers were patrolling the perimeter."

Sonny cracked his knuckles. "A'ight, as soon as the sun goes down, we runnin' up in that mu'fucka, and we killin' *everything*."

When Easy looked at his son and saw the pain and frustration in his eyes, he realized how much he truly loved him. He made a vow to himself that he would do anything to protect him.

"Yo, we gotta murder these niggas, son," Breeze stated, while strapping on a bulletproof vest.

Sonny looked at him and nodded his head. "Did y'all figure out a way to get pass the gate and into the building?"

"Yeah," Zaire responded. "I got us some hand grenades."

"Hand grenades?" Sonny asked. "How the fuck did you pull that off?"

Zaire smiled. "You remember the bul Benny Blanko from Franklin and Berks?"

"Yeah, you talking 'bout Shakill. That's my mu'fuckin' ol' head. He used to fuck wit' Mook back in the day."

"Well, you remember when his spot got raided back in '03, and the cops found all them rocket launchers and hand grenades?"

"Yeah, I remember," Sonny shot back.

"A'ight, well let's just say that Shakill wasn't the only nigga that was on deck."

*****

Later That Night...

The cold February weather sent chills down their spines as they climbed out of Sonny's Escalade and scoped out the scene. "Sonny, are you ready?" Easy asked.

Silence.

When they approached the gate that surrounded the building, they were immediately greeted by the barking and growling of the two Doberman Pinschers.

"Breeze," Sonny looked at his cousin. "Shut 'em the fuck up!"

Breeze raised his 9mm and screwed a silencer to the barrel. He aimed the pistol at the dogs and fired.

Beaw! Beaw! Beaw! Beaw!

After a few seconds of body spasms, both dogs were laid out with a puddle of blood surrounding their heads. Easy reached inside of his jacket pocket and pulled out a bottle of sulfuric acid. After twisting off the top, he poured the liquid over the deadbolt lock that secured the gate. As the acid sizzled and burned through the steel, breaking down its components, Breeze aimed the 9mm and fired.

Beaw! Beaw! Beaw!

The lock cracked down the middle and fell to the ground. Sonny kicked the gate open, and one by one they crept toward the warehouse with assault rifles clutched in their hands. Aside from Grip's money green Escalade, the parking lot was deserted. They noticed a door on the side of the building, and approached it cautiously. Easy checked the doorknob, and astonishingly discovered that it was left unlocked. He cracked it open, and then motioned for Zaire to come closer. Behind him, Sonny and Breeze were looking back and forth, looking for any signs of a sneak attack. Easy held his index fingers to his lips, signaling for them to remain quiet.

"Zaire," he spoke just above a whisper. "Hand me one of those grenades."

Zaire removed the book bag he was wearing, reached inside, and carefully removed the pineapple. He handed it to Easy, and then took a step back. Easy pressed his thumb on the spoon, and then extracted the pin.

"Listen, I need y'all to take cover behind that truck," He nodded toward the Escalade. "'cause this shit is about to get hectic."

In unison, they nodded their heads and did as he

suggested. Easy waited a few seconds, then in one swift motion he lifted his thumb from the spoon. He tossed the grenade inside of the warehouse, and then ran to take cover behind the SUV. Approximately ten seconds later, the grenade exploded.

KaBoom!

A blast of fire shot from the door and a cloud of smoke seeped into the parking lot. Hoping to catch Grip and his cohorts off guard, they stormed inside of the building with their guns blazing.

Brrrroc! Brrrroc! Brrrroc! Brrrroc!

Almost immediately, Easy noticed that nobody was shooting back so he yelled for everybody to stop shooting. Their ears were ringing, and the smokefilled atmosphere was burning their eyes and lungs. Sonny was enraged, and the realization that nobody was in the warehouse drove him over the edge.

"Y'all mu'fukas wanted to go to war, so let's get it! He shouted at the top of his lungs, and then let off a barrage of gunfire.

Brrrroc!

"Y'all niggas gon' kill my girl and my baby on some fuck shit, and now y'all wanna hide! Naw, fuck that!"

Brrrroc!

"Grip, don't hide now pussy! You wanted me right! Well, now you got me mu'fucka!"

Brrrroc! Brrrroc! Brrrroc! Brrrroc!

"Sontino, calm down!" Easy shouted, but the look that Sonny gave him was a clear indicator that if he got in his way he could get it too. "Baby boy," he continued in a softer tone. "I know you're feelin' fucked up and frustrated, but them niggas ain't here!"

Sonny broke down crying and trembling with rage. "Naw, pops, them niggas is here! I can feel it!" He shot back. "So you can talk until ya face turn blue 'cause we ain't leavin' this mu'fuckin' warehouse until we find 'em!"

Easy shook his head in defeat. "A'ight, Sonny, if it'll

make you feel better, you and me can search the second floor and Breeze and Zaire can search down here." He looked at Breeze and Zaire. "Search everything, and if y'all find something, let off a few rounds to let us know." They nodded their heads, and then began searching.

Sonny and Easy cautiously crept to the second floor, and after searching just about everything they came up empty handed. There was, however, a door at the end of the hallway that they hadn't searched. Slowly, they crept toward it with their weapons aimed and ready to fire. Sonny used the barrel of his AK-47 to open the door, and when he realized that the office was empty his frustration grew immensely. As he looked around the office, he noticed that a single sheet of paper was lying on what appeared to be Grip's desk. He picked it up and saw that it was a letter from Grip, addressed to him.

Sontino,

By the time you find this letter, I'll be out of the country so don't bother looking for me. When I heard the news about your fiancé and unborn child I knew that you would come here. I need you to know that I did not sanction that hit! I gave all of my men specific orders to keep you in one piece. Trust me, if I wanted you dead, you would have been buried and forgotten. Throughout our minor misunderstanding, I've known your every move. Do you remember the two Cuban women that you and Rasheed took to the Marriott Hotel? Maria and Michelle? Well, unbeknownst to you, I call them Murder and Malice, and they are the head enforcers of my family. I knew all about Riana and her mother Mary. They live in a little town called Crestmont, and it's right next to the Willow Grove Mall. I also knew about the woman that you kept on the side. Her name's Daphney Rines, and her father is an old friend of mine. I even knew about your house in Cheltenham. I drive pass it every day.

The only reason that I didn't take your life is because

you're my grandson. The biggest mistake that I've ever made was not being there for your grandmother when she was pregnant with your father. I was young and arrogant just like you! I let my pride trump my judgment, and as a result I lost the only women that I've ever loved. Not only did I miss the opportunity to be a father to my only son, I miss the opportunity to be grandfather to you, my grandson. When I first saw you at that restaurant, I immediately recognized you. However, it wasn't until the day that I spoke to you on Fairhill Street that I realized your true potential. It was then, that I decided that I wanted yon to be the heir to my throne. Not just because you're my grandson, but because of the fire that I saw in your eyes. It was the same exact fire that burned in mines over fifty years ago when I was forced to start my own family. The Moreno Family.

Now, for the last time, will you please take your rightful place as the boss of this family, and allow me to retire as a wealthy old man? As a token of my love, the two assholes responsible for what happened to Riana and my great grandson are tied up in the basement awaiting your final judgment. You'll also find a briefcase down there, and inside I left you $2,500,000. I know that it can't replace Riana and the baby, but like I said it's a token of my love!

Always and forever,
Gervin 'Grip' Moreno

P.S. You were destined to be the boss!

As soon as he finished reading the letter, gunfire erupted from the ground floor. "Yo' Sonny! Uncle Easy!" Breeze shouted from the bottom of the stairs. "It's two niggas tied up in the basement!"

When Sonny and Easy entered the basement, and saw Monster and Lil' Buggy hanging from the ceiling butt ass naked, goose bumps covered their skin.

"Go outside and wait for me in the truck!" Sonny snarled through clenched teeth.

Without uttering a word, the three men did as he instructed. "Hey, yo' pops, hold up," He grabbed Easy by the arm. "You got some more of that sulfuric acid?"

"Yeah," Easy replied. "I got two of 'em left."

"Lemme get 'em."

Easy handed over the brown bottles, and then left the basement.

As the door shut behind him, Sonny circled the two men hanging from the ceiling. "Y'all gotta be the dumbest mu'fuckas in the world!" He antagonized them.

In unison they both attempted to plead their cases and beg for their lives, but the gray duct tape that covered their mouths wouldn't allow it. Sonny opened the first bottle of acid and tossed the liquid on Monster's bare skin and immediately the acid sizzled and ate through his flesh.

"Ummmm! Ummmm!!!!" He cried out. His muffled screams depicting the excruciating pain he was forced to experience.

Sonny opened the second bottle and gave Lil' Buggy the same treatment, eliciting the same response.

As both men slipped in and out of consciousness, Sonny threw on a pair of gloves, and then grabbed the hot barrel of his AK-47. He held the assault rifle like a baseball bat, and with all of his might he repeatedly struck their bodies until his arms grew tired. After a good sixty seconds had passed both Monster and Lil' Buggy were barely breathing. The sulfuric acid had burned their bodies so bad that a puddle of bloody flesh had accumulated on the floor beneath them.

In a silent rage, Sonny removed the depleted magazine from his AK and replaced it with a fresh one. After cocking back the lever, he took a few steps back and fired relentlessly. He filled both bodies with the 50 round clip.

Brrrroc! Brrrroc! Brrrroc! Brrrroc! Brrrroc! Brrrroc!

As the bullets ripped through their mutilated bodies, chunks of flesh and bone flew across the smokefilled room. After emptying the clip, Sonny scooped up a handful of shellcasings, ignoring the heat, and placed them inside of his jacket pocket. He then headed toward the briefcase sitting on the far end of the basement. He popped it open, and just like Grip had stated in the letter there were rubber banded stacks of one hundred dollar bills. Exasperated, he closed the briefcase and left the basement.

Chapter Twenty-Nine

A Week Later…

The First Baptist Church of Crestmont was filled with the family and friends of Riana Smalls. It was a sad day for everyone who knew and loved her, and this was predicated by the loud wails and controlled sobbing that filled the sanctuary.

The pastor of the church was assuring her loved ones that she was now in the presence of her Lord and Savior, and just below his elevated pulpit, her flower covered casket was accompanied by the gold picture stand that held her picture.

A cold chill entered the sanctuary causing everybody to turn around toward the door. Standing in the doorway, dressed in a triple black Armani suit, black Armani shades, and a black Armani trench coat, Sonny took a deep breath, and then headed up the aisle toward her casket. When he approached the pulpit, the pastor looked down at him and said, "Ah, excuse me young man, but you're gonna have to take a seat until I'm finished with the eulogy."

Silence.

The look that Sonny gave the man was so ferocious he almost pissed in his pants. *Oh, my Lord Jesus, this nigga ain't nothin' but the devil,* the fat, black T.D. Jakes looking man thought to himself as he pulled out a handkerchief and wiped the sweat from his brow.

Ignoring the man, piece by piece, Sonny removed the floral arrangement from the top of the casket. A handful of her family members voiced their displeasure, but nothing or nobody was going to stop him from seeing his soul mate one last time.

"Sontino?" Her mother questioned his actions from the first pew.

He looked at her and removed his Armani shades. With tears streaming from his eyes, he said, "I'm sorry, Ms. Mary, but I gotta give her somethin' before she leaves." He returned his full attention to the ivory casket with white gold trimmings and opened the lid. He couldn't believe his eyes. Aside from her swollen head, the right side of her face was caved in, and her once light complexion was now a purplish blue. He broke down crying. *Damn, man, look at the way these niggas did my baby!* He thought to himself as tears continued to pour from his eyes. He took a deep breath, and then fixed his eyes on the ceiling of the church. "Yo, how could you even let some shit like this happen? How?"

He reached inside of his Armani slacks and pulled out a purple Crown Royal bag. He loosened the gold colored string, then reached inside and pulled out the casings of the bullets he used to avenge her murder. After placing them inside of her casket, he reached into his coat pocket and pulled out her engagement ring. He then lifted her cold left hand, and put the diamond ring back in its proper place. He bent forward and softly whispered in her ear. "I love you, Riri, and no matter whatchu go through in the next life, just know I'ma always love you and you'll always be my wife." He wiped the tears from his eyes, and then stood erect. Slowly, he closed her casket and put the flowers back in position. After taking a few seconds to regain his composure, he threw his shades back on and quietly left the church.

*****

Later That Night...

Attempting to blow off some steam, he drove to Erie Avenue looking to find a dice game. Ever since he first started getting money with Mook, just like his slain big homie, gambling became one of his favorite past times and he desperately hoped a couple hours of shooting dice would ease his mind.

It was 10:45 p.m. when he pulled up on Park Ave. and Butler Street. He was a couple of blocks away from Broad Street Eddie's and uncharacteristically the block was essentially deserted. The orange street lights that normally illuminated the block weren't working, making a dark night appear even darker. A strange silence filled the intersection, and the only thing moving was the large North Philly rats that scurried from one side of the street to the other. Normally, this would have been a clear indicator that something wasn't right, but he was too caught up in his stress filled thoughts to take notice.

After retrieving the $15,000 that was stashed in his glove compartment, he climbed out his SL 550 and closed the door. As he turned to walk up the block, a dark, shadowy figure in a black hoody appeared from out of nowhere and placed a snub nosed .357 to the side of his face.

"Nigga, you know what the fuck it is!" The man snarled, and then nodded his head toward the brick of money that was clutched in his hands. "Run that!"

Yo, this shit is crazy! He thought to himself as he caught a glimpse of the man's face. Aside from his piercing blue eyes, the face under the hoody was analogous to his own. He had lightskin, a chiseled face, and a thin mustache.

"Yo, why the *fuck* is you lookin' at me like that, dawg?"

"Naw, that's my bad, fam. I ain't mean no harm," Sonny quickly replied, while handing him the $15,000.

"Take that jewelry off too!" He nodded at Sonny's iced-out 'NP' charm and his Brietling.

After removing his jewelry and handing it over to his little brother, Rahmello smacked him in the side of his head with the .357, and then took off running.

To Be Continued...

Blood of a Boss **II**
Coming Soon

Coming Soon From Lock Down Publications

GANGSTA CITY

By **Teddy Duke**

STREET JUSTICE

By **Chance**

A DANGEROUS LOVE **IV**

By **J Peach**

BONDS OF DECEPTION

By **Lady Stiletto**

LOVE KNOWS NO BOUNDARIES **III**

By **Coffee**

BLOOD OF A BOSS **II**

By **Askari**

DON'T FU#K WITH MY HEART **II**

By **Linnea**

BOSS'N UP **III**

By **Royal Nicole**

LYING LIPS **III**

By **Mahaughani Fiyah**

THE KING CARTEL **II**

By **Frank Gresham**

RICH MAN'S WOMAN, POOR MAN'S DREAM

Askari

By **Kanari Diamond**

THE DEVIL WEARS TIMBS **III**

By Tranay Adams

Available Now

LOVE KNOWS NO BOUNDARIES **I & II**

By **Coffee**

SLEEPING IN HEAVEN, WAKING IN HELL **I, II & III**

By **Forever Redd**

THE DEVIL WEARS TIMBS **I & II**

By **Tranay Adams**

DON'T FU#K WITH MY HEART

By **Linnea**

BOSS'N UP **I & II**

By **Royal Nicole**

A DANGEROUS LOVE **I, II & III**

By **J Peach**

CUM FOR ME

An **LDP Erotica Collaboration**

LYING LIPS I & II

By **Mahaughani Fiyah**

Blood of a Boss

THE KING CARTEL

By **Frank Gresham**

BOOKS BY LDP'S CEO, CA$H

TRUST NO MAN

TRUST NO MAN 2

TRUST NO MAN 3

BONDED BY BLOOD

SHORTY GOT A THUG

A DIRTY SOUTH LOVE

THUGS CRY

THUGS CRY 2

TRUST NO BITCH

TRUST NO BITCH 2

TRUST NO BITCH 3

TIL MY CASKET DROPS

Coming Soon

TRUST NO BITCH (EYEZ' STORY)

THUGS CRY 3

Blood of a Boss

BONDED BY BLOOD 2

Made in the USA
Coppell, TX
11 December 2020